W9-BCW-424

The Body in the Billiard Room

By the same author

Inspector Ghote Novels

Go West, Inspector Ghote
The Murder of the Maharajah
The Sheriff of Bombay
Inspector Ghote Draws a Line
Filmi, Filmi, Inspector Ghote
A Remarkable Case of Burglary
Bats Fly Up for Inspector Ghote
Inspector Ghote Goes by Train
Inspector Ghote Trusts the Heart
Inspector Ghote Breaks an Egg
Inspector Ghote Plays a Joker
Inspector Ghote Hunts the Peacock
Inspector Ghote Caught in Meshes
Inspector Ghote's Good Crusade
The Perfect Murder
Under a Monsoon Cloud

Other Crime Novels

Is Skin Deep, is Fatal
Death of a Fat God
The Dog it was that Died
A Rush on the Ultimate
Zen there was Murder
Death and the Visiting Firemen
Mrs Craggs, Crimes Cleaned Up (short stories)

Novels

The Strong Man
The Underside
A Long Walk to Wimbledon
The Lucky Alphonse

As Evelyn Hervey

The Governess
The Man of Gold
Into the Valley of Death

Non-Fiction

Murder Must Appetize
Sherlock Holmes, the Man and his World

The Body in the Billiard Room

H.R.F. Keating

VIKING

VIKING
Viking Penguin Inc.
40 West 23rd Street
New York, New York 10010, U.S.A.

First American Edition
Published in 1987

LIBRARY OF CONGRESS CATALOGING IN PUBLICATION DATA
Keating, H. R. F. (Henry Raymond Fitz-Walter), 1926–
The body in the billiard room.
(A Viking novel of mystery and suspense)
I. Title.
PR6061.E26B6 1987 823′.914 87-40038
ISBN 0-670-81744-9

Printed in the United States of America by
Arcata Graphics, Fairfield, Pennsylvania
Set in Baskerville

Author's Note

The setting for this story is not so much the South-Indian hill resort of Ootacamund, familiarly Ooty, as Dream-Ooty, a mingling of Ooty as it ought to be with some of Ooty as it is and as it was. Consequently, none of the people portrayed – not even Inspector Ghote himself – is anything other than an upswelling of imagination.

The Body in the Billiard Room

1

Kringg-kringg, kringg-kringg, kringg-kringg . . .

The strident shrilling of the telephone at last penetrated Inspector Ghote's head. He came to with a start, pushed himself up from the lotus position in which he had been seated on the floor and made his way stiff-legged towards the faded black, quiveringly vibrating instrument.

Had he, he asked himself, been in a proper state of dharana, as defined in Dr Joshi's book on yoga in daily life? Had his thoughts stopped running after objects of enjoyment and focused solely on the point at the tip of his nose? Was he making progress in clearing his mind of its accumulated rubbish so as to perform his task in life all the better?

Or had those thoughts been wandering vaguely in swirling trails as they so often turned out to have been when he sat to meditate?

He could not be sure.

Kringg-kringg, kringg-kri—

He picked up the receiver.

'Ghote, is that you? Inspector Ghote?'

He recognized at once the incisive voice: the Assistant Commissioner, Crime Branch.

'Yes, sir. Yes, ACP sahib. Ghote here, sir.'

'Ah, Ghote. Good. Now, listen. I have received a request for your services. To act in the capacity of OSD.'

'An Officer on Special Duty, sir?'

What could this be? He had plenty-plenty on his plate already, even if nothing of Number One priority. But why was he being made an OSD? And what special duty could this be?

'You're to go to Ooty, Inspector.'

'To go on duty, yes, sir. Which duty, sir?'

'Not duty, Inspector. Ooty. Ooty. Ootacamund. Don't tell me you've never heard of Ooty.'

'No, sir. Yes, sir. Yes, I am very much hearing of Ooty. Hill station, sir. South India. Very high up in Nilgiri Hills. Most popular resort, sir.'

All the same, could he have heard the ACP correctly? Was it possible he was to be sent to a place as far away as Ooty? Damn it, it was more than a thousand kilometres from Bombay, right down in Tamil Nadu. It came under a different state force altogether.

At the other end of the line the Assistant Commissioner coughed sharply.

'It seems, Ghote,' he said, 'that you have an excessively high reputation. In certain quarters.'

A high reputation? Ghote felt his heart give a lamb-joyous leap.

'It appears you once made an arrest in a theft and murder affair in which some British novelist fellow had an interest, and he afterwards went about singing your damn praises.'

'Yes, sir?'

Quiet caution seemed the only possible response. What could this be about?

'Well, all that tamasha eventually came to the ears of a very influential gentleman long resident in Ooty, and there's been a Section 302 business down there.'

'Murder, sir?'

'Yes, man. Murder. Murder. And this gentleman, one

Mr Surinder Mehta MC, considers you, Ghote, are the only person capable of finding the perpetrator.'

Ghote felt another waft of rosy pleasure rise up in him. But there was a tiny thorn among the roses.

'Please, sir. MC? You were saying after Shri Mehta's name the letters MC, no?'

'Yes, yes. They stand for some sort of British medal, a Military Cross or something. The gentleman – he's pretty old – won it in the Second World War. I gather he likes the letters put after his name whenever he's written to, etcetera. And there is one other thing.'

'Yes, sir?'

'You had better call him Your Excellency. He became an ambassador after Independence, Indian ambassador to some damn place in Europe. I don't know whether he's still properly entitled to be excellencied, but he likes it, I'm told. And you'd better do it.'

'Yes, sir. Your Excellence. I would remember, sir.'

'Your Excellency, Ghote. Excellency. Get it right.'

'Yes, sir. Excellency. Excellency. But, sir, what exactly is this gentleman wanting?'

'He is wanting you to present yourself in Ooty and solve his damn murder for him. The body on the billiard table. That's where the victim was found. On the billiard table in the Ooty Club. Very famous place. I think he sees it all as a kind of sacrilege, and wants the very best man there is to deal with it.'

Ghote felt himself swallow. Was he really the very best man there was? By the sound of it the murder was not some simple killing during the course of a quarrel or anything like that. There must be some special circumstances about it for this ambassador to have used his influence to call someone all the way from Bombay.

To call him himself. As the very best man. And he was not truly that. Oh, yes, he had had his successes. There was the business that had brought him kudos from the

British author. But he was not, in fact, the very best man there was. No.

'Sir,' he said tentatively. 'Sir, are you one hundred per cent certain it is right for me to be going? I mean, sir, for one thing only, what about the local fellows? They would resent an officer from another force coming into their territory, isn't it?'

'Ghote, you have been asked for. By name. I am not going to refuse to send you, whatever I may think. And in any case you are to go in a private capacity. There will be no question of treading on any toes. Besides, I expect the Tamil Nadu wallahs will have it all wrapped up even before you get there.'

'Yes, sir. But if I am to be in a private capacity, sir, what kind of powers will I be having? Sir, it would be most difficult.'

'Not at all, Ghote, not at all. Damn it, there are private detectives, aren't there? They clear up cases sometimes. Or I suppose they must. Well, you will be a private detective down in Ooty. That's all there is to it.'

'Yes, sir. But—But, sir, what about my present workload?'

'You can pick up whatever you're doing when you get back. As I said, no doubt you'll find the whole thing's been dealt with before you even arrive.'

'Sir, but—'

'Damn it, Ghote, you're being offered a stay in one of India's finest hill stations. Right out of the heat. Bloody fine climate. Top-class holiday place. And you're making every sort of damn difficulty.'

'Yes, sir. I am sorry, sir.'

Yet, Ghote could not help reflecting, January in Bombay was the coolest and pleasantest month of the year. Now, if he had been offered a trip to Ooty in May or October . . .

'Right then, there's a plane that leaves for Coimbatore Airport at twelve noon exactly. I'm having you booked on to it. See that you're there.'

'But—'

*

The Ooty bus, when Ghote came to board it stiff-limbed after the flight to Coimbatore, looked as if its every seat was occupied in advance of his arrival. Already having to fight back a feeling of muzzy disorientation at finding himself at such short notice in a place where even the voices around him were jabbering all the time in barely comprehensible Tamil, he shook his head in blank bewilderment.

How was it that, when the flight had been scrupulously on time, the bus taking passengers onwards was already jammed full?

It was just part of the illogicality of everything, he supposed. That feeling, from the sheer strangeness of his surroundings, was invading his mind more and more with each passing moment.

Why could things not be simple? Why did life never go to plan?

Except with this last Indian Airlines flight?

Sharply he pulled himself together, swung up on to the entrance-step of the bus and from there made out that there was a small gap right at the back between two ample ladies dressed in rich silky South Indian saris. He took a last look at his hastily packed suitcase waiting to be stowed in the baggage compartment and pushed his way forward along the packages-crammed aisle. Somewhat to his surprise the two ladies, without a pause in the clackingly loud conversation they were having in mysterious Tamil, shifted apart just enough to allow him to sit.

He had barely wriggled himself into place when the bus abruptly set off. Within minutes they were speeding with slewing recklessness through the bare countryside, its monotony broken only by the repeated clusters of villages where dogs and children scattered squealing or barking at their approach.

Inside, at least, it all ought to have been peaceful. Things were now going to plan again. There was nothing to do but sit and be delivered to Ooty some fifty kilometres away up among the distant blue Nilgiri Hills, occasionally to be glimpsed beyond the driver's impassive head.

But Ghote could not bring any peace to his thoughts. The prospect that awaited him up in the resort ahead, which he had read about over the years here and there but never expected to see, was too full of unknown hazards. What sort of a person would this Mr Surinder Mehta MC be, someone with so much influence he could summon at no notice an inspector of the Bombay CID? And, more, what was the exact nature of the crime – the murder – he had been hurried all this way to solve?

He knew almost nothing about it. The Assistant Commissioner had given him hardly a single detail. Except that there was a body. A body on a billiard table. What was he actually expected to do in Ooty? And where, where, would he get boarding and lodging when at last he arrived there? He had been issued with no instructions whatsoever. He had not even been given expenses and allowances. How would he pay his way?

In the large, stinkingly hot shed-like structure that served as the airport lounge at Coimbatore, waiting for his bag to come off the plane, he had spotted, on the floor, a brightly coloured brochure for one of Ooty's tourist hotels, formerly a maharajah's palace. But its thumping claims had filled him only with dismay: rooms *exuberating with luxury*, a restaurant *decorated beyond-the-words* and a Lovers' Lane *intimately private for the needy couple*, what had all that to do with him?

He made an effort to attain once more the calm which he had occasionally achieved in recent months in following the precepts of K. S. Joshi, MSc, MA, PhD, author of *Yoga in Daily Life*, Hind Pocket Books, price Rupees 3. But, concentrate as he would on the point at the tip of his nose, his thoughts only whirled faster and faster, more and more uselessly.

Mr Mehta. He must not forget to call him Your Excellency. Or Your Excellence? Which? Whichever was it?

A deep flush of embarrassment came over him in the steamy hotness of the packed, racketing bus. Which title had the ACP given him such a strong advice about? Excellency? Excellence?

Much as he repeated the two, trying them out again and again for sound and suitability, neither one seemed more right than the other.

The tip of his nose. The tip of his nose. Concentrate. Concentrate.

He became aware that the nature of the countryside had changed. The bus had slowed in its wild rush and was beginning to climb upwards. Now on either side there could be seen plantations of palm trees in long, ordered rows that ought to have been calming to the spirit, only they seemed somehow inhuman, unlike the random palms of other places.

Excellence? Excellency? Good evening, Your Excellency? Good evening, Your Excellence? Excuse me, is it that you are His Excellence Mr Surinder Mehta? His Excellency? Why, oh why, were there strict rules of precedence and protocol?

Damn it then, when the time came he would just say whichever came first to his lips. And if it was wrong, it would be wrong.

But all this was nothing compared to the real business that awaited him. Summoned as the very best man there was to investigate – what? A murder. A dead body on a billiard table in a club, some sort of sacred club apparently. It would be full of Englishmen, of white sahibs.

But no. No, surely all or most of those had long ago gone back to the UK. And even those who had stayed on would, many of them, have died off by now. It was more than forty years since Independence after all. Things had changed. Time had bit by bit battered away at the old rules and regulations, the order and dignity of the British Raj.

Outside now there were in the distance tea and coffee gardens, with bushes in long neat lines. The wildness tamed.

Yet, it seemed, this body in the billiard room was still considered so important that he himself had been brought here, with the fearsome reputation he had earned only through one success that happened to have been witnessed by a British writer of crime novels. So, surely there must be special circumstances about this murder – but who was it even who had been murdered? – that made the case a difficult and especially complex affair. Otherwise the CID from Madras, or even the Ooty police themselves, would surely have been capable of handling it.

Now the climbing road had begun to wind instead of charging straight ahead. The bus's engine had taken on an unvarying, determinedly chugging note.

And would not the business up there in Ooty be as twisted and tortuous as the road? And even their ultimate destination had now become, in a way, less clear. The signpost he had last glimpsed said in English letters above the meaningless, to him, Tamil script, not *Ooty* or even *Ootacamund* but *Udhagamandalam*. To what mysterious place was he going?

But no point in letting his thoughts go aimlessly round and round. Better to prepare himself internally for what might lie ahead, in so far as he could. What other techniques besides concentrating on the tip of the nose had Dr Joshi recommended so as to arrive at that state of purely concentrated dharana in which the mind gathered to itself its true strength? Concentrating on the mid-point between the eyebrows? On an attractive idol of Lord Shiva?

No hope of getting at the book in his suitcase somewhere underneath the steadily grunting bus.

And in any case unremitting concentration did not seem

possible with the sudden doubling-back twists in the road now coming every few minutes, sending the soft flesh of either one of the ladies on each side of him – both had lapsed into light sleep – flooding warmly against his own bony body.

He looked out of the windows ahead.

The landscape had changed once more. The neat tea gardens had abruptly ceded to jungle. At either side a wildly growing mass of creepers obscured and confused the tangled trees in a chaos of different greens and sudden bright flowers. Overhead, high branches cut out the light.

And in that riotous jungle would there be tigers lurking?

Well, perhaps not. But there would be panthers certainly. Panthers waiting to spring. And snakes. Venomous, unpredictable snakes.

Again he could not help feeling it was into something like this jungle that he himself was going. He saw trails of logic that would peter out almost at once as other trails superimposed themselves. He imagined sudden glimpses of the bright flower of suspicion, but no way of telling what plant it sprang from. He envisaged a mysterious darkness over all, and somewhere in it a murderer, a person past all the rules.

A gloom equal to the greenish mist under the tall trees' shade settled into his mind.

Time passed. The bus engine roared unceasingly. The sleeping ladies on either side swayed into him and away again as the road hairpinned yet higher.

Then he saw, with a dart of apprehension, a large roadside notice boldly warning in English *Sleeping While Driving Is Prohibited.* He raised his head and peered at the outline of the driver in front. Was the fellow fully awake? Was prohibition only enough to stop sleep overcoming him?

He could not tell.

They must have been going now, he calculated a little desperately, for two and a half hours, or three. Perhaps more. He would have liked to look at his watch. But his left arm was wedged down by the weight of the silkily sari-clad lady beside him.

He tried once again to think of the tip of his nose.

But, almost imperceptibly, another change was manifesting itself. Ghote felt it first as a gradual lightening of the spirit. He then realized what the cause must be. They had climbed into coolness. The heat of the turbid plains, trapped in the bus, was at last yielding to the clear air outside.

That he had read of. It was the great thing about Ooty. The wonderfully cool and fresh air.

Perhaps, after all, he would get on well enough there. Damn it, he was a Bombay CID officer, and was not Bombay hailed as 'India's capital of crime'? Its CID was the best. They had to be. He himself might not be the very best that that fool of a British writer had made him out to be, but he was not altogether inefficient. Perhaps it would turn out that the case ahead was simply one that the police in Ooty could not cope up to, but which he, with all he had learnt over the years about ways of criminal humanity, would be able to see his way through to the end easily enough.

The snoozers on either side woke and began at once to clack out their incomprehensible conversation. Ghote eased his trapped arm free and rubbed his hands briskly together.

Soon the long climb began to level out. The jungle melted away and above the sky was clear and blue.

To either side of the road, now running straight there was extraordinary countryside. The famous Ooty countryside that was said to look so like distant England. Miles of sweet shorn grass, rising up in little rolling hills with the swelling lines of darker woodland here and there nestling among them.

So this was it. Ooty. Had someone not called it paradise? Well, he was in paradise then. Even if it was a paradise with one snake in it.

But he was here to find that snake. To catch it by the

tail, twist and turn how it might. And he would do it. He was a thoroughly experienced police officer, and he would do it.

Then, abruptly turning a corner, there was a brightly painted signboard. *Welcome to Ooty Queen of Hill Stations.*

And welcome, he thought, to the body in the billiard room.

Out of the window to his right he caught a glimpse of the statue of a familiar figure, the stooped, emaciated, radiantly benevolent form of Gandhiji himself. Somehow it disconcerted him. Was the Queen of Hill Stations then not as regally separate as they said from the cares and troubles of the world? Had everything that Gandhiji stood for, the fight for Independence, the uplifting of the downtrodden Untouchables, the healing of the clash between Moslem and Hindu, had all that, still by no means fully achieved, penetrated up the 7,000 feet or more from the everyday, turbulent plains to this paradise after all?

No time, however, to ponder the riddle.

'Charing Cross, Charing Cross,' the driver sang out. The thrum of the bus engine died away and they came to a halt.

Already the more experienced Ooty-goers had risen to their feet and were pushing and shoving their way along to the exit at the front.

Ghote decided to sit where he was until the crush had worked itself out. There was still the question of boarding and lodging. He would have to make inquiries. Better to wait till the first arrivals had dispersed.

The ample ladies on either side of him heaved themselves up as one. He shivered as the soft warmth that had penned him in for so long was withdrawn.

Now the way was clear for him to get out.

He pushed himself upright and made his way, awkward-legged, along the length of the exhausted bus. As he stepped down on to the ground, he was at once overcome by a fit of trembling as the cold air struck his thin cotton shirt and hardly less thin cotton trousers.

Then a tall figure detached itself from the crowd around the bus, a distinguished-looking elderly man, face leathery behind a neatly trimmed white moustache, dressed in a suit of fine tweed, its elbows patched with leather, gleamingly polished brogues on his feet.

'At last', he exclaimed, coming straight up to Ghote. 'The Great Detective steps on to the scene.'

2

The Great Detective. Ghote felt the confidence which had blossomed inside him with the first exhilarating whiff of cool Ooty air go spiralling sharply away.

He was not any sort of a Great Detective. He was, he hoped, a good police officer. A competent detective. But it seemed to be just as he had feared when over the telephone back in Bombay he had heard the Assistant Commissioner say that the influential figure in Ooty considered him 'the best there is'. He had been puffed up by that bloody British author into something far beyond his true status.

A Great Detective. What was a Great Detective? Some super-best character like Sherlock Holmes? Someone who – his mind scrabbled among dimly remembered stories read as a boy – had solved, sucking at a pipe, mysteries baffling all Scotland Yard. Someone who with a lofty 'Elementary, my dear Watson' had casually made clear utterly inexplicable events.

Could he at once tell this Mr Surinder Mehta, ex-ambassador, one-time distinguished soldier in the British ranks, that he was no such thing as a Great Detective?

He looked more closely at the tall figure confronting him with such easy assurance. In the lean, leathery face, immaculately shaved even at this late hour of the day, he saw a pair of disconcertingly fierce eyes. He was aware too that, though perhaps into his eighties, the former soldier's bearing was still awesomely erect and commanding.

'Well, but Your Excellency,' he began. 'That is, Your Excellence. Your Excellency, I am not . . .'

He came to a halt.

What had this influential person made of his stutterings?

He appeared hardly to have heard them. The cool eyes in the lean face were looking at him still with an expression of simple expectancy. Waiting for the first pronouncement of the Great Detective.

Ghote swallowed hard.

'But, Your Excellence,' he said, in lame substitution for the declaration he had found it not quite possible to make. 'Your Excellency, I am not at all sure where I am to find boarding and lodging in Ooty. In Ootacamund, that is.'

'Oh, all taken care of, my dear fellow. You'll put up at the Club, of course. Only possible place really. I mean, you must be on the spot, mustn't you? You remember how Poirot had to stay at that dreadful guest-house in *Mrs McGinty's Dead*?'

'Poirot?' Ghote asked, repeating two unfamiliar syllables, completely baffled.

'Hercule Poirot, old chap. Your distinguished predecessor, as it were. You're India's answer to Hercule Poirot, and to Lord Peter Wimsey and the others. Brilliant piece of work that double murder case you solved.'

Then a sudden quick, almost suspicious look.

'You have read your Agatha Christie, haven't you?'

'No,' said Inspector Ghote.

'No? No? Not read Agatha Christie? My dear chap, you don't know what you've been missing. We'll have to remedy that. We'll have to remedy that. Why, when I was in the UK – I was Ambassador to Yuroglavia, you know, just after Independence, never actually got out to that pretty forsaken spot, just had an office in India House in London – well, when I was there, I tell you, I acquired such a liking for those books. Liking? No, such a love for them, it's lasted me the rest of my life.'

'But, yes,' Ghote answered, feeling himself beginning to be swept away on this flood of warm reminiscence, 'I am remembering now. I was once as a young man going through a book by that lady. It was called – It was called – Yes, *The Murder of Robert Ockrent*, I think. But, I am ashamed to say, I was altogether failing to discover who had committed that murder. And so, as one about to enter the police service, I did not attempt any more of those books.'

'Well, I should imagine *Roger Ackroyd* would baffle even you, my dear chap. Especially if you were only a novice then. But you must battle it out with Dame Agatha again now. We'll see to that. I can lend you a dozen at any time. Or there are plenty in the Nilgiri Library.'

'Well, that is most kind. But if I am to be engaged in the investigation of a murder, I am doubting whether I would have much of time for light reading.'

'Oh, but you mustn't say that. Light reading? Agatha Christie and the others are much more than that. Those books, you know, show you the world as it ought to be. My dear fellow, when I read them first in England, I felt as if I was seeing things straight for the first time in my life. A world where the evil man, or the evil woman, by Jove, is always brought to justice in the end. That's as things should be, you know. As things should be. Not like our wretched India today, I can assure you.'

'Well, but—'

'No, my dear chap. Those books are just marvellous. The worst of crimes uncovered by the best of men, Sherlock Holmes, Lord Peter, Mr Albert Campion, Hercule Poirot. Heroes every one.'

'But,' Ghote managed to break in, seeing a tiny chance of putting the objection he had wanted to make when he had first been hailed as the Great Detective. 'But, Your Excellence—'

He came to a stop. At the word *Excellence* he had seen the ex-ambassador stiffen minutely.

So he had got it wrong. It was a black mark. But, come what may, he must say what he had to say.

'Your Excellency,' he began once more, with heavy emphasis. 'Please, life is not at all as it is seeming to be for Mr Poirot and those others in books. What I am meaning is this: things are not always at all ordered in the life which we are living. You see, in that case of mine you were mentioning, I—'

'But that's just my point, old boy,' His Excellency interrupted. 'From everything I heard, you brought the bad hat to justice there in absolutely classical style. And I warn you you're up against just such a diabolically ingenious opponent here, too. A diabolically ingenious murderer.'

The aged, erect, imperious figure turned away.

'But, come along, my dear chap. Mustn't stand here gassing all night. We'll walk up to the Club, it's only a step, and I'll send a servant for your baggage. Then I can put you properly in the picture.'

'Thank you,' Ghote said, acknowledging to himself defeat but resolving that it would be only temporary.

They set off in silence through the rapidly gathering dusk. There was a school, called Bucks, on the left, very British in style with its roof, made out of corrugated iron, mounting to a peak. On the right there was some sort of a Christian church, and there was another with a squat tower further on at a little distance up a turning behind double gates. There was also, as a noticeboard outside proclaimed, the Collector's Office, arcaded and much hung with balconies. It was all very much Ooty, Ooty as he had read of it. A quiet English town in the middle of teeming India.

Soon His Excellency directed him into the turning of a lane.

'The Club,' he said.

And there at the crest of a small hill it lay, the scene of

the crime. In the fast-fading light Ghote could still see the long, low white building, distinguished by four tall, very British pillars rising up at its centre from a flight of wide steps. Away to either side ran fine lawns, their expanse broken here and there by huge old trees.

Then he noticed close at hand an inconspicuous sign reading *Private – Members Only*. It was, he felt, all the more of a barrier for its very lack of threat. It was enough for the members of this awesome institution just to give the briefest message to outsiders that this was forbidden territory.

Territory which he, simply because one of those members had taken it into his head that Inspector Ghote of Bombay was another Sherlock Holmes, was about to be introduced into.

And then, just behind the sign, he saw something else. A yogi was sitting on the ground there, sitting so still in meditation as to be almost invisible, streamingly white-locked and white-bearded, bare of chest, impervious to the sharp chill of the evening air.

A holy man in a state of dhyana, Ghote thought in sudden envy. One whole step beyond the dharana he himself had such difficulty in getting near. With every impurity of thought banished. Or the stock-still figure might even be in samadhi, all consciousness of self obliterated.

'Come on, old chap,' His Excellency said. 'Want to have our chat before they sound the dinner gong.'

'Yes, yes.'

He hurried after the ex-ambassador up along a tree-lined drive. And, before he had time fully to prepare himself, they were mounting the ancient steps, passing between the white pillars, through the portico, where a huge gong waited to be struck, and were inside the Club itself.

It appeared to be altogether deserted. There were dark-wood painted rolls of honour on the walls, deep sofas covered in blue and white linen and a pervasive smell of resin from the polished floor at their feet. But no bustle of activity. No members doing whatever it was that members of such a Club did within its sacred walls.

'Koi hai?' His Excellency called.

Silence.

Ghote looked about him more closely. Just near there was a green baize board for notices, the scraps of paper pinned to it mostly yellowing with age. He read one. *Wanted – Good Home for Three Adorable Puppies Not Pedigree.*

Well, he thought with a dart of irreverence, so even here nature can thrust aside the rules.

'Koi hai?' His Excellency called again.

And now there did come the patter of feet in soft chappals and a bearer, in cripsly starched blue uniform, appeared.

'Sahib?'

'Ah, Patiyar. Is there anyone about? Mr Iyer? Major Bell?'

His Excellency turned to Ghote.

'Iyer's our Assistant Secretary,' he said. 'Does the work, you know. Major Bell is Club Secretary, one of the last few Europeans in Ooty. We gave him the post two or three years ago, though of course he's been a member for decades.'

He dropped his voice.

'Otherwise he would have ended up among the flotsam of the Friend in Need Society, I'm afraid,' he said. 'Sad thing when a fellow's been part of Ooty life so long, sidesman at the church and all that.'

'Please,' the bearer said, 'Mr Iyer is at own residence and Major Sahib is taking Dasher for customary evening walk.'

'Ah, well, never mind. Just wanted to get Mr Ghote here booked in as a Temporary Member. But it'll wait. It'll wait.'

His Excellency turned again to Ghote, who had been

wondering whether he could ask what a sidesman at a church was and had decided he had better let it pass.

'We'll go into the Reading Room. If Ringer Bell's out with that desperate old dog of his – fellow knows it's high time the beast was put down – then he won't be having a snooze in there. And no one else will disturb us.'

'Very good,' Ghote said.

He began preparing in his mind a few phrases for the declaration he felt he must make before he got embroiled any further in the ex-ambassador's detective-story scheming. 'A police officer is working very much by knowledge of locale' and 'almost to one hundred per cent murder cases are altogether simple affairs not requiring much of detection, only routine inquiries'; even 'there is no room for amateur effort in dealing with whatsoever sorts and kinds of crimes'.

His Excellency ushered him into a large echoing room. Clusters of leather armchairs were drawn up here and there, the seat of one near the door showing a wide white split. Writing tables marched down the length of the room at well spaced intervals, each with a neat pile of pale green notepaper at its exact centre. On the deep shelves along one wall there was a line of tall green books. Ghote glimpsed the title of one of them, embossed in gold, *Ootacamund Hunt – Hounds Breeding Records – 1920–25*. And away at the far end there was actually an open fire, quietly glowing in a wide fireplace.

Yes, this was truly Ooty. The unchanging order. The keen, clear air of paradise warmed by the cheerful glint of burning wood.

'Damned fire,' His Excellency said. 'Thing's half out. Trouble is you can't get the logs nowadays. Too many people in the place, always scrounging for firewood. You know what they did to old Ringer Bell one night?'

'No, Your Excellency.'

'Crept into his garden and dug up a whole damn cherry tree. There when he went to bed. Gone in the morning.

Still, I didn't bring you in here to talk about how Ooty's going downhill.'

Now would be the moment. Jump in at the start and tell the old man, however influential he might be, that he had not summoned any sort of a Great Detective, that this was not the way murder cases were cleared up. That—

'Right. Well, you know, of course, that the Club billiards marker, fellow by the name of Pichu, was found dead first thing yesterday morning, sprawled out bang in the middle of the billiard table?'

'Oh, yes,' Ghote put in quickly, seeing a way of making his case with the ex-ambassador from a sympathetic angle. 'It was altogether sacrilege, isn't it?'

'Sacrilege? Don't know about that. Point is, old Pichu was definitely murdered. Stabbed to the heart. No weapon nearby. Clear case.'

'Yes. Yes, Your Excellency. But if it is being such a clear case, why cannot Ootacamund police deal with same?'

'Ah, you've put your finger on it. Right on it. Expected as much from you. And, of course, that's it. The police here have bungled the business. Always do, the local chaps, don't they? Have done ever since the days of Inspector Lestrade.'

'Inspector Lestrade?'

Who on earth was he? An officer from British days?

'Chap Sherlock Holmes was always putting right, you know.'

'Oh, yes, sir. Yes.'

'Well, we've got a fellow here with some long damn Tamil name – Meenakshisundaram, that's it – and all he could do, when he came up here hotfoot when the crime was discovered, was to say it must be a dacoity. Simple robbery, I ask you.'

'But is that not—'

'Well, of course, it can't be anything of the sort. I mean, is it likely that a dacoit, intent on doing no more than lay hands on the Club's silver trophies, would commit murder?'

'Well, no, I—'

'Exactly. Knew you'd cotton on to that at once. But Inspector Meenakshisundaram can't see further than the end of his nose. Why, even when I pointed out to him that the body was absolutely in the centre of the billiard table, laid out flat on its back, he couldn't see what that must mean.'

Ghote felt the challenge.

'Yes,' he said. 'If the man had been killed in the course of a dacoity it is most unlikely his body would have landed up in such position. And also it may have been placed in that manner by way of making some sort of statement.'

'Of course, my dear chap. Of course. But it takes a fellow of your stature to appreciate a point like that.'

Ghote cursed his impulsiveness.

'But, sir,' he said, hoping to regain lost ground, 'it could have been mere chance only also.'

'Well, suppose it could have been. . . . Perhaps. But you and I know better, don't we? The Great Detective and his trusty Watson, eh? Or, as Poirot once said of Captain Hastings, the detective and his stooge. I hope you're going to let me be your stooge, Ghote. I mean, go round with you as you investigate. Not sharing your thoughts, of course. But asking the odd question every now and again.'

'Yes, sir—But, Your Excellency—'

'Knew you'd see it that way. Good man. So let me tell you about the suspects.'

'Suspects? There are suspects already?'

'Well, yes, I haven't been idle, you know. Made a few discreet inquiries in advance of your coming. And one thing's quite clear.'

'It is?'

'Yes. Quite plainly, Pichu was murdered because he was blackmailing somebody. Only possible motive. And the fellow was a damn rogue, after all. Mustn't speak ill of the dead and all that, and he had been a Club servant for half a century or more. But the truth is he was a nasty piece of work. Wouldn't have put blackmail past him any day.'

'If you are saying it.'

'Yes, yes. Can't be any doubt. But, and this is the thing, we can go one step further in narrowing it down. I mean, who would you point the finger at in the first place in a case like this?'

Ghote considered. Briefly.

'In such cases we start by surmising on the servants,' he said.

'No, no, my dear chap. First rule of the game that. You know what Hercule Poirot says. In *Dumb Witness*, I think it is: "I eliminated the servants. Their mentality was obviously not adapted to such a crime." '

'But, Your Excellency, in the case you were giving me so much of credit for, it was a servant who was one of the murderers itself.'

'Ah, different matter that. Different altogether. No, here in the Club you can take it there's no question of a servant being involved. All neatly tucked away in their quarters, for one thing. Locked out. And that's the point, you see, the place was properly snowbound.'

'Snowbound? You are saying there was snow two days ago in Ooty? It is very, very cold, I am knowing, but I have seen no sign of snow.'

'No, no, my dear fellow. I didn't mean real snow. I meant what you might call metaphorical snow.'

'Metaphorical?'

'Yes. Just like in the books. The circumstances that make it clear that only a limited number of suspects could have committed the crime. I mean, in *The Sittaford Mystery* it was real snow. House on Dartmoor surrounded by snow, no footprints leading away, bound to be one of the people inside who'd done it. But just who was Dame Agatha's secret, eh?'

'It is an Agatha Christie story?'

'You've got it in one, old man. Got it in one: the situation here is precisely that of a Christie story. You see, Pichu was killed some time during the night when all the doors were locked, and, since we're certain that the missing Club trophies and the forced window in the billiard room were only intended to deceive—'

'But, please,' Ghote broke in.

'No, no, let me finish. Since we're certain of that, it follows the murder must have been committed by someone inside the building. And it's out of season now, you know. I mean, if this had happened in Planters' Week when every tea-estate manager for miles around comes flocking into the Club, it would have been a different matter altogether. But, you see, on the night of the murder there were just five people inside the locked premises.'

'Five only?'

'Yes, my dear fellow. Five. I mean, I know that in all the best detective stories there are six suspects, or seven. There's a book actually called that, you know. *Seven Suspects*, by Michael Innes. But here we shall just have to put up with having only five.'

Ghote blinked.

'And Inspector Meenakshisundaram has questioned each of these persons?' he asked.

'No, no. Of course not.'

'Of course not? But why?'

'Because he's Inspector Lestrade. And what we want here is Sherlock Holmes. Or Hercule Poirot. You, in short, old chap.'

'But, sir. But, Your Excellency—'

What Ghote might have managed to say at last he never knew. Because at that moment through the empty premises of the Club there came, booming and reverberating, the sound of a mighty gong stroke.

'Dinner,' said His Excellency, rising briskly to his feet. 'Dinner, and with any luck all five of your suspects neatly lined up in the dining room for you.'

3

With the sound of the great gong in the portico still humming in the air, Ghote rose up from the edge of the wide leather armchair where he had been sitting. He felt trapped, and he felt foolish. How could the Assistant Commissioner have agreed to him being sent here? To take part in what seemed to be some sort of a detective story? But then he knew the answer. He had been sent because a person of influence had asked for him.

Yet, here in Ooty, paradise Ooty, hell Ooty, how had it come about that he had allowed himself to be engulfed in that influential figure's unlikely theory? He thought he knew the answer to that, too. It was because he could not, when it came down to it, fly in the face of someone with so much influence and authority.

And perhaps he had been sensible not to have done so. After all, if he had, word would soon enough have got back to whatever high-up old friend the former ambassador had gone to in the first place. It might be a Cabinet Minister even. Or the head of some huge industrial empire with contacts at the top. Or some very, very senior civil servant. And when they got to hear his career might be blighted for ever.

No, it was best, in a way, to let this ridiculous business go on. And, besides, it might not be altogether ridiculous.

There was just something in what His Excellency had said. The circumstances of the murder were not one hundred per cent consistent with a killing in the course of a dacoity, as Inspector Meenakshisundaram had assumed was the case. The body being in the very centre of the billiard table, if it truly had been so, was certainly an odd circumstance. And murder was by no means the modus operandi of the ordinary dacoit.

So, let matters continue a little longer. See what happened, and take the first chance possible to have a talk with Meenakshisundaram. He might be able to put the whole thing straight with just one word.

But first His Excellency's five suspects, so-called suspects. To be confronted with them at dinner in this posh club . . .

'Come along, my dear chap. I'm certainly peckish, even if you're not.'

Yet getting a meal did not prove as easy as Ghote, who found he was very hungry, had assumed it would be. At the door of the big dining room a Club servant barred their way.

The fellow looked at His Excellency with an expression of mingled determination and dismay.

'Sahib, it is By-law 13,' he said.

'By-law 13? Oh, no tie. No tie. Yes, of course.'

His Excellency turned to Ghote.

'Frightfully sorry, old chap,' he said. 'Never took in that you weren't wearing a tie. And, of course, no one's allowed in the Club dining room in European dress without one. But don't despair. Just hold on a tick.'

He disappeared.

Ghote stood just outside the dining room staring in at its dark wainscoted walls and the round tables dotted about. At which of them were the five suspects seated?

He did his best to ignore the blue-uniformed bearer who

did not seem altogether sure that he would make no further attempt to breach By-law 13. He tried, too, to dismiss the decidedly appetizing odours that floated through the open doors.

Luckily, His Excellency reappeared within a couple of minutes, carrying dangling in his hand a long silk tie, plain green in colour.

'Not much of a match for your shirt, I'm afraid,' he said. 'But it's the only one I've got that doesn't belong to some club or regiment you wouldn't be entitled to wear.'

'Thank you all the same,' Ghote confined himself to saying, as he wound the luxurious silk round the neck of his by no means expensive pink-checked cotton shirt.

Once he was properly attired the bearer stepped aside and with a salaam permitted them to enter.

'Ah,' His Excellency said in a low voice, 'I'm glad to see we've got a full complement, every single suspect present and correct. You'll be able to give them a good looking-over, and then when we've eaten I'll introduce you and you can chat to them. You remember what Hercule Poirot says about talk?'

'No,' Ghote said, unable to suppress a little swirl of resentment at once again hearing the name of Agatha Christie's detective. 'No, I am not at all remembering.'

'Oh yes, forgot you don't know the works. Have to see about that before the night's out. But what Poirot said is something like this: it is a profound belief of mine that if you can induce a person to talk to you for long enough, on any subject at all, sooner or later they give themselves away. Pretty clever, eh? Always remembered that.'

'But—But . . .'

Ghote decided to abandon objection to this curious method of detection. He was, after all, more or less under His Excellency's orders, however odd, or alarming, they were.

He buried himself in the menu card where, he saw, lamb cutlets jostled with vegetable curry and roly-poly pudding and apple crumble matched kheer and kulfi. But he found his appetite was not as sharp as he had thought. The prospect of parading round the dark, impressive room contriving conversations with members of this exclusive institution, whom he was also expected to regard as potential murderers, sat heavily on his stomach as if he had already consumed a monster helping of that roly-poly pudding.

'Well now,' His Excellency said, swiftly discarding his own menu and looking eagerly round the room, 'where shall I begin? Hm, yes. The couple over there in the corner. Maharajah of Pratapgadh and his Maharani, the second or third maharani, I believe.'

Ghote looked in the direction his host – and his Dr Watson – had indicated.

He saw a handsome, straight-nosed man of forty or so, slightly running to fat, dressed in a gold-buttoned blue blazer and wearing a tie which, from its combination of ugly stripes, could only be that of some exclusive sporting organization. A typical Rajput, he thought.

His wife, the second or third, was dressed in a deep blue silky blouse covered with a variety of gold chains and a pair of extremely tight white trousers. On her lap she was nursing a fluffy and dyspeptic-looking pekinese. The word 'voluptuous' came clicking into Ghote's mind.

'The Maharani?' he asked His Excellency. 'She is one of your five? There are ladies also staying in the Club?'

'Yes, yes. There's accommodation for married couples, and for single ladies. Which brings me to that person over there, Mrs Lucy Trayling, widow, long-time resident of Ooty, staying here temporarily owing to the illness of her ancient ayah, single servant she still has.'

Ghote looked at Mrs Trayling.

She was very much the British memsahib he remembered from his earliest boyhood, if a rather older version. She wore an aged tweed suit of an indeterminate browny-green colour. Iron grey hair straggled all round her head.

And a large handbag lay dumped on the table to one side of her, wide open and sprawlingly tilted. On her other side was an even larger knitting-bag made out of some thick, flowery material. A sturdy pair of needles stuck out from a ball of pale mauve wool at its crammed top.

A murderer, Ghote thought. Surely not. And yet, old women did commit murders sometimes. And Mrs Trayling looked wiry and strong enough, for all her age.

But the next candidate His Excellency presented for inspection seemed almost as unlikely.

'Now, two tables further along. Little fellow with his head stuck in that damn great book. Name of Godbole, some sort of academic. Not been here very long, about ten days. But in the Club all right on the night in question.'

Ghote dutifully turned his gaze in the direction indicated. He saw a small, spry, almost monkey-like man with a cap of wavy black hair and large hornrimmed spectacles perched on a hooked nose. A Maharashtrian brahmin by the look of him, coupled with that name. He was, as His Excellency had said, deeply absorbed in a large, leather-bound volume, almost crouching over it. As Ghote discreetly observed him, he picked up a strong ivory-bladed paperknife and slit apart two of the book's pages as yet unseen by any prying, curious eye. In front of him a vegetarian dish of phool gobi ki bhaji stood neglected.

Well, Ghote thought, surely one suspect who is hardly a suspect at all. An academic, a typical absent-minded professor type. And a new arrival. No, one of His Excellency's five at least could be dismissed out of hand.

A bearer at his elbow was murmuring something.

'What? What?'

'Sir, I am requesting: military or brahmin?'

A feeling of dazed bewilderment came over Ghote. Was the fellow asking him which was the most likely murderer of the billiards marker? The Maharajah, military descendant of a long line of warlike Rajput princes, or the stooping brahmin pedant?

'Means do you want the English menu or the Indian', His Excellency explained. 'Always use those terms here. Come from the British days, of course.'

'Oh. Oh, yes. Vegetarian. Er—brahmin. Yes, brahmin.'

'Very good, sahib.'

As soon as the bearer was out of earshot His Excellency leant forward and once more murmured in Ghote's ear.

'The big Moslem over there.'

Ghote turned, trying not to look as if he were doing so.

'Name of Habibullah, Mr Ali Akbar Habibullah. Been here in Ooty a year or more. Lives at the Club. Retired railways officer.'

Mr Habibullah looked like a balloon, as if at any moment, despite the roly-poly pudding he was already cheerfully tucking into – but why was he already eating the last course? – he might rise up and float gently away. Dressed in white, from the round lacy cap on his head to the elephant-sized muslin trousers on his legs, he certainly hardly had the air of the ex-official His Excellency had said he was. He looked indeed, with the stout ebony silver-headed walking stick leaning on the chair beside him, more like an Urdu poet, if of a more earthy nature than many – how he was enjoying that pudding – and it was hard to think of him too as any sort of killer.

Not that murderers could be detected by their physical appearance, Ghote thought. He had seen too many mild-looking men sent to Thana Gaol to be hanged on the second Thursday of the month to be in any doubt about that.

'Well, there you have them', His Excellency said. 'Five suspects.'

Ghote sat in silence. The bearer returned with bowls of celery soup, a dish apparently both military and brahmin. The bowls, which were smoothly thick and white, had on them, Ghote saw, the Ooty Club crest. They seemed to gleam with assurance.

'And you are certain, Your Excellency,' he asked, 'that

one of these five persons only must be the murderer of the said Pichu, billiard marker in this Club?'

'Ah, no, my dear fellow, you don't catch me out that way. Five suspects, yes. But not just one of them may have committed the murder. Agatha Christie's taught me better than that. Remember *Evil Under the Sun?* Two in combination, eh? Perhaps the two who seem least likely to have any connection between them? Mr Habibullah, retired officer of Indian Railways, who worked, if I remember rightly, in Cochin a good many miles from here, and, say, Mrs Trayling, who to my knowledge hasn't left Ooty since she and Brigadier Trayling retired here when he left the Indian Army? Or . . . Or, no, there's always *The Orient Express.*'

'Mr Habibullah has some connection with such a train?'

'Quite right, my dear fellow. Him and Mrs Trayling and the Maharajah and Maharani and little Godbole, all in it together, eh? It's a possibility. It's a possibility we shouldn't altogether neglect. But, assuming in this case there's just one solitary murderer, who are you going to point to now you've seen the field, my dear fellow?'

'I would not be pointing anywhere whatsoever,' Ghote managed to say at last.

'Quite right, quite right, old chap. The Great Detective never gives his thoughts away, not even to his Watson.'

But Ghote felt determined not to be prevented once more from saying what he had begun.

'Oh, that is not at all what I was meaning,' he declared. 'I was meaning that no detective would fasten upon any criminal without evidences.'

'Quite right, my dear chap. Quite right. Observation as well as logical deduction, eh? Right then, as soon as we've finished going the rounds here, we'll take a look-see at the billiard room.'

'That would be a very, very good idea,' Ghote said, thinking that actually setting eyes on the scene of the crime might even produce some evidence that was more than extraordinary ideas out of books.

'Yes,' His Excellency went on, 'and there you'll see what all the rest of us have missed, eh? The observance of trifles. What none of us thought was even significant.'

Ghote felt a new depression settle within him as if he, too, was eating the weighty plain boiled potatoes that accompanied His Excellency's military lamb cutlets.

But more immediate trouble was about to break over him.

They had been eating in silence for a while when His Excellency suddenly looked up.

'Habibullah,' he exclaimed.

'Mr Habibullah? You have thought of some circumstance that is telling against him?'

'No, no. No such luck, my dear fellow. Or not unless you think it's a sign of guilt sometimes to eat only the pudding.'

'Pudding? It is roly-poly, yes? That is some sign of guilt?'

'No, no. But it does mean that the chap is going to get up and wander away at any moment. Seen him do it times without number. Unpredictable, you know. Unpredictable. So it's up Guards and at 'em, eh?'

'You mean I should talk to him? Now?'

'That's the ticket, my dear chap. The Poirot technique. Look forward to seeing you at it.'

And His Excellency jumped up and plunged off in the direction of the table where, sure enough, the big Moslem was rising to his feet.

Ghote followed.

But what was he to say to this retired railways official? What exactly was it that was the profound belief of this Poirot fellow His Excellency kept bringing up to the fore? Talk for long enough on any subject and the suspect in question will let out some damning fact? Yes, but on what subject? And for how long?

He had hit on no answer before he found himself face to

face with the enormous, white-clad Moslem. His Excellency performed brief introductions.

'Mr Ghote,' he concluded cryptically, 'is here for a few days at my invitation.'

'Ah,' Mr Habibullah replied, a wide, dreamy smile appearing on his air-blown cheeks. 'I trust you will find Ooty as altogether pleasant as I do myself, Mr Ghote. It is, you know, pure unreality.'

'Unreality?' Ghote echoed, wondering where on earth a conversation that had started this oddly would go.

'Yes, yes. You must already have noticed as much, in however brief a time you have been with us. It is England here, my dear sir. England, is it not? And we are, or so we suppose, in India. There's unreality for you. Delightful, disconcerting unreality.'

'Well, yes,' Ghote cautiously agreed. 'I am noticing many things that seem most English. So, yes, there must be some unreality. Yes. I am quite able to see what you are meaning.'

The balloon-like Moslem's eyes lit up.

'You are? My dear sir, a fellow soul. This is a happy chance. A happy chance in a world that often seems to me altogether too much regulated, too much ordered.'

He beamed at Ghote.

And Ghote, whose belief on the whole was just the opposite, did not have the heart not to smile agreement.

Besides, he needed to keep the Poirot conversation going.

'I am supposing,' he ventured, 'that it was your daily tasks that gave you this feeling? You were working, I understand, for the railways.'

'Indeed it was, my dear sir. Indeed it was. You know, it was I, I myself and no other, who was responsible when I was in Delhi for framing the chapter on "Disallowances and Objections" in the handbook known as *Indian Railway Administration and Finance*?'

'No,' Ghote said, 'I was not knowing. May I offer

congratulations? It must have been a most comprehensive undertaking.'

'No, sir, no. Congratulations are not proper. Commiseration would be much more gratefully received. Sir, such order, such regulation, such devising of rules: it warped my life. Absolutely. Indeed, it was only the thought that the majority of those rules were destined to be consistently ignored and regularly flouted that saved me at times from a suicide's grave.'

'Yes, I am seeing that,' Ghote replied, unable to think of any way at all, subtle or not, of moving the conversation nearer to the murder in the Club's billiard room.

He could, he thought, have mentioned how his own life was ruled for the most part by attempting to see that the Indian Penal Code with all its sections and sub-sections was strictly adhered to. He could have added that this often could be managed only by discreetly ignoring the equally strict provisions of the Criminal Procedure Code. But His Excellency, by the way he had carefully omitted to mention that the guest he had brought to Ooty was a detective, had put that out of court.

'A friend, a sympathetic soul,' the balloony Moslem intoned.

Well, Ghote thought, at least I have put myself on good terms with the fellow. With this suspect. But so far he has in no way betrayed himself as any sort of murderer. So what next? What more to say?

'Any family?' he shot out at last, aware that too long a pause had already occurred. 'That is—That is, you are having your family members here with you in Ooty also?'

'Oh, no, no, my dear sir. I had children. Yes. Three. Perhaps four. Let us say four sons. But they went their ways. To tell the truth, I found the duties of a father somewhat too much. After long days striving to regulate the comings and goings of the altogether unregulatable passengers of Indian Railways I was not able to face regulating the comings and goings of my sons. So they went. Yes, they went. I do not know where.'

Ghote felt more than a little puzzled. Could any father be so lacking in responsibility? Was Mr Habibullah really so? Or was this some blown-about fantastical joke? And again he wondered how, how, could a conversation which had taken such a turn be continued?

He swallowed.

'And Habibullah Begum?' he inquired. 'She is here?'

'No, no, my good friend. A wife who insisted endlessly in the house on a place for everything and everything in its place? No, no. Once I was freed of my chains in the railways I stood before her and pronounced *Talaq, talaq, talaq.*'

'Divorce? Moslem divorce?' Ghote stammered out, wondering more and more whether what he was hearing could be true.

'My dear sir, the only possible course. Away with all cares. Away with all chains. And then, Ooty. Magical, unreal Ooty. Oh, you cannot tell how greatly I enjoy my life here.'

Enjoyments of Ooty, enjoyments of Ooty, Ghote thought. What to say about them? Golf. There was golf. And tennis? Walking also? And was there not a big, big Flower Show? And horse racing in the season? What was there to ask about the enjoyments of Ooty?

But he need not have racked his brains.

With a sudden doubly beaming smile the big Moslem had somehow stepped aside and was now propelling himself out of the room with his heavy, silver-topped stick.

Ghote gave an anxious glance at his Watson and here in Ooty, his boss. But he was spared criticism of his performance as a Poirot.

'Always the same,' His Excellency said with a shrug. 'Start talking to the fellow about something really interesting, detective stories or something, and what happens?

Bang in the middle he just drifts off. Extraordinary. Extraordinary.'

Extraordinary enough, Ghote thought. Perhaps altogether too extraordinary. So, was what the fellow had been saying – his mind began to race – was it all a show? Had it been done to convey a feeling to all and sundry of complete irresponsibility, just in order to conceal the committing of a well-planned deadly act?

Perhaps, after all, he himself was not such a bad Poirot. Only there were four more such conversations awaiting him.

4

It soon proved, however, that the time for further Hercule Poirot conversations had not yet come. While Ghote was working apprehensively through a large plate of creamy rice kheer and His Excellency was putting away a noble piece of apple crumble a youngish man dressed in a neat, tight-buttoned European suit, complete with tie, his face with its trim moustache partly concealed by a pair of large dartingly shiny spectacles, came into the room.

'Ah, Iyer,' His Excellency at once barked out. 'Word with you, if you please.'

He leant confidentially towards Ghote.

'The Efficient Baxter,' he said. 'Ooty version.'

'Please?'

'Ha, don't know your P. G. Wodehouse any more than your Agatha Christie, eh? We shall have to see to your education. Efficient Baxter, secretary fellow in the great man's works. Iyer's just like him, always poking his nose in everywhere. Club nearly lost a damn good cook once because of him totting up supplies in the kitchens.'

'Ah, yes, I am understanding,' Ghote said.

And then the Efficient Baxter was with them, gleaming spectacles brightly inquiring, hands washing and washing themselves in an overwhelming desire to see something done down to the last detail plus a little extra.

'Iyer,' His Excellency said, 'my friend, Mr Ghote here, would like to become a temporary Member. He's up in Ooty for a few days. On holiday. On holiday, you understand. Nerves a bit out of order. Taking a break. Recommendation, as you might say, of Dr Moore Agar, of Harley Street.'

He turned to Ghote with a covert wink.

'I make no doubt you at least know your Sherlock Holmes,' he murmured. 'Adventure of the Devil's Foot, if I'm not mistaken. Holmes sent off to Cornwall to avoid a complete breakdown from overwork.'

Ghote smiled, palely.

'Ah, yes, yes, Temporary Member,' Mr Iyer said, redoubling the speed with which he was washing his hands. 'I will fetch the necessary form immediately, and see it posted up on the notice-board for full scrutiny by existing Members before tomorrow dawns. Yes, yes, before tomorrow is in any way dawning.'

And he darted away.

Ghote turned to His Excellency.

'Sir,' he said, 'I am noting that you are telling all and sundry I am here as a person recovering from illness only. But, sir, if I am to investigate into the murder of the man Pichu I do not at all want that.'

'Eh? Not want it? But it won't do to let the murderer know the Great Detective is on his track. Or her track.'

'Oh, but, yes, sir. In so far as I am this person it would be altogether better if the miscreant is knowing there is someone besides Inspector Meenakshisundaram investigating. Then he would no longer be laughing in his sleeves all the time but would perhaps make some move that would show him up for what he is.'

'By Jove, you're right, of course,' His Excellency said, looking, to Ghote's secret pleasure, somewhat abashed. 'Damn silly of me. Exactly what Poirot said in the Mrs

McGinty case. Flush the murderer out, eh? But then you and Poirot are two of a kind, aren't you?'

Ghote's secret pleasure evaporated.

But he was saved from pursuing the subject by the speedy return of Mr Iyer, flourishing a Form of Application for Temporary Membership.

It took some time to get it filled in, largely because of Mr Iyer's excess of zeal.

But the long-drawn-out business gave Ghote the opportunity of making a quiet assessment of the Club's assistant secretary. He was, he thought, a type he knew: the painfully over-conscientious type, which would possibly make him an extremely useful witnesss.

So when at last the form was complete down to the last comma he put out a hand and detained him.

'One moment,' he said. 'His Excellency has referred to Mr Sherlock Holmes and the matter of a devil's foot, a story in which that most notable detective was sent off to recover from some sort of nervous illness. I suppose, however, that this was a case he was also investigating into and solving with uttermost brilliance.'

'It was indeed,' His Excellency put in.

Ghote looked steadily at the Efficient Baxter, waiting to see if his point had sunk in.

'So perhaps,' he added, 'it would not be much of surprise to you if I myself am asking questions about the murder of one Pichu, billiards marker at this Club.'

But it did seem to surprise Mr Iyer, despite Ghote's carefully planted warning.

He started back from the table as if he had dropped the soap from his ever-washing hands and it had landed on his toe.

'But—' he said. 'But—But I was understanding that Pichu was done to death by a dacoit only. That is what Inspector Meenakshisundaram was saying. But—But is it that now it is suspected that some person—Some person in the Club is the culprit? That it is a Member even?'

'You are very much astonished at such a possibility?'

'But no one is becoming even a Temporary Member without the recommendation of one who is already a Member.'

Ghote put on a smile of heavy cynicism.

'Perhaps,' he said, 'such is not invariable guarantee of always first-class behaviour?'

Mr Iyer swallowed.

'Perhaps you are correct, sir,' he said in a voice so low it was almost a whisper.

A look of swift calculation came on to his face. Ghote imagined that his machine-like mind was running through the total list of the Ootacamund Club membership.

'So,' he said, 'tell me, Mr Iyer, can you think of any circumstance whatsoever, that is in any way unusual, concerning any Club member who was sleeping in these premises during the night in which Pichu was killed?'

The look of calculation on the assistant secretary's face settled suddenly as if the whirring wheels in his head had locked together in one particular combination.

'Well?' Ghote said sharply.

Mr Iyer bent forward even more over their table.

'I was reading article in *The Hindu* newspaper about one year back,' he said.

'Yes?'

Mr Iyer gave a strangulated cough.

'Yes, Mr Iyer?' Ghote said.

'Well, I am not at all knowing if it is in any way relevant to the matter under discussion.'

'You are bound to tell,' Ghote said.

Mr Iyer swallowed. Once.

'It was a case of smuggling,' he stuttered. 'The smuggling of drugs. In Cochin. There was a consignment of catfish, most strongly smelling, as you no doubt know. But, thanks to an informer, the Cochin police were able to raid that place and discover rupees three crore worth of heroin concealed therein. Only . . .'

He gave another strangulated cough.

'Only the mastermind of the whole affair was absconding under the MISA,' he said.

'MISA?' His Excellency interrupted. 'Never can remember what that is. See it often enough in the damn newspapers.'

'It is Maintenance of Internal Security Act,' Ghote explained, furious at the loss of impetus in his questioning.

'And the said absconder,' Mr Iyer mercifully went on, 'was described as being a Moslem gentleman of considerable size and weight.'

His hands, which had twisted and turned as he had come out with his story, now dropped to his sides.

'That is all?' Ghote asked.

'Yes. No.'

'No? What more is there?'

'It is that Pichu, the late Pichu, had always to my feeling too much of money for one in such lowly occupation. He was the possessor of one transistor radio of great power wherewith he was able to obtain Test match commentaries from foreign. And I myself was constrained to show him certain favours to be able to listen also.'

'I see,' Ghote said.

So, he thought, perhaps His Excellency has more weight to his case than I was believing. It seems altogether likely now that Pichu's behaviour is stinking of a blackmailer, and had been such for possibly many years.

'There is one thing more,' Mr Iyer whispered, bending yet closer.

'Well, you are bound to state whatever you are knowing to fullest extent.'

'It is drink. Pichu was frequently partaking of spirituous liquors. Perhaps from some illicit source in the Bazaar, perhaps even from one of the Club bars.'

'Good God,' said His Excellency.

'I was never able to obtain one hundred per cent proof,' Mr Iyer went on, 'or otherwise it would have been a question of instant dismissal. But I had my most strong suspicions. Every night that I was in a position to do so I have smelt alcohol on that fellow's lips when he was retiring to his sleeping place.'

'That is finally all now?' Ghote asked.

'That is everything.'

'Very good. You have done well to say what you were knowing. Very well.'

The assistant secretary smiled, bowed, gave one last quick wash to his hands and left them.

'Well,' His Excellency said, 'Habibullah arriving about a year ago; that drugs affair taking place at much the same time; the fellow, the mastermind, escaping; and Pichu here needing money for drink I suppose, and confirmed as a blackmailer. It all adds up, you know. It certainly all adds up.'

He gave Ghote a look of quick admiration.

'Had a small bet with myself,' he said, 'That you'd have the whole thing wrapped up within twenty-four hours, Ghote, but I never thought—'

'But,' Ghote broke in firmly, 'a police officer is never proceeding on allegations only without checking the veracity of same.'

'Quite right, my dear fellow. Quite right. And what steps do you propose by way of doing that?'

'I shall talk with Inspector Meenakshisundaram in the morning,' Ghote replied.

His Excellency blinked.

'Meenakshisundaram? That tomfool? My dear chap, I don't think—'

'But, yes, it is necessary. And, besides, it is my bounden duty when I am in his territory.'

His Excellency pulled a long face.

'Well, I suppose you're right,' he said. 'So you won't want to go talking to the others who were on the list now, will you?'

'No,' Ghote said, trying to contain his relief.

And then, almost without willing it, he added something.

'But what I would be liking to do,' he said, 'is to examine scene of the crime itself.'

'The billiard room?'

'Yes, the billiard room.'

'The observance of trifles, eh?' His Excellency said. 'The final nails in the case? I look forward to seeing a Great Detective at work on that. Yes, indeed.'

Ghote cursed his own over-conscientiousness. It had occurred to him that if Inspector Meenakshisundaram had really been completely fixed on the crime being the work of a dacoit, he might have overlooked some useful piece of confirmatory evidence in the billiard room. But he had not at all counted on having to give a demonstration of observing trifles, whatever that implied.

Sullenly he followed His Excellency out. He had a fleeting impression of dark walls with animal heads hanging from them, of pictures everywhere, pale views of Ooty and group photographs of cheerfully grinning white faces, or of hunting scenes with Englishmen dressed in red coats happily falling off horses. And then they were at the door of the billiard room.

There His Excellency paused.

'Wait for the stroke,' he said, repeating the words of a warning notice fixed to the wide door.

He bent forward and peered through a small glass inset panel.

'Yes, all right.'

He opened the door and preceded Ghote into the room.

It was totally unoccupied.

There was just one table, its bare, once brilliant green baize noticeably faded under the light pouring down on it from a long fringed shade. Round the walls more animal heads looked down on the silent scene, great horned bison and a score of other lesser creatures brought down by the guns of white sahibs long ago. There were pictures here, too, mostly scenes commemorating feats of arms in distant days and very distant places.

Stepping further in, Ghote saw 'The Battle of Tel el Kabir', 'The Defence of Rorke's Drift', 'The Charge of the Light Brigade'.

'Yes,' said His Excellency, catching him peering at this last in which all the blood and mess of long ago had been turned into a never-changing scene of military glory. 'Yes, some pretty historic things in here one way and another. You know that it was in this very room, on this very billiard table, that the rules of Snooker were finally hammered out, to be passed on through the years and over the world for ever?'

'No,' Ghote said. 'No, I was not at all knowing.'

'Yes, yes. It was here, on this self-same spot, that one Lieutenant Neville Chamberlain, later as Sir Neville to be Prime Minister of Great Britain, the man who tried to stem the tide of war by coming to an agreement with Hitler at Munich, it was here that he named his version of a primitive game called Black Pool as Snooker.'

He seized Ghote by the arm, swept away by enthusiasm. 'Come over here. It's all written up and framed.'

Ghote found himself propelled towards the long cue-rack – two of the cues in it were broken and others bent – where His Excellency read out for his benefit Sir Neville's account of the historic moment.

' "One of our party failed to hole a coloured ball close to a corner pocket, and I called out to him 'Why, you're a regular snooker'." You see, my dear chap, at the Royal Military Academy in England first-year cadets were called snookers. It all fits in.'

'Most interesting,' Ghote said.

The lack of interest in his voice apparently did not impinge on His Excellency.

'I tell you what, old chap,' he said. 'You must play a few shots on the table here and now. Just so that you can say you've actually put cue to ball on the very table on which Snooker was invented. Tell your grandchildren.'

Ghote, though he had no doubts about acquitting himself with a billiard cue, since an eye for a ball was one of the gifts he had been luckily endowed with from birth, prickled violently at His Excellency's suggestion.

It seemed to him to be all a part of an attitude of airy frivolity which he had had hints of already. It went with looking on murder, not as the killing of a living person, but as a reason for writing concocted tales.

'No, excuse me, sir,' he said firmly. 'As of today's date I am investigating a most serious crime.'

'Quite right, quite right, my dear fellow,' His Excellency somewhat unexpectedly replied. 'No doubt the secret of your success. Unremitting concentration, what?'

Ghote turned away and looked at the billiard table, as bare and monumentally still as when he had first seen it.

'And the body of the marker, Pichu, was at the exact centre?' he asked.

'Saw it with my own eyes, before they took the poor fellow away. Lying there on his back, stab wound in his chest, little patch of blood on his white jacket. In the very centre of the table. He can't have been put there for any other reason than the murderer, so to speak, saying "He deserved to die." It's a case of revenge against a blackmailer all right, take my word for it.'

'But how was it that Pichu was in this room in the middle of the night only?'

'Ah, forgot to explain that. Simple really. You see, he slept in here.'

'In here?'

Ghote looked round. There were certainly the benches from which in past days no doubt groups of eager sahibs had watched thrilling games. There were some comfortable wicker chairs, too, if now dry and broken here and there. Near him there was even a sturdier affair in dark wood, with on it a brass plate recording that it had been presented in the year 1875 by Captain Winterbotham of the Madras Sappers. Pichu could have slept in moderate ease on any of them.

'But you were telling that the Club has quarters for all servants,' he said. 'That none of them could have had access to the scene of the crime.'

'Quite right, my dear fellow. Can see there's nothing much gets past you. Ha. But Pichu was an exception to the rule. Slept in here to guard the Club trophies. Had done for countless years. Lay down on the shelf in front of that cupboard there where they were kept. You can see where the murderer forced the doors to make it look like a dacoity and deceive that idiot, Inspector Meenakshisundaram.'

'These silver trophies were most valuable?' Ghote asked.

'Well, my dear fellow, they did have a certain value, yes. But that wasn't why old Pichu slept here to guard them.'

Ghote felt puzzled.

'Not because of the value of those objects?'

'No, no. Or only because of their sentimental value. You see, some of them had the names of competition winners engraved on them, on little silver shields, you know, going back a hundred years or more.'

'They were rolling trophies?'

'Yes, yes. You kept the one you won for six months or so, and then it came back to the Club to be contested for again. Some historic names on some of them, you know. Major Jago, for one, after whom the Jago Room here's named. Lots of others.'

'Major Jago?'

'You haven't heard of Major Bob Jago?'

For a moment His Excellency looked as if he was beginning to doubt the brilliance of the man whose skills he had used all his influence to acquire, and Ghote felt a tiny leap of relief. But the moment did not last long.

'Well, suppose a chap from Bombay side might not know

about Jago,' His Excellency conceded. 'Was Master of the Nilgiri Hounds. One of the great hunting men of all time.'

He threw back his head and broke into a curious sort of chanting. Ghote realized, just in time, that it was verse.

'Oh, it's jolly to hunt with the Nilgiri pack, Major Bob with the horn and a straight-going jack.'

'Please,' Ghote said, after a properly reverent pause, 'what is a straight-going jack?'

'Oh, a jackal, old boy. Jackal. Can't hunt the fox here, you know. But hill jackal's always made a pretty good substitute. Not like his brother of the plains, nothing sneaky about your hill jackal.'

Ghote did not feel he had any comment to make.

His Excellency grunted.

'Not that there's all that much hunting nowadays,' he said. 'Not with the factories they've put up on the Downs, and nobody much with the money either except a few Army wallahs from the barracks over at Wellington.'

He sighed deeply for a past that had gone, days of leisured regularity and ordered existence.

Ghote, anxious to get down to some proper police work, moved away from him and went to the window which, from its still empty panes, must have been the one the thief had broken. Or the one that had been broken in order to lay a false trail.

He looked hard at the damaged area. But all the remaining pieces of glass had been removed and every trace of any splinters swept up. Nothing to be gained.

He then moved on to the cupboard from which the trophy with Major Jago's famous name on it and the others had been taken.

'If you want to grasp the real sentimental value of what's gone,' His Excellency said, joining him, 'you ought to talk to old Bell. His name's been on a trophy ever since he won the snooker contest back in the early fifties, though that was in a damn poor year actually.'

A gleam of gossipy malice lit up his leathery features.

'Yes,' he went on, 'lot of chaps still away after the war then. Why, I don't suppose anybody even saw his triumph right through to the last frame. And old Ringer's never put cue to ball since. Daren't, I suppose.'

But Ghote was busy examining the ravaged cupboard. Would it be possible to tell whether any damage had been caused by a real dacoit, or by some amateur imitator?

It was a sturdily-built piece with glass doors on its top section and a broader bottom half forming a wide shelf. Certainly it was clear that the top doors had been recently levered apart. The wood round the lock was splintered and still light-coloured and fresh. It looked, too, as if some sharp, pointed instrument had been used.

But, again, it was impossible to tell whether the harm had been done by a determined thief or an ingenious faker.

But could it really be true, Ghote thought, that the theft had been a subterfuge only? After all, despite what His Excellency had said, silver was actually valuable. It was by no means unlikely that some local dacoit would have heard of the rich haul to be made here: if firewood looters could steal a whole tree, then trophies at the Club could no longer be considered safe.

And His Excellency's theory, looked at in a calm light, was surely too fantastic. To murder an old man for some reason and afterwards to break open the cupboard of trophies, pretend to force the window and take away all the silver cups and bowls just to make it look like a killing in the course of a dacoity. Really, there was too much of elaboration there.

So could it be – the idea slipped traitorously into his head – could it be that His Excellency simply wanted there to be a mystery here at the Club? A mystery for a Great Detective to come and solve?

'You can see the grease mark where old Pichu laid his head,' His Excellency said abruptly, causing Ghote to give a little jump of surprise. 'No amount of polish will ever remove that, I dare say.'

Ghote, recovering, turned to face him.

'The cupboard is cleaned every day?' he asked.

'Oh, yes, definitely. The Club still keeps up its standards, you know. Damn great army of sweeper women come up from the lower town at crack of dawn each day.'

'Then there will not be much of clues remaining.'

'Well, no. No. Dare say not.'

Then His Excellency's face brightened again.

'But it's the psychology we've got to rely on here,' he said. 'Unless of course, you yourself have already noticed something the significance of which has escaped everybody else?'

Ghote turned to his wistful companion and looked him straight in the eye.

'As you have said yourself, sahib,' he replied. 'The Great Detective is never giving away his thoughts. Not even to such a person as you were calling his Watson.'

5

For half a second His Excellency had looked disconcerted at such a sign of rebellion from the Sherlock Holmes that, Watson though he was, he had had summoned here to solve the mystery. A tiny flush of anger had begun to come up on his leathery cheeks. But it was quickly suppressed.

'Well,' he said mildly, 'that seems to be about all then, for the time being. I dare say you're tired, Inspector. Travel and all that.'

Ghote, though well knowing that an excuse was being made for barely acceptable behaviour, realized that he was in fact extremely tired. Worn out. Being a Great Detective was decidedly a strain.

'Yes,' he said, 'I would very much like to sleep early.'

But he did not get to bed in the enormous room he had been allocated – the contents of his suitcase were ridiculously put to shame by the two huge almirahs he distributed them between – before he had admitted at a knock on the door a salaaming servant saying 'Hot-water bag, sahib' and had watched that object being carefully placed in the wide, white-sheeted, blanket-covered bed.

Nor did he finally secure peace and privacy without being presented by His Excellency with a copy of Agatha Christie's *Mrs McGinty's Dead.*

'Thought this would be best for you to begin on,' the old man said. 'Poirot in top form for one thing, and then there's a remarkable similarity to the present business. In both, you see, the vital question is: what was the weapon that was used?'

Ghote had almost replied that here in Ooty there was no question at all about what the murder weapon was. In all probability it would be whatever the dacoit who had broken in and stabbed Pichu had happened to be carrying. But he was too exhausted to risk venturing into a dispute.

'Weapon?' he said simply.

'Yes, old man, the sharp instrument. As opposed to blunt instrument, ha. That fool Meenakshisundaram kept going on about the crime having been committed with a sword. Had to say that, of course, just to back up his absurd notion of a dacoit being responsible.'

Ghote smothered the groan that rose up inside him.

'But I prefer,' His Excellency went bouncing on, 'to think of that weapon simply as a sharp instrument. A sharp instrument of as yet some undetermined sort. Something that the murderer had to have immediate access to, and could equally hide away rapidly once it had been cleaned of blood.'

To this Ghote was too tired to do more than offer a temporizing reply.

'Then tomorrow it would be most important to look into the matter.'

And he had ushered His Excellency out, clambered up into the big, blanket-covered bed and, with a grimace, opened *Mrs McGinty's Dead*. But he was able to get through only its first two pages before, his head filled with Hercule Poirot's lamenting the lack of order and method in the world, sleep welled up over him.

The next thing he knew he was being wakened by a soft-footed servant bringing him – wholly unaccustomed luxury – bed-tea. And it was not any thoughts about what unlikely weapon might possibly have been used to kill the Club billiards marker that came into his mind then but the simple necessity of seeing as soon as he could Inspector Meenakshisundaram, local representative of the rough simplicities of everyday police work. A few hard facts from a fellow professional might well send all His Excellency's speculations sky-high.

The earliness of the hour, and the chance of consuming an enormous English breakfast, a little delayed the consultation. But before long Ghote set off for the Urban Police Station, fortified by a steaming bowl of porridge (peculiar, and darkly reminiscent of a fact learnt at detective school, that it was the only substance in which white arsenic could be concealed), followed by fishcakes (less peculiar and scarcely needing the Dipy's Tomato Ketchup thoughtfully provided) and a large rack of freshly made toast, served with thick marmalade from somewhere in the UK called Dundee (demolished in its entirety).

The Police Station, another British-looking building not far from the ornate and impressive Collector's Office, had each of the pitched roofs of its three sections studded by a high round window set in solid white stone. They seemed to Ghote, as he stood outside gathering himself together, like three watchful benelovent eyes looking out over the calm and quiet order of the town around.

Would Inspector Meenakshisundaram in his office behind one of them be somehow equally Ooty-like and British-patterned? Not, of course, a British police officer of the old days, but a true Indian successor, reserved, just, dignified?

Two minutes later he found out.

Meenakshisundaram, seated at a table in front of the Crime Board found in all police stations, with its disposition table of *Personnel Available, Personnel on Casual Leave, Personnel on Annual Leave, Vehicles Available, Vehicles Under Repair, Dogs Available, Dogs in Kennels*, all carefully enumerated, proved to be a big, sprawling man running noticeably to fat.

And an enthusiastic greeter.

'Wah, a Bombaywallah. It is good to see. You boys up there know how to run things.'

Ghote wagged his head deprecatingly.

'Oh, I have heard the stories,' Meenakshisundaram boomed, throwing himself back in his heavy chair. 'Hand-outs and hafta on a super-class scale. A son to educate, a daughter to get married, and what trouble is it to you fellows? Money from above is seeing to it in one minute only. Colour TV right from the beginning. Video also. Foreign liquor like buffalo milk only to you fellows.'

'No,' Ghote exploded. 'No, no, I am telling you.'

'Oh, with me there is no need to hide, man. I am doing all right myself. But it is the opportunities that you have I am envying. All those criminals needing to keep you sweet, and all the money-punny in Bombay. Crime capital of India, isn't that what they are calling?'

'Well, criminals we have I am not denying. And, yes, bribes are offered and bribes are taken also, that again I am not denying. But officers who will not take are there. That also I am stating.'

Inspector Meenakshisundaram gave a rich laugh.

'Well, well,' he said, 'it is taking all sorts to make one world, that is the old British saying, isn't it? But you, I am sure, Inspector, you are not standing back when there are chances put at your feet.'

Ghote's immediate reaction was hotly to deny the specific suggestion. But at once it occurred to him that he needed to be on friendly terms with this fellow. He needed to find out man to man, with nothing held back or concealed, the full strength of the dacoity explanation of the murder. He would hardly succeed in doing that if Meenakshisundaram regarded him with contempt.

So he wagged his head ambiguously once more and produced a little smile which he hoped looked somehow sly.

'But tell me, man,' he said quickly before the subject of

bribes and bribe-taking could go any further, 'what is this I am hearing that the murder in the Ooty Club was not at all a dacoity?'

Meenakshisundaram gave a deep belly laugh.

'You have been talking-palking to that Surinder Mehta fellow, I see,' he said. 'Crackpot-whackpot if ever I saw. He was telling, isn't it, that the billiards wallah was victim of blackmail attempt that was coming unstuck? That one of those sahibs at the Club is secret-weekret murderer? I ask you, man, what more of nonsense could be there?'

'Yes, certainly that is sounding a nonsense story,' Ghote said tactfully. 'And you have good evidences for dacoity, Inspector?'

'Evidences-shevidences in plenty. Look, man. You have, Number One, a window forced. Then, Number Two, cupboard doors forced. Number Three, one lot of silver cups and what-all missing. So, that fellow gets himself killed while all this is happening? What could be more likely?'

But on this last point Ghote had reservations. Pichu had been a very old man. Despite his nights of sleeping across the cupboard doors, it was not very likely that he would have put up a strong fight to preserve the Club silver. But, even if he had stood between this dacoit of Meenakshisundaram's and the loot, surely one good blow to the head would have dealt with him. Murder by stabbing was not the most likely outcome, by any means.

'Mr Mehta was telling,' he said, sounding as casual as he could, 'that you were stating the victim was killed with a sword. Any confirmation from the post-mortem?'

'Post-mortem, piss-partem,' Meenakshisundaram replied cheerfully. 'The fellow was dead-dead, isn't it? What for would I go through all that business? He had been stabbed-stabbed. I am not needing some damned medico to tell me that.'

Ghote took this in.

'Tell me, man,' he said, 'is there a name you can be

putting to this dacoit? Are you hoping to nab the fellow shortly?'

'Name-shame. What does one name matter? There are ten-twelve I could be pulling in if I am wanting. Fifteen-sixteen.'

'So you don't expect to make an arrest straightaway?'

Meenakshisundaram shrugged.

'Oh, if things are getting too hot I can pick up some fellow in one jiffy. And be beating confession out of him in jiffies two.'

Ghote thought then that he had learnt enough for the time being. He turned the talk back to less contentious matters, even going so far as to imply that he owed his own refrigerator to a slice of someone's black money. But at length he ventured on a cautious approach to the matter of the particularly fat Moslem said to be absconding under the MISA following the big heroin raid in Cochin.

'I suppose you were not having anything to do with that business, Inspector?' he asked.

'How I am wishing I was,' Meenakshisundaram replied. 'That Moslem fellow who was absconding, he must have paid and paid to be knowing in advance what was coming.'

'No doubt. No doubt. And where is he now? Are there any gossips on that?'

'Oh, yes, plenty-plenty. He is seen in Madras every day. So they are saying.'

Ghote wondered how much reliance was to be placed on that. But he decided there was nothing to be gained from any further probing and asked instead where in Ooty he could get the good warm pullover he had realized, walking to the police station with his breath pluming out in the chill morning air, that he would certainly need if his stay was to last any longer.

Then, noting with scrupulously false care the exact location of the pavement hawker in the Bazaar who, Meenakshisundaram had claimed, would hand over in fear and trembling a first-class pullover at the mere mention of his own name, he left.

He did not, however, make his way straight back to the Ootacamund Club, scene of the crime.

He felt he had too much to think about.

So he wandered about the town and its outskirts, gratefully warm in the thick green jersey he had begun by obtaining in Chellaram's department store from among all the souvenirs waylaying tourists there. He had thought of buying one of the bracelets made by the original inhabitants of the area, the Toda tribe, as a gift for his wife. But somehow he suspected he would not relish the idea in the years to come of being reminded too vividly of Ooty: paradise Ooty, hell Ooty.

So he strode about among the other striding inhabitants of the Ooty of old, in their well-dubbined walking shoes, their flourished walking sticks, their tartan scarves and their obedient, heel-trailing dogs. And he thought.

Every now and again the beating of his mind up against the dilemma which, more than ever since his meeting with Meenakshisundaram, confronted him would be halted by some unusual sight. The name of one of the neat little houses that reminded him, with their tiny turrets or decorative boarding or windows criss-crossed with diamond panes of pictures of faraway Britain: Iris Cottage, Rosemead, Hillside, Apple Cottage. Or there was 'Rembrandt and Vandyke, Photographers', with sepia portraits of British officers of long ago stiffly at attention in elaborate uniforms, their ladies beside them almost as military in long ballgowns.

A post-box stopped him once and sent him into a long transfixed reverie. Startlingly different from Bombay's squat, tinny, domed affairs with their dangling padlocks, it stood sturdy and upright, a tall iron pillar painted scarlet and topped by a little iron pineapple and with even, yes, a British crown raised up from the ironwork of its door still visible beneath the layers of painting and repainting over the years. Under it, only just to be made out, were the initials VR. Queen Victoria, Empress of India, she they must denote. He thought of all the decades of quiet peace and order there had been as mail had been confidently despatched to all parts of the world through the box's rain-protected mouth.

But less pleasant ideas forced themselves back into his consciousness all too quickly. The body in the billiard room. And the two explanations he had been given for its presence there.

And, however hard he thought, he could not contrive to come to any conclusion about them.

Certainly His Excellency showed every sign of having concocted his detective-story theory simply to please himself in his irresponsible old age. But on the other hand it clearly looked as if Meenakshisundaram was not the diligent investigator he ought to be. Far from it. So what was more likely than that he had jumped to the easy conclusion which the mere outer signs indicated?

Neither explanation was wholly satisfactory. But neither was wholly to be dismissed. And each was plainly contradictory of the other.

They could not, they could not possibly, both be right. Yet which was? Which was?

6

Ghote sighed. It was plain that no amount of solitary walking and hammering thought was going to produce a solution to his dilemma. There was nothing for it, after all, but to go back to the Club, meet His Excellency and tell him as little as he could of Inspector Meenakshisundaram's beliefs.

In fact, he encountered the ex-ambassador well before reaching the Club. He heard his name called out and looked up to see his unwished for partner, clutching a book on his way to the Nilgiri Library, just by the deep veranda and dark, rich interior of Spencer's Stores.

'Ah, Ghote. Something given you furiously to think, as old Poirot says?'

Something had, Ghote reflected sourly. But he was damned if he was going to say what it was.

'No, no, Your Excellency,' he answered, stammering slightly. 'It is that I was taking some time to look over this spot of Ooty.'

'Hah, lie of the land, eh? Feeling the atmosphere? Suppose you read that bit near the beginning of *Mrs McGinty's Dead* last night where Poirot says it was a case for once where it was not the voice of the silent dead that interested him, since the victim was only a charwoman, but the personality of the murderer himself. Just as here where we've got a servant as the victim.'

His Excellency looked at Ghote, head cocked to one side in birdlike expectation. Ghote said nothing.

'So,' His Excellency asked at last, 'you learn anything about any Moslem absconders from the plodder Meenakshisundaram?'

'Yes, sir, I did,' Ghote answered, twisting the strict truth, with a small jet of pleasurable spite. 'There is one thing I am able to tell you. Inspector Meenakshisundaram is stating that the Moslem person wanted under the MISA has been reported sighted in Madras.'

His Excellency looked gratifyingly disconcerted.

'So not our friend in disguise after all,' he said. 'Well, well.'

Then at once he became a great deal more cheerful.

'So, all to play for still, eh?' he said. 'All five of them still possible.'

'Perhaps you should be saying now four,' Ghote said, disliking the cheerfulness. 'Four only.'

'Oh, no, old chap. We all know about the one who's cleared in the early stages, don't we?'

'Please?'

'Always means that everything is not as it seems about whatever it was that cleared him, doesn't it? So I don't think we can regard our friend Habibullah as being altogether out of play. No, indeed.'

'Ah,' Ghote said, light breaking in, 'it is detective-story books you are referring?'

'Well, yes, I suppose it is.'

But His Excellency's embarrassment lasted only for an instant.

'But, you see, old man,' he said, 'this business is a detective story. A detective story come to life. Never thought I'd live to see it, but there it is. Perfect situation. Body on the billiard table, weapon missing, false trail laid and seven suspects. Well, no, five actually. But amounts to much the same thing.'

'Yes,' said Inspector Ghote.

'And,' His Excellency added with relish, 'you brought in, eh? India's answer to Hercule Poirot.'

'Well, but—'

'And, by Jove, here's a chance to see you in action. Look who's going into Spencer's.'

Ghote turned, with a sinking of dismay, towards the dim interior of the big grocery shop. He saw, just disappearing into it, a wiry tweed-clad back which he recognized, chiefly from the iron-grey hair escaping in every direction from a stout green cotton waterproof hat, as that of Mrs Lucy Trayling.

'Yes,' His Excellency said, 'Lucy must be going back to live at her house and needing supplies. That ancient ayah of hers will be on her feet again no doubt. If you ask me, Lucy's only waiting for the old thing to pop off before she goes home.'

'But if—If her ayah is popping off,' Ghote said, once more bewildered, 'would not Mrs Trayling be staying in the Club?'

'Ah, no, my dear fellow. By home I mean Home. England. From all I hear Lucy wants nothing more than to go back Home, though I think she's in for a pretty nasty shock when she gets there. England isn't like it was in the Christie books any more, you know.'

'But Trayling Memsahib is staying on, staying on in Ooty, because of her very aged ayah?' Ghote asked, pricked by a dart of curiosity.

'That's what I hear. You see, when old Spot, her terrier, had to be put down a few months ago she did nothing about getting another dog. Significant, what? No, I tell you what it is. Lucy feels she can't let an old servant down, not when she's been with the family ever since the Traylings had that boy of theirs. See her point, of course, more or less, though Lucy's a damn sight more loyal than most of us would be. But that's the British for you.'

'Oh, yes,' said Ghote politely.

If Mrs Trayling, barely possible though it seemed, was a suspect as the wielder of the 'sharp instrument' that had ended Pichu's life, it did not appear to be very likely that the coming death of her ancient ayah, or the recent popping off of her dog, Spot, had anything to do with it.

'Yes,' His Excellency went on, warming to his gossip in true Ooty style, 'damn loyal woman, Lucy. Loyal to that frightful husband of hers through thick and thin. Thick and thin.'

'Brigadier Trayling was a frightful person?' Ghote inquired, scenting the faintest possibility of something not quite as it should have been.

'Well, mustn't speak ill of the dead,' His Excellency said, 'but it was common knowledge that Roly Trayling was knocking it back to a fearful extent in his latter days.'

'The knocking back of alcoholic liquors?'

'Whisky,' said His Excellency. 'Indian whisky, most of the time. Cheaper than Scotch as a deadener, and poor old Roly seemed to feel the need for a deadener more and more. Didn't like Ooty life as a permanent thing, you see. That was the trouble. Had been an active man. Army. Commanding troops. Field exercises. Spot of real war from time to time. And then he ends up here. And what's there for him to do? Take the dog for walks, come to the Club and see the same damn people every night, go to the Culture Circle on the last Saturday in each month and listen to some damn talk about art or something. Well, you can see how he came to his sticky end. And, of course, the fellow didn't care for detective stories, unlike Lucy who's almost as keen as I am. And she had the Flower Show, too. Her pelargoniums won year after year.'

'The Brigadier was coming to some sticky end?' Ghote asked sharply, cutting through the floral reminiscence.

'Well, suppose that's not quite the word, sticky end. He

fell in the Lake one night, actually. On his way home from the Club. Drunk as a coot, of course.'

'That is certain.'

'Oh, yes. Bar steward gave evidence at the inquest, and so did old Pichu, come to that. Saw the poor chap staggering along by the Lake. And there was the medical evidence. Full to the gills, full to the gills. Still, that's all keeping us from the matter in hand, eh?'

'What matter is that, please?' Ghote asked.

'Why, stepping into Spencer's and talking to Lucy Trayling, of course. Thought that was what this was all about. The old Poirot technique, get 'em talking and something comes out. Something comes out, eh?'

And, seizing Ghote firmly by the arm, the ex-ambassador strode off towards the wide veranda of Spencer's Stores.

Apprehensive thoughts ran round and round in Ghote's head like so many garishly painted horses on a wooden roundabout at a mela. He had succeeded in talking with Mr Habibullah, for a short while, and he had even found what was said had given him grounds for some vague suspicions. But what was he to talk about to this British memsahib? Her dead dog? Her dying ayah? The amount her dead husband had drunk?

He had a fleeting impression of a clutter of people and objects on the shop's wide veranda under the ornate ironwork brackets. There was a blackboard with prices chalked on it, a wide-smiling boy with a big, leaf-fringed basket of bright strawberries, a sign saying *Dogs Not Allowed*, a monster thermometer four feet high advertising Stephen's Ink, a squatting man clutching a small aluminium case and looking sly as a pickpocket. And then they were inside and His Excellency was greeting Mrs Trayling in a voice that rang round the high interior of the shop with its long polished counter dotted with pairs of bright brass scales and attended by a row of assiduous clerks.

And a moment later Mrs Lucy Trayling was thrusting out a hand to be shaken.

'Saw you at dinner at the Club last night,' she said. 'Any friend of Surinder Mehta's is a friend of mine.'

'Most pleased,' Ghote replied.

But he could think of nothing to add. What would Hercule Poirot have found to say in such circumstances, he asked himself.

'It is a very nice place you are having here in Ooty, no?' he brought out at last. 'I am greatly enjoying. Here you have very much of order and method.'

'Good of you to say so,' Mrs Trayling replied. ''Fraid I'm not much of a one for order and method myself. Or so my friends are always telling me. Aren't they, Surinder?'

His Excellency laughed, roguishly.

'Yes, yes,' he said. 'We are always telling Lucy she's left something or other behind. Or dropped something. Or she's telling us there's something she's forgotten.'

Then another thought came to Ghote, and he began to wonder whether he might not after all possess something of Hercule Poirot's art of making conversation flow.

'But His Excellency was telling that you are thinking of going to Home,' he said. 'And after all leaving Ooty.'

'Well,' Lucy Trayling answered, 'Ooty's going to hell, you know. I mean, just look at what they sell in this place nowadays. Beach balls. Beach balls, big, vulgar, plastic beach balls in Spencer's Stores. Beach balls and nasty little aluminium picnic chairs.'

Ghote looked.

And, yes, putting into the shade the bottles of Rose's Lime Juice and the tins of Scottish shortbread on the shelves behind the counter was a high-piled display on the floor of big, brightly coloured beach balls. Perhaps Ooty had begun to go to hell, or at least become just another holiday playground.

His Excellency seemed to think so as well. He joined in now to denounce aspect after aspect of life in the town in the past few years, the huge factory on the outskirts making film stock for the torrential production of song-and-dance spectaculars from the Bombay and Madras studios, the new houses and high-rise blocks being built with no consideration for the traditional British-looking Ooty style of architecture, the people from what he called 'the weaker sections' setting up hovel homes in the public streets.

Ghote listened, thankful that the burden of talking for long enough on any subject at all had been taken up by someone else. But nothing of any significance seemed to be being said. Not the least sign of anything bearing even remotely on the Club billiard room and the corpse that had desecrated its historic table. Soon his mind slipped away to thinking once more about what he had learnt from Inspector Meenakshisundaram and whether, despite the Tamil's deplorable attitude, his account of the crime might not be, more or less, what had actually happened.

But then a development in the talk caught his ear.

'Yes,' Mrs Trayling had said, 'and there's that Maharani of Pratapgadh's. She certainly would never have been allowed in the Club in the old days.'

'Extraordinary woman,' His Excellency agreed, if without thoroughgoing conviction.

Ghote thought that here at last was something useful, even if it was not revealing anything about Mrs Trayling. But it seemed as if His Excellency was throwing the chance away. Well, if Watson was not up to seizing it, then the Indian Hercule Poirot was.

'Please,' he said, thrusting himself in. 'Please, why for would Her Highness the Maharani of Pratapgadh be not allowed upon Club premises in days of old?'

Mrs Trayling gave him a sharp look.

'Hm,' she answered, 'less said about that the better, I think.'

'Well, yes,' His Excellency added, traitorously aligning himself with his own suspect. 'No talk about ladies in the smoking room, you know.'

'But, please, we are not at all in smoking room. And I

am asking, why is the Maharani a person who would not have been welcomed?'

Mrs Trayling gave him a look now that was quite clearly disapproving, and turning to the patiently waiting clerk at the counter resumed giving her order in a particularly loud and emphatic manner.

After a moment Ghote took advantage of her firmly turned back to whisper urgently to His Excellency.

'Sir, what is it that would stop the Maharani staying in the Club in old days? Sir, it is important to consider, no?'

His Excellency, who had become deeply interested in the display of brightly coloured picnic chairs, turned to him reluctantly.

'Dare say it is important in a way, old fellow,' he said. 'But, the truth is, I don't really know myself. Dare say old Lucy's picked up some gossip somewhere.'

Ghote came to a decision.

Abandoning His Excellency, he stepped outside onto the veranda and placed himself squarely in the path Mrs Trayling would have to take when she came out.

As soon as she appeared he challenged her.

'Mrs Trayling. Please, I am most interested in the Maharani of Pratapgadh. Would you kindly tell what it is you are knowing to her detriment?'

'Certainly not,' said Lucy Trayling.

And she swept past and marched down to the sunlit, bracingly chilly street below. To be followed a moment later by one of the counter clerks waving above his head the knitting-bag she had left in the shop. From it there fell with a tinkling jangle like a long glissando from some film hit-song a stout knitting needle. It rolled all the way down into the road where a band of urchins fell on it with cries of delight scenting baksheesh.

Ghote stood on the veranda next to the tall tin-backed thermometer with its alarming figures rising up to 150 degrees Fahrenheit and its bold lettering pointing to *Blood Heat* and *Fever Heat.* He felt such rage that he might almost have reached this last state himself. Rage against Mrs Trayling for her hinting and withdrawing, but more rage against himself for the way he had mismanaged the talk that should have produced revelations.

And then he felt a tugging at the sleeve of his new jersey.

He swung round in quick irritation. Beside him, down on the wooden floor of the veranda, he saw the sly-faced man he had half-noticed squatting there before, the man with the little aluminium case. He saw now that painted in shaky red letters on its side were the words *A.T. Ramamirtham Diseases of Dogs (All Kinds) Treated By Best Homeopathic Methods.*

The fellow was still plucking at his jersey.

'What is it you are wanting?' he said to him furiously. 'Are you thinking I am having a diseased dog?'

'No, no, sahib. It is to tell what you are wishing to know that I am wanting.'

'Are you a fortune-teller also? Such I am not needing. My fortune is too bad altogether.'

'Sahib, I bring you good luck only. It is about one diseased dog I am altogether curing by my methods that I would tell.'

'I am not interested in any dogs, cured or not cured, by your methods or any others.'

He pulled his arm from the fellow's grip and made for the steps down to the street.

'Sahib, not if it is the dog of the Maharani of Pratapgadh?'

Ghote turned in an instant. He looked quickly from side to side.

'If you have anything to tell,' he said, 'follow me till I find somewhere we would not be seen together.'

7

Glancing back to make sure the dubious dog doctor was following, Ghote made his way quickly down towards the Bazaar. He hoped that among the jumble of humanity there, which till now he had been aware of as little more than the sound of innumerable jangling bicycle bells, furiously tooting truck horns and the wail of music from countless conflicting sources, he could find a place of concealment. It would never do, he thought, for anyone from up at the Club to see the pair of them, Great Detective and wretched dog doctor, apparently, as the saying was, going together like dal and chapattis. A chance observer of that sort might gossip, and give his suspect an opportunity to cover any tracks.

He had hardly got down into the noisy clutter of the lower town when he saw what he wanted. Behind a huge hoarding painted with a film advertisement – over which someone had already plastered a bright yellow handbill – there was a conveniently hidden patch of ground.

He gave one more quick look behind, saw the man with the little aluminium case was within sight and stepped sharply into hiding.

In a minute his possible informant joined him.

'Well,' he asked him at once, 'what is it you have got to tell?'

'Sahib, I am a poor man. At this moment itself I should be giving one treatment to the dog of a guest of a most posh hotel.'

Ghote sighed, poked two fingers into the top pocket of his shirt and drew out a note, just far enough to see that it was an orange twenty-rupee one. He left it peeping out of the top of his new jersey.

The dog doctor promptly put on a face of woebegone disappointment.

'Not one paisa more,' Ghote said, already regretting he had not fished out something smaller.

The dog doctor gave a resigned shrug.

'Sahib,' he said, 'I was hearing what you were asking Trayling Memsahib. Trayling Memsahib went always to that Western-science vet they are having, so that her dog by the name of Spot was at once dying—'

'Dying of old age,' Ghote interrupted brutally. 'Now, what have you got to tell that Trayling Memsahib would not?'

'Sahib, it is this. You must go to Bengal Vegetarian Hotel. There you would see a certain person.'

'What person? That is not enough.'

Ghote made a pretence of stuffing the orange note back into his pocket.

'Sahib, he is called Mr Amul Dutt. He is coming all the way to Ooty, sahib, from Calcutta though he is student only and not at all rich.'

The dog doctor came to a halt, plainly hoping to have given enough to cause the twenty-rupee note to appear again.

'Go on,' said Ghote sharply.

'Sahib, you must be asking why he stays in such a third-class place. And also whose was one pekinese dog I was seeing him making unholy fuss over.'

Ghote pulled the note right out. In a flash the dog doctor's sly hand folded over it.

Ghote let the fellow go. He felt he had learnt enough. He would go at once to the Bengal Vegetarian Hotel, wherever it was, and see how true what he had been told might be. After that he could perhaps face seeing His Excellency once more.

Thank goodness, he thought, I have succeeded to leave him among those Scottish shortbreads and beach balls.

He stepped out from the shadow of the big hoarding – it was advertising, he saw now, a police story featuring a come-and-gone star called Sarla Kumar, a notorious flop picture in Bombay a year or more ago – and made his way further downhill. The Bengal Vegetarian Hotel sounded as if it was hardly likely to be up in old Ooty.

Sure enough, as soon as he began to make inquiries he was directed, not without one or two contrary pieces of advice, to a lane at the far end of the Bazaar.

He made his way along towards it, noting with momentary exasperation that the Tibetan refugees squatting there beside arrays of woollen garments were calling out prices about half the amount he had paid for his almost identical jersey.

Then as he made his way through the crowds clustered round stalls piled high with vegetables and fruit – he recognized the fine quality, Ooty quality, the fruits of paradise – he came to an abrupt halt.

At a banana stall, bargaining over a small, still greenish hand of fruit, there was an elderly, red-faced European wearing a faded sola topee against the bright sun and a tweed suit not unlike the one His Excellency had sported that morning, though plainly a great deal more threadbare. Slumped in a patient, panting heap at his feet was the most ancient of woolly-looking dogs.

Major Bell. He did not quite know why he was so certain that this must be the Ootacamund Club secretary. But he was certain. The man fitted the description His Excellency had given of him when he had first arrived, right down to the 'desperate old dog' that ought to have had its life mercifully ended.

Dasher, that was its name. A first-class joke now, however right once.

Then a cold sweat broke out over him. What if Dasher's master had seen him talking with that dog doctor? What if he had not had the good sense to hide behind that hoarding? A person like this Major Bell – if this was Major Bell – would be just the sort to go gossiping at the Club. Gossiping perhaps to the Maharani, whose pekinese had been seen in a hotel in this insalubrious quarter of the town.

What an escape.

He slipped behind a stall piled high with little pinkish potatoes, crept with head bent past another heaped with big orangey tomatoes and a third on which the stall-keeper, in a heroic attempt to impose a pattern upon disorder, had tirelessly arranged long curly pale green gourds so that their rounded ends placed together made a whole wall some three feet high.

Then he reckoned he was beyond the danger point.

He straightened up and made his way swiftly to where the consensus of opinion had stated the Bengal Vegetarian Hotel was to be found.

The consensus was right, though he missed the place at first, so unprepossessing was its appearance. It seemed to have been built not many years before, in the flat-roofed, square block style so frowned upon by His Excellency and Mrs Trayling. But, for all that it could not be very old, it was already shabby. Its white front was now stained with long greenish streaks and its cement outer coating had flaked away here and there in dark irregular patches. The V of 'Vegetarian' was missing from its once bold and colourful signboard and the rains and mists of Ooty had reduced the rest of it to something little more than a mere random pattern.

On the broken pavement outside a circle of young men squatted, happily playing cards. Beside them a knife-grinder had set up his apparatus constructed chiefly out of an old bicycle and was making the air around shriek each time he touched a blade against his whirring stone.

Ghote stepped into the building's constricted lobby.

Behind a counter on which the red plastic covering had become wavy as an ominously swelling sea, a little fat man wearing a dingy white kurta under a much-mended fairisle pullover sat slumped in a doze. His almost completely round face was the sepia colour typical of Bengal.

Ghote thought for a moment, then coughed loudly and went up to him.

'Good morning, do you have any accommodations?' he asked in English.

'Oh, yes, sir,' the fellow said, jolting awake and brightening rapidly by the moment. 'Most certainly, yes. Very, very good rooms, most spacious and modern. Highly respectable also. No hanky-pankies allowed. And in dining room very best Bengali cooking. Oh, you would enjoy, sir. Also my wife and three daughters are all the time singing most sweet Bengali songs. You are following Bengali?'

'Unfortunately not,' Ghote said. 'But, tell me, do you have many Bengali persons residing at the present time?'

'Oh, yes, sir, yes, yes. My rooms are full-full with happy guests from my distant native-place.'

'Ah,' Ghote said, seizing on this way out of the consequence of his first pretended inquiry, 'then you are not having any rooms available after all?'

'My dear sir, no, no, no. Exactly the opposite. You would have best room in all hotel, with bathroom attached. Almost with bathroom attached. We have just only one person staying at this exact moment, and he is not at all a first-class guest. He is having our cheapest room only.'

'Oh, yes? And may I ask his name? I have a young Bengali friend who spoke of coming to Ooty, and I am sure that if he is here he would stay at this hotel.'

The fat little proprietor rubbed his hands together.

'Then you will stay also?' he said. 'Perhaps you would like your friend, Mr Amul Dutt, to be having a better room next to your own, sharing same bathroom, and not much of extra cost?'

'Perhaps, perhaps,' Ghote answered.

Then, leaning forward across the wavy red counter, he gave the proprietor of the no hanky-panky hotel a broad wink.

'Tell me,' he said, 'is my friend seeing that lady he was hoping would come, very modern, very beautiful, somewhat more old?'

The proprietor returned his wink.

'Oh, sir, that is occurring. From time to time, yes, that is occurring. A most posh lady with one very fine pekinese dog. You are having similar arrangement also?'

For a moment Ghote wondered whether, in the interests of his investigation, he had got himself in deeper than he had counted on. Then inspiration came.

'So,' he said, 'my friend Mr Dass is most happy here.'

'Oh, yes, sir, yes. Mr Dutt is very, very happy to be in my beautiful, first-class, altogether vegetarian and pure hotel. You would be also. Please, what is your good name?'

He began hauling a battered register from beneath the time-warped counter.

But Ghote was ready for him.

'Dutt?' he said. 'Dutt? Did you say Mr Dutt?'

'Yes, your good friend, Mr Amul Dutt.'

'But the name of my friend is Mr Amar Dass. You were altogether hearing wrong. I must look for him elsewhere. Yes, yes, elsewhere definitely.'

And, rather more hurriedly than was perhaps dignified, he made his way out into the noisy street.

The scream of the knife-grinder's wheel sounded loud in his ears, but he endured it happily. He had, at last, discovered a fact that might well prove a step towards solving the mystery of the death of the old billiards marker.

If Pichu truly had had a taste for blackmail, and from the evidence of Mr Iyer it seemed that His Excellency's bald assertion earlier had some substance to it, then what was more likely than that Pichu had somehow found out about the Maharani of Pratapgadh's secret love affair with a poor Bengali student in a third-class hotel and had threatened to tell the wealthy Maharajah? And that this had brought about his sudden demise on the billiard table?

Yes, now it would be possible to go to His Excellency with something worth telling. Perhaps now he could even bear to be hailed as a Great Detective, however much what he had learnt had been wormed out of a witness by the somewhat dubious methods ordinary detectives employed on occasion.

He set off with a light step to go back up to the Ooty of old.

The former ambassador, he remembered, had been carrying a book when he had met him outside Spencer's. No doubt he had been on his way to the Nilgiri Library. He would see if he could find him there.

He located the Library without difficulty, just past the shop of a Chinese shoemaker, a tall old building in brick with prominent white stone surrounds to its narrow windows that made him think of Bombay's older Christian churches. Inside, he was greeted by a fierce-looking lady wearing a coat draped over her sari against the sharp Ooty air, seated at a gleamingly polished wooden counter.

How different, he thought, from my last encounter at a reception desk. He felt a quiet burgeoning of contentment.

'Good morning, you are wanting for to join up to the Library? Fee is now Rupees 10, and you may borrow out books straightaway.'

He swallowed.

'I should very much like to be becoming a member,' he said. 'But I hope I will be in Ooty for a short time only. That is – That is, I am afraid that my stay here would not be for more than two-three days.'

'Then what is it you are wanting?'

'I – I am believing that His Excellency Mr Surinder Mehta is in this building, and I am wishing to communicate with him most urgently.'

He received at this a long severe look through the pince-nez spectacles the Library's guardian was wearing. But he seemed to pass the test.

'Yes, Mr Mehta is inside. You may go in. But kindly observe strict silence at all times.'

'Yes. Yes, very good. Thank you,' he whispered.

He crept in, pushed open with great caution a pair of double doors and found himself in a lofty chamber lit by five tall arched windows on each side and an even taller one at the far end. A picture of the Queen of England presided over the whole, only rivalled – he saw as he tiptoed further in – by the head of a large bear, rather ant-eaten, suspended over the entrance doors. Ancient glass-fronted cases of books ran along the walls and on round tables with green-shaded lamps there were laid, with scrupulous neatness, a few newspapers and magazines. A number of sadly sprawling armchairs added to the atmosphere of dilapidated comfort.

There were three people present. Two of them, men in tweedy suits, were talking to each other, in rather loud voices. The third, a girl in a deep-green muslin sari wearing a pair of huge-lensed spectacles, was standing beside one of the tables reading what looked like a newspaper from the UK.

But nowhere could he see His Excellency.

Then he spotted a small door at the far end. Tiptoeing still, though the sound of the two talkers' voices almost drowned the creak of his shoes, he made his way down the length of the room.

Yes, it was an English paper the girl with the big spectacles was reading. *The Sunday Times.* For a date at the end of November of the previous year, two full months ago.

Beyond the small door he found a flight of steep stairs

and mounting them step by careful step he came into the Library's upper storey. Here there were book stacks rising up to the ceiling containing, he saw, volumes on every subject under the sun. He even noticed a copy of the much-trusted *Criminal Investigation* by Dr Hans Gross, as adapted by John Adam MA, Crown and Public Prosecutor, Madras, and J. Collier Adam, Public Prosecutor, Madras, that he himself possessed. It stood between Alfred Swaine Taylor *On Poisons*, 1848, and a collection of famous British trials.

Then, rounding a stack towards the far end of the room, he saw His Excellency. He was sitting perched on a pair of tall library steps, plunged deep in a book.

Ghote went up to him.

'Mr Mehta. Sir. Your Excellency. I have made a discovery.'

His Excellency looked up from his book – it was another copy of *Mrs McGinty's Dead*, the one he had said was so much like this case itself – and at once put a finger to his lips.

Ghote felt an onrush of guilt. He had broken the rules. He had failed to observe silence. And His Excellency was justly rebuking him.

He wondered whether quietly murmuring 'Sorry, sir' would add to the offence or mitigate it.

But then he saw that His Excellency was jerking his thumb over his shoulder, past the bookstack in the direction of the end of the room.

He looked.

There was a portrait of Victoria, Empress of India. There were two enormous black leather armchairs like obediently crouching elephants. And, almost invisible in the gloom, sitting cross-legged on the further one of them not unlike the elephant's mahout, if a mahout could be absorbed in an immense leather-bound volume, was Professor Godbole, his broad-bladed paper-knife glinting whitely on the arm of the chair beside him.

Ghote understood. The professor, after all, was still one of His Excellency's list of suspects.

He leant down towards the ex-ambassador and spoke softly.

'Your Excellency, I have succeeded to discover that the Maharani of Pratapgadh is having secret rendezvous with a young Bengali student by the name of Mr Amul Dutt at a third-class hotel in the Bazaar. You are seeing the significance?'

His Excellency looked up. A beaming, joyous light shone in his eyes.

'I knew it,' he said in an echoingly loud voice. 'I knew it. No sooner does the Great Detective arrive than mysteries begin to be unravelled. Splendid, splendid.'

'Ah,' came a high-pitched voice from beneath the benevolent gaze of Victoria, Queen-Empress, 'the Great Detective. A most interesting phenomenon. And really of considerable importance.'

And Professor Godbole hopped down from his sprawling armchair and came over to them, grinning all over his monkey-like countenance.

'I did not have the pleasure of a formal introduction when I saw you in the Club dining room last night,' he said to Ghote. 'My name is Godbole, and I am by occupation a professor of English literature.'

He gave a sudden sharp sideways smile.

'Oh, yes, my dear sir,' he said, 'I am well aware that this makes me, so to speak, a character in a world-famed novel by the late Mr E. M. Forster. Such was my fate from my earliest years. A devotee of English literature in all its wayward glory, I wanted nothing more than the academic life and, indeed, a professorship to crown laborious days. So sooner or later I was bound to become Professor Godbole, a figment from a novel, and, worse now, a pasteboard representation in a cinematograph film.'

Ghote, washed over by this incomprehensible flood of

words, and half-suspecting that behind them lay some sort of joke, could do no more than murmur a reply.

'Most unfortunate. That is – most fortunate. I mean – But, in any case, I am most pleased to make your acquaintance.'

'And I to make yours,' the professor replied. 'The Great Detective himself. Oh, we have heard all about you, my dear sir. Word goes round, you know. Servants listen, and servants speak.'

'But – But I—'

His Excellency broke in.

'Exactly, my dear Professor,' he said, in a manner so heavy with threat that Ghote looked over at him in sharp surprise, until he recalled that the excitable little academic was still if only marginally one of the five marked-out suspects.

'Exactly. The Great Detective here to solve the mystery of the body in the billiard room.'

But if His Excellency had hoped by these tactics to bring a betraying look to the professor's face, he was altogether unsuccessful.

'Ah,' the little brahmin exclaimed, eyes bright, 'but more even than a solver of this particular mystery, my dear sir. The Great Detective is a mythical figure, no less. Yet, here he is, a living example in front of us.'

'A mythical figure?' Ghote blurted out, too astonished to keep silent. Who was he being labelled as now? Some personage out of the time-encrusted legends of the Mahabharata?

'Oh, a myth, yes, indeed,' Professor Godbole said to him. 'That is what you are, my dear sir, no doubt about that. You see, I am by way of being an authority on the subject of detective fiction. Some years ago, you know, I was misfortunate enough – or perhaps fortunate enough, who shall say? – to be given the task of supervising a student seeking the degree of PhD who had taken it into his head to make his thesis subject *The Detective Story in*

England from Conan Doyle to Peter Dickinson. A subject that would hardly have won the approval of the Board of Studies except that the candidate in question happened to be the nephew of none other than our Vice-Chancellor.'

He stopped abruptly and cocked an inquiring eye up at them both.

Ghote felt that no comment, however, was needed.

'Yes, you see,' Professor Godbole launched out again, 'the Great Detective, first adumbrated by that flawed genius, Mr Edgar Allan Poe, has become a figure known throughout the world, if only through the representations of the curving tobacco pipe and deerstalker headgear of his later avatar – if I may so put it – Mr Sherlock Holmes. His features appear, you know, at least once a month in advertisements in the Indian papers, the vernacular press almost equally with the English-language. And why is that? Because Holmes is a person, a super-person one might say, of a unique sort. He is a man able to combine at the highest level the intuitive powers of the poet with the powers of logical analysis of the mathematician. He unites in himself, to borrow from popular psychology, the thinking of the left-hand side of the brain, that is to say the part of the mass of grey matter—'

'Hah,' His Excellency interrupted the word flow with explosive force. 'Hah, the little grey cells of Hercule Poirot.'

But any such hastily thrown-up dam was instantly swept away.

' . . . that part of the brain which thinks logically, with the thinking of the part which makes the leaps of intuition of the poet, the right-hand brain.'

The professor did halt for a moment now, just time enough to give a quick smirk of self-satisfaction.

'The part of the brain which is most developed in my own case,' he added. 'The part that has produced some of the greatest discoveries of all, I may say, of the greatest poems. Now, you see, it is a person combining these sides to the utmost that Mr Poe put before us in the shape of the Great Detective, and after him Sir Arthur Conan Doyle and a whole tradition, as we may say, of lesser lights. Now you can see why this figure has gripped the imagination of the world. He, and he alone, putting himself into a state of trance, often induced by the inhalation of tobacco smoke – "Quite a three-pipe problem" Holmes is once made to exclaim – from a trance induced, then, often by an ounce of tobacco, the Great Detective produces at last that altogether startling answer to the apparently insoluble problem, what Mr Poe called "that which has never occured before".'

But the repeated word 'trance' had set off in Ghote's head a diverging train of thought. Dr K. S. Joshi, he recalled suddenly, I have altogether forgotten your *Yoga in Daily Life*. Ever since I was stepping out of that bus into the clear air of Ooty I have not given you one moment of attention.

Yet his instant resolution to amend the negligence petered into nothingness almost at once. What Professor Godbole had gone on to say caught his ear.

'I tell you, gentlemen, it is not just the power of thought that the Great Detective possesses. He is also capable of actually uncovering the mysteries put before him. He acts. He performs for us that which we all want to see done: to have uncovered, in the words of Mr Charles Dickens, "the naked truth without disguise".'

To act. To bring out the truth.

Ghote forced himself to concentrate with all his might on what the professor was saying. Was he himself not, at least in Ooty and according to His Excellency, just such a Great Detective? And was it not his bounden duty then to uncover that naked truth without disguise?

'The Great Detective,' Professor Godbole was torrenting on, 'puts himself, in order to perform this feat, wholly into the minds of others. We have, remember, Mr Sherlock Holmes disguising himself by plunging into the very personality of an assumed character, varying, as Dr

Watson is made to say, his very soul. We have Mr G. K. Chesterton's Father Brown declaring that he does not know who a murderer is until – I am quoting kindly note – "I have bent myself into the posture of his hunched and peering hatred." We have—'

But once again, His Excellency hurled himself into the turbulent flood.

'We have Miss Marple,' he almost shouted out, his aged fluting voice echoing round the book-stacked room. 'We have Miss Marple in her very last case, if I have it right, saying she actually feels ill when she finds herself in the shoes of the murderer.'

But a dark cloud of depression now filled Ghote's mind. How could he, just only a CID officer, do what these towering figures did? Get into the souls of murderers? Into their hunched and peering hatreds? Feel altogether ill by seeing who had committed a crime?

'But, no,' he broke in with abrupt rebellion, 'that is not the way offences under Section 302 of Indian Penal Code are dealt with. I myself have never acted like any Great Detective.'

Professor Godbole took a step backwards in something like astonishment.

'You have never acted as a Great Detective?' he repeated.

'No,' Ghote said simply, wishing that he could make the declaration bolder but intimidated a little in the presence of His Excellency.

Professor Godbole looked at him.

'Well then,' he said, 'it seems as if I have been casting such pearls as I have before—'

He checked himself.

'Well, before you two gentlemen, let me say.'

For a moment he looked almost abashed. Then he perked up.

'But I must be getting back to my work,' he said. 'The

demands of scholarship. A world I understand. Remote though it may seem. Good day to you.'

He turned, scuttled back to his battered elephant armchair, jumped on to it and immediately resumed his study of the large volume that had rested on his knees.

His Excellency took hold of Ghote by the arm and almost dragged him out on to the steep stairway.

'My dear chap,' he said, 'I suppose you must have had some good reason for issuing that denial. But Godbole was talking away, you know, and Poirot did say, after all, that talk will ultimately reveal all a man's secrets.'

Ghote felt simultaneously infuriated at having Hercule Poirot and his methods thrust in his face once more and disgraced by his failure to have triumphed in Poirot's way. He attempted to account for his action. 'But, sir, but, Your Excellency, nobody can be thinking truly that Professor Godbole is the murderer of Pichu. He had not been staying in the Club for long enough to become in any way whatsoever the subject of blackmail.'

Surprisingly His Excellency did not seem offended at this uncompromising removal of one name from his declared list of suspects.

'Ah, but, my dear fellow,' he said, 'you're forgetting.'

'What forgetting?'

'The Least Likely Person, old boy. Godbole's the perfect example.'

Ghote thought hard, but still felt baffled.

'The least likely person to have committed the murder, yes,' he said. 'That is what I am stating. Professor Godbole is altogether unlikely to have had anything to do with the matter.'

'Which, as you will recall,' His Excellency answered happily, 'is why, in the end, it may very well turn out that he is the murderer.'

8

Despite Ghote's renewed attempt to renounce the title thrust on to him, His Excellency's opinion of him seemed unchanged. It was, he said in a friendly manner, almost the tiffin hour and they ought to be getting along to the Club to eat, 'at the scene of the crime, eh? At the scene of the crime.'

So they walked together through the curious, English-looking town with its spacious shops and pretty, tin-roofed cottages to the little hill on which the Club stood, cool and white under the cheerful blue sky. Mercifully, His Excellency seemed temporarily to have run out of detective suggestions, and they parted outside Ghote's room with nothing more about the case having been said.

Entering the dining room as soon as the gong in the portico had boomed out, Ghote, this time properly dressed, saw there were more people present than on the previous evening. Evidently various Ooty inhabitants, Indian or aged English, took lunch there from time to time. Making a quick survey, he located under the numerous photographs of former Masters of the Ootacamund Hunt, thickly-moustached and rock-unshiftable on their huge horses, only three of His Excellency's suspects.

There was Mr Habibullah eating – curiously, already –

steamed ginger pudding with so much enjoyment that it seemed to radiate out from him in circle after circle. And there was the Maharajah of Pratapgadh with his Maharani. She was wearing trousers as brilliantly red as the post-box seen on his solitary walk following his meeting with Inspector Meenakshisundaram. The little dog on her lap, confirmation that it was she who had been the secret visitor to the Bengali student at that disreputable hotel, looked every bit as much in need of a homoeopathic purge as ever.

Mrs Trayling, he remembered, had returned to her own house now that her servant had recovered from her illness. How was that going to affect his investigation, he wondered. If it should turn out that she had been blackmailed by Pichu and had stabbed him to death because of it, little likely though that seemed, how was he going even to see her now? Let alone to question her?

And Professor Godbole, the even more unlikely candidate for all His Excellency's ideas about that making him somehow more likely, was evidently not in the dining-room because he was still studying whatever it was he had been reading in the Library.

He took a second quick glance at Mr Habibullah. Was he really no more than the retired railways officer he gave himself out to be? Or was he, just possibly, that absconding king-pin of the Cochin drugs-smuggling racket? After all, Meenakshisundaram's belief that the absconder had been sighted in Madras had been based on gossip only. And if he had been surely there would have been an arrest.

But he had no time to ponder further. His Excellency had come to join him, and as they went over to their table he murmured something in an undertone.

'Excuse me, I was not quite hearing.'

'I said: better not discuss anything here. Walls have ears, and all that.'

'Yes, yes, first-class decision,' Ghote answered, grateful for another respite.

But he did not have long in peace. Barely had he finished his stewed pears and custard (not very nice) when His Excellency whisked him off into 'Major Jago's Room'.

'Bound to have it to ourselves,' he said, 'when everybody's on ration in this damned dry Tamil Nadu of ours.'

'Yes,' said Ghote.

In the dark-panelled room with its rows of semi-forbidden bottles behind the bar they settled themselves underneath the glass case in which for ever Bob Jago's hunting whip, once so vigorously wielded, lay in calm repose.

'Well now,' His Excellency said, 'let's just see where we've got to.'

Ghote felt that this was hardly how a Watson should address a Holmes. But if he was not such . . .

'Yes,' he said.

'Hah. Well, Number One in my book at this moment is the Maharani. If you're right about her having an affair with some damned Bengali student somewhere down in the Bazaar, then she's got something to hide all right. And, pretty woman though she is, I wouldn't put it past her to stick a sharp instrument into old Pichu. There's a lot of weight there, you know, a lot of weight.'

Ghote, contemplating for a moment the well-filled trousers, pure white or startling red, wagged his head in agreement.

'But, trouble is,' His Excellency went on, 'just what was that confounded sharp instrument? I mean, if she did deal with Pichu, she probably did it at pretty short notice. So she would have had to have availed herself of whatever she could get hold of easily. So what was it? What was it, eh?'

He gave Ghote a look that seemed to combine uncomfortably acute inquiry with due respect.

Ghote scrabbled hard for some brilliant answer. But nothing came.

'Well, Your Excellency,' he said at last, 'it is always best in these matters to continue to suspect everyone.'

To his surprise His Excellency answered this feeble attempt with a sudden joyous smile.

'Quite right. Quite right. Just what I'd expect. Quotation for you. Not Poirot, but Poirot's occasional colleague, that very shrewd Superintendent Battle. Said something like this once: if you were to tell me that a dear old maiden lady, or an archbishop, or a schoolgirl was a dangerous criminal, I wouldn't say no. Hah.'

Ghote reflected that never in any of the cases that had come his way had an archbishop or any other top-ranking Christian holy-man been the malefactor. Nor had any old lady, nor even one single schoolgirl. But he thought it safest to let His Excellency's remark pass with merely a look of deep interest.

'Yes,' the ex-ambassador went on, 'I agree we mustn't lose sight of any of the others. I mean, there's the Maharajah. Fellow used to getting his own way, if ever there was one.'

'And perhaps,' Ghote suggested, happier now, 'such person would also somehow defy the law in order to obtain that own way. And thereby he would fall into the clutches of a blackmailer.'

'Exactly. High on the list, then. And Habibullah, mustn't forget him. I dare say he seems to have been cleared if what that fool Meenakshisundaram told you is right. But as I said before, clear a suspect early in the story and. . . . After all, blackmail doesn't have to be at the root of the business, you know.'

'It does not?' Ghote asked, trying hard to work out why his domineering Watson should seem to be reversing something he had so definitely stated earlier.

'No, no,' His Excellency said, 'it's a possibility I don't at all like to raise, but, you know, murder can be committed for the strangest of reasons. Or even none at all.'

'Well, yes, that is so,' Ghote agreed cautiously. 'In Bombay we have had cases of killers running mad.'

His Excellency pulled a long face.

'Not very satisfying,' he said. 'I mean, if there's going to be no logical reason for a murder, you can't hope to fathom out who's done it by purely logical steps.'

Ghote wanted to say that murder was seldom logical. But he did not think the observation would be well received.

'However,' he ventured, 'such things are sometimes happening.'

And if that was what had happened here in Ooty, he thought, if the business was caused only by one of the unpredictable twists of life, then it certainly was not an affair that merited summoning him all the way from Bombay.

But this, again, was a thought he felt it wiser not to share.

'A murder for no good reason, or out of mere malice,' His Excellency went on in a ruminative way. 'Habibullah might fit as a spur-of-the-moment murderer. It is possible, I suppose. Just about possible.'

Then visibly he shook the notion off.

'But, no. No, we can't think of it. It would spoil—That is, it is really most unlikely. Most unlikely, wouldn't you say?'

He looked at Ghote almost piteously.

And Ghote, though he resisted the pleading look, had in justice to agree that murder from such a cause was in fact unlikely indeed.

'So that is leaving from those on your list just Mrs Trayling,' he said. 'And you yourself were already stating that even dear old maiden ladies must fall under suspicion. I am supposing same would apply to ladies who are widows only?'

'Oh, yes, yes. No favouritism. Lucy Trayling was in the Club that night, and must stay on the list. And, do you know, I've just thought of something. A couple of months ago she tried to get Pichu sacked.'

'Given a sack? But why was that?'

'Well, it seems that ever since old Roly Trayling fell into

the Lake she's had some idea that Pichu, who saw it happen, might have saved the old boy. I don't know why she waited this long to do anything about it. Something to do with making up her mind to go Home perhaps. But try to get Pichu sacked she did. Only of course, old Ringer Bell wouldn't hear of it. Knew when the Club had got a good servant.'

'So you are thinking,' Ghote said, 'that Mrs Lucy Trayling was instead plunging some sharp instrument into the said Pichu?'

'Hit it in one, old boy. Question is again, though, what sharp instrument? That's what we—That's what you, Ghote, have got to concentrate on. The hidden sharp instrument. Something staring you in the face all along, just like that chopper thing in *Mrs McGinty's Dead.* Was recalling that only this morning. Poirot saw the chopper looking just like some oriental ornament, but when the time was ripe he fell into that sort of trance little Godbole was talking about and he connected it up straight away with the missing murder weapon. Marvellous.'

Ghote swallowed. Once again more was being expected of him than he felt he could produce.

But an answer came.

'When the time was ripe,' he quoted. 'And I am thinking the ripe time has not yet come.'

'Hah. Then what happens between then and now, eh? What does India's Poirot do next?'

For a longer moment Ghote was as stuck for a reply. But an answer came.

He rose smartly to his feet.

'I do not know what would be doing such a person,' he said. 'But the investigating police officer would do just only one thing.'

'And what's that?' His Excellency asked, looking startled.

'He would be conducting rigorous search of the quarter occupied by the suspected blackmailer with a view to finding evidences. I am correct, no, in thinking such procedure has not been carried out by Inspector Meenakshisundaram?'

'Well, no, old chap. Damned fellow was so stuck on his dacoity theory he just wasn't interested in anything else.'

However, for all Ghote's determination for once in this rarefied atmosphere to engage in a simple piece of investigation, he did not find it easy even to locate the quarter the dead billiards marker had occupied.

His Excellency, of course, had no idea where it was. He did not even know exactly where, among the Club's outbuildings, the servants' quarters were. And when, emerging from Major Jago's Room, they found Major Bell, red-faced and puffing, followed by his dog Dasher, thickly woolly and panting, he was able only to direct them vaguely in the right direction. He had, he said, no idea which of the quarters was Pichu's.

'Have to ask Iyer that,' he grunted, subsiding onto one of the blue and white sofas. 'Iyer deals with all that sort of thing. Makes a hell of a fuss about it, but does keep an eye on what's going on.'

He issued an enormous wheeze then, and they left in search of the Efficient Baxter.

Who made difficulties.

'Yes, yes, I have the keys to the billiards marker's allotted quarter. But I do not think I should permit access. It has yet to be subject of police inspection.'

'Hah,' His Excellency said. 'Just what Mr Ghote here thought. And all the more reason why we should get a look at it.'

'Yes, but, Your Excellency,' Mr Iyer answered, soaping his hands at top speed, 'I am not sure that you yourself examining the quarter would not be ultra vires.'

Ghote could stand the bureaucratic rigmarole no longer.

'Get me that key,' he snapped. 'At once. Or there will be a question of obstructing a public servant in the exercise of his duty.'

Whether it was because of his own bureaucratic jargon, or because of the sharpness of his tone, the reprimand had its effect. Mr Iyer scuttled away, to return almost immediately holding a large iron key. He then led them through the Club kitchens – Ghote caught a glimpse of that night's roly-poly pudding being placed in a huge metal contraption of ancient vintage labelled *No 6 Pudding Boiler* – and out to the servants' quarters. There Mr Iyer stiffly pointed to Pichu's door.

'Thank you, that would be all,' Ghote said firmly.

He waited until the Efficient, and inquisitive, Baxter had disappeared. Then he inserted the heavy key into the lock, turned it and pulled the door open.

Pichu's private territory was by no means extensive. It measured a little more than two metres each way. Its floor was bare stone, and its only furniture was some shelves on the far wall.

These, however, were not lacking in contents. Dominating everything there was the transistor radio Mr Iyer had spoken of with such envy, an expensive and formidable object well capable of receiving Test match commentaries from England or Australia. Ranged beside and below it there were tins and old boxes of every shape and size.

With a sigh Ghote went over to them, took down the first one in the top row, a carton that had contained Liril soap tablets, opened it and began examining the contents. Finding nothing of interest, he replaced the carton – *Liril Soap with the fresh tang of limes* – and took down the tin next in line. With the same result.

After he had been working with equal system for about a quarter of an hour His Excellency, who had been standing in the doorway watching, gave a little cough.

'Don't know how Dr Watson stood it,' he said. 'Somehow in the stories this sort of thing flips by in a flash.'

Ghote, cross-legged on the floor with the sixth box, *Quink Ink, 2 doz. bots.*, open in front of him, was going through the packets and packets of cigarettes it contained, enough to have provided Pichu with secret enjoyment for a long time to come. Nor were they the cheaper brands, let alone the leaf-rolled bidis a servant might be expected to smoke. Here instead were Charms, Panama Filters, Regent Kings.

He looked up.

'Please,' he said, doing his best to conceal his immediate feeling of relief, 'if you are having anything else you should be doing, kindly go. I will inform of any findings I may make. Be assured.'

'Well, I do have one or two things I should be seeing to.'

And Dr Watson, mercifully, wandered away.

Just at the moment that, from between two packets of Four Square Kings, there fell a greasy, much-stained visiting card. Ghote picked it up and gave it a quick glance. Then he looked at it more carefully, interest aroused. *Shri B. K. Biswas*, it read, *Proprietor Bengal Vegetarian Hotel, Ootacamund. Best Accommodations All Bathroom Attached.*

Thoughtfully he put it into his wallet.

But when at length he had completed his search he had discovered nothing more that was in any way significant.

Wearily he got to his feet and stretched.

The only thing for it now was to go back to His Excellency and tell him that the move had hardly advanced matters. There was the card belonging to the proprietor of the Bengal Vegetarian Hotel which seemed to show he had more of a connection with the Club than might have been expected. But it was difficult to see what line of progress that indicated.

So how would he look now in the eyes of the influential person who had specially summoned him to Ooty?

Perhaps some kudos could be gained from the factual confirmation he had gathered of Pichu's more than ordinary wealth. Some credit, too, could be had from pointing out how that visiting card indicated that the Maharani was definitely likely to have been a blackmail victim. But neither discovery was the sort of expected revelation of that 'something that had never occurred before'.

He took one last look round the little box-like quarter.

And an idea came to him.

Quickly he went over to the big shiny radio, lifted it from its place and turned it round. Yes, its plastic back was secured by large flat screws which could be undone with a coin. And there were pale scratches round them that indicated that this had been done more than once.

He dipped into his trouser pocket, found a big, wavy-edged ten-paisa piece, hoped it would do and set to work.

The screws yielded easily. The radio's back came away. And, stuffed inside, he saw a roll of shiny paper, evidently from some magazine.

He dropped down to the floor again and carefully spread the roll out.

It appeared to be a cutting from a film gossip magazine. A year or more old.

Sarla Kumar, star of the upcoming Prem Putla, has a new hero in her private, private life. Hero from the old, old days, almost British Raj. Yes, none other than a maharajah, and one who in youth (how long ago was that, Highness Pratapgadh?) was a real champion at the old sport of pig-sticking. And we predict that, wife, wives or no wives, the beauteous Sarla will have the chance to retire before Prem Putla hits the screens. Which, if all we hear is true, would be one good move.

Sarla Kumar. The name rang a bell. Yes, of course, *Prem Putla*, Love Doll, was the film that had been advertised on the front of that hoarding where he had had his twenty-rupee talk with the dog doctor.

And there was something more. Something teasing at the edge of his mind.

Got it.

On the painted hoarding someone had plastered a bright yellow handbill. And it had said – although at the time it had made no particular impression – *ToNite Sarla Kumar in Person Willingdon Talkies.*

So, Sarla Kumar, a star whose name had been very clearly linked to the Maharajah's, was in Ooty. And Pichu had thought it worthwhile to cut out that piece from that old magazine and, more, to hide it carefully away. If ever anything stank of a blackmail attempt this was it. Then the boot could, after all, be altogether on the other foot when it came to illicit love affairs. If the Maharani would want to keep from her husband her meetings with Mr Amul Dutt at the Bengal Vegetarian Hotel, equally he would surely want to hide Sarla Kumar from her. If she knew, as perhaps Pichu had, that his affair with the star of *Prem Putla* had been renewed, it would give her a very strong hold over him.

9

Reluctantly Ghote decided that before going to the Willingdon Talkies and seeing if he could discover where Sarla Kumar was to be found, by way of checking out what he had learnt, he had to report his discovery to his looming, inescapable Watson. He had promised him he would let him know the outcome of his search of Pichu's quarter, and he could hardly go back on that. Especially not to someone on whom his future career probably depended.

He found His Excellency sitting at ease in a long wicker chair out on the portico.

'Sir,' he said, endeavouring to put some excitement into his voice, 'I was most urgently looking for you.'

'Hah. A clue among all that stuff Pichu had collected up?'

'Yes, sir. I was discovering eventually, most carefully concealed, a cutting from a filmi gossip magazine wherein it was stated that the Maharajah of Pratapgadh was at one time having illicit affair with a certain star by the name of Sarla Kumar, a lady who is just only now in Ooty itself.'

'Ah ha. And the cutting was concealed no doubt in a whole batch from similar magazines?'

'Excuse me?' Ghote asked, again blankly puzzled.

'The purloined letter, old boy. Expect you penetrated the ruse just as the Chevalier Dupin did.'

Ghote decided that a straight question was the only way he was likely to make out what on earth His Excellency was talking about.

'Please, what letter is this?'

'The Edgar Allan Poe story, old fellow. You must remember it. Where your illustrious predecessor found the stolen letter which the best police detectives in Paris had not been able to locate because he guessed that it would have to be hidden in a letter-rack, the most obvious place.'

'Well, yes, sir. But, I am assuring, if I had been asked to find a certain letter, the first place I would be looking as a simple CID wallah would be any letter-rack.'

'Ah, no, no. I venture to suggest that you'd do that precisely because you're a Great Detective of today,' His Excellency said with unruffled cheerfulness.

Ghote, in a burst of inner fury, contemplated making off without further comment in the direction of the Willingdon Talkies and his possible lead to where Sarla Kumar might be found.

'And what did you deduce from this cutting about our princely friend and this – what was her name? – Sheela Kumar?' His Excellency went on.

'No, sir, it is Sarla Kumar. She was a famous film star for some months about one year past, and she was even making personal appearance last night at Willingdon Talkies.'

'Hah. And making personal appearance for Pratapgadh somewhere round about here, eh? That your thinking?'

'Yes, sir.'

'By Jove, you know I believe this is the best yet. Fellow like Pratapgadh might well go to considerable lengths to keep a business like this from his Maharani, and if Pichu stood in his way . . . Yes. Yes, it's strong, very strong.'

He came to an abrupt halt.

'Of course, though,' he added, 'a strong motive thrust

under one's nose often means the suspect is innocent after all. We all know that. But, still, this wasn't exactly thrust under our noses, was it? No, I think you're on to something, Ghote. And now's just the time to put it to the test.'

'Yes, Your Excellency, it is most necessary to check the veracity of any such lead. I was just on my way—'

'Now, it so happens I was chatting to Pratapgadh not ten minutes ago, and he told me he was off to play golf and was looking everywhere for a partner. Couldn't oblige him myself. Golfing days over, I fear. Anno domini, you know. But you could step into the breach, my dear fellow. First-rate opportunity for Poirot-style talk.'

'But—But—Please, I am not at all able—'

And at that moment there stepped out on to the portico the Maharajah of Pratapgadh himself, tall, boldly handsome, and just a little paunchy. His long golf-bag was slung carelessly over his shoulder.

'Ah, Pratapgadh, my dear chap, just found someone for you to play with.'

The Maharajah came strolling over.

'It is Mr Ghote here?' he asked. 'The Bombay detective we've all been hearing so much about. I'm not sure about playing against you, old boy. You might worm all my filthy secrets out of me as we go round.'

'If you are not wanting . . .' Ghote snatched at the excuse with more than a little eagerness.

But the Maharajah's eyes took on instantly an aggressive glint.

'No Pratapgadh ever refused a challenge.'

'Well, but I am afraid I am not having any golf clubs,' Ghote said.

'Never mind. Share mine. Only a friendly round, after all. Although it'll give me a slight advantage, eh? Unfamiliar clubs.'

The Maharajah laughed.

'Well, yes,' Ghote conceded dismally. 'You would have a most great advantage.'

'Then come along, old boy. Let's be on our way.'

And, almost before he had time to take it in, Ghote found himself sitting up beside the Maharajah in his jeep, careering out of the town and through the rolling hills and wooded valleys of the countryside.

'The course is out at Fingerpost,' the Maharajah shouted, as he swerved past a flock of sheep meandering along the narrow twisting road. 'Pretty well the best in India, you know.'

'Oh, yes?' Ghote shouted back.

Then they were there.

The Maharajah brought the jeep to a screeching halt outside the long, low, tin-roofed clubhouse building, jumped out, tossed his golf-bag to a little wizened man who had emerged from beside the building at the sound of the jeep's engine, and led the way out on to the course.

Ghote, following him, strove to remember anything he could about the game that he was on the point of playing. It was not much. He had seen golfers in action only once, on an occasion when he had been at the select Willingdon Club back in Bombay pursuing inquiries.

He felt a leaden lump of depression settle somewhere in his chest. And it was not lightened when he reminded himself that the actual object of this sudden diversion was, not to play this mysterious game, but to extract from the breezily confident Maharajah any additional evidence he could.

'Well, old boy,' his opponent said cheerfully, 'what handicap do you play to?'

'My handicap is that I am not at all acquainted with the game of golf,' Ghote replied, deciding that the truth was in any case bound to come out very soon.

But the Maharajah took the disclaimer as the funniest of jokes.

'I can see we shall get on,' he said, spluttering with laughter. 'I like a chap who can joke about serious subjects.

So let's play stroke for stroke, shall we, and see how we get on? I'll tee off.'

Ghote was relieved to find that this meant that the Maharajah would be the first to do whatever had to be done. He watched intently as his opponent, if such in golfing terms he was, went over to the wizened bag-carrier and took from a pocket in the bag's side a little, bright red plastic stick, pushed it into the fine turf at his feet and then balanced a white golfball in a cup at its head.

The little bag-carrier – was he what they called a cuddie? Or just a coolie? Or, no, a caddie? Yes, a caddie – removed from the deep bag a club with a leather pouch over its head. This he untied and then offered the club to the Maharajah. The Maharajah addressed himself with it to the poised ball. He wiggled his shoulders, changed his stance by a quarter-inch two or three times and at last took a whirling swing and sent the ball flying for some distance down the long swathe of cut grass stretching out in front of them.

'Your tee-off, old boy.'

Ghote swallowed.

The Maharajah handed him a ball and he placed it on the little red stand. Then the caddie offered him the club which the Maharajah had used. He took it and hastily, for fear of now exposing his total ignorance before there had been any time for the talking he knew he had to engage in, he went through a quick imitation of the shoulder wiggling and stance-shifting he had seen the Maharajah perform. Finally he swung the club high and brought it swishing down. He felt a smack of impact as its head came into contact with the heavy little white ball. A not unsatisfactory sensation.

'By God,' said the Maharajah, 'I can see I shall have to pull my socks up.'

Ghote looked down the length of crisp cut grass in front of him, dotted to either side with low dark-green bushes sprinkled with yellow flowers and a few tall spindly pale-trunked unfamiliar trees. The ball he had hit had travelled about half as far again as the Maharajah's.

'Away we go then,' the Maharajah said, rather grimly.

He set off at a wide-striding walk. Ghote, keeping up with some difficulty, decided that he must now begin the business of talking like Shri Poirot.

'It it that you are often coming to Ooty?' he ventured.

'Hm?'

'I am asking do you visit Ooty very, very often?'

'Hm? Oh, yes. Yes, I suppose I do. Family used to have a palace here, you know. In what they call Rajahs' Square. Good many princely families used to come in the season and had places there. Most of them shut up now, of course.'

Ghote began to feel that, despite his fluke shot with the golf club that had seemed to upset the Maharajah, he was now getting on to easy terms with him.

'And is it that you have many friends here?' he said, hoping that he was not being too hurried in leading the talk towards the possible presence somewhere in or near the town of Sarla Kumar.

'Hm?'

'Are there many friends of yours in Ooty now?'

The Maharajah stopped suddenly in his striding walk and turned to him.

'I say, old boy,' he said, 'do you mind not actually talking while we're playing. Spoils the concentration, you know.'

'Oh, yes. Not at all, not at all. I am sorry.'

Glumly Ghote walked on towards the little white specks of their two golfballs. And to think, he said to himself, that I have let myself in for this most curious ritual, when I have no idea at all of its proper rules and regulations, and all to no purpose.

They arrived at the Maharajah's ball. It was resting in a slight depression in the springy turf. From what he recalled of the game, Ghote expected the Maharajah to take another of his clubs from the deep bag under the weight of which their caddie had tramped along and with it hit the ball as near as he could to the pole with a little flag on it he could see in the distance.

But instead the Maharajah went and stood at a distance of a few feet and watched while the caddie, dumping the heavy bag down, picked the ball up, looked about and then placed it on top of a convenient tuft of grass from which, clearly, it would be a great deal easier to hit it effectively.

Perhaps, Ghote thought, his own vague understanding of the rules of this game was at fault. Or was it permitted to those of princely blood, however unrecognized elsewhere in republican India, to flout such rules at golf? Or perhaps there was a special rule here, up in paradise Ooty, that things could be made easier than they were elsewhere?

The Maharajah, after even more preliminaries than with his first shot, swung the new club the caddie had handed him, hit his ball off its tuffet and sent it to a spot just short of the circle of trimmer grass surrounding the pole and its flag.

They marched off again, in silence, to where Ghote's ball had finished its run. It, too, was lying in a depression in the springy turf, a rather deeper depression. Ghote wondered if the caddie would do the same kindness for himself as he had done for the Maharajah.

The wizened old man looked up at the Maharajah questioningly. The Maharajah gave an almost imperceptible shake of his head. The caddie dipped into the golf bag and handed Ghote in a pointed manner the club he was evidently to use on his half-sunken ball.

A small fire of resentment began to burn in Ghote's mind.

He gritted his teeth, stood astride beside the ball, swung the club back and, by dint of bending sharply at the knees and achieving a sort of scooping action, succeeded in making a fair-and-square hit.

He tried to keep any expression of triumph off his face

as he saw the ball land inside the circle of close-cut grass round the pole and trickle a foot or two onwards.

'Jolly good shot,' said the Maharajah.

Bitterly.

They walked on again to where the Maharajah's ball lay, and once more the caddie altered its position slightly before handing over a club.

The Maharajah's shot was better this time. His ball ran across the smooth grass surrounding the flag in its hole and looked as if it might even strike the pole and plop in.

In the event it came to a stop some six inches away.

'Jolly good shot, sir,' Ghote said, guessing that this was what was required of him.

'Not bad, not bad. Let's see what you make of your putt. Pretty long one, of course, twenty-five feet if it's an inch.'

They walked across to Ghote's ball. It was certainly twenty feet from the flag. The caddie handed him a club with a flat iron head to it. He supposed that it would be more efficient at sending a ball in a straight line across the very short grass.

The caddie went up to the flag in its hole and, after another quick glance at the Maharajah, removed it. Ghote now had some difficulty in making out exactly where the hole was. But he made up his mind he would do his best. He took a look along what he thought was the line his ball should go, gave it a firm tap with the club and watched the result.

The ball ran fair and true, slowed at its approach to the hole, almost came to a stop, reached the lip of the hole a little towards the right-hand side of it, teetered there for an instant and at last dropped in.

The Maharajah did not say 'Jolly good shot'.

Instead he picked up his own ball and muttered 'One up to you, then.'

Well, Ghote thought, if I am not a Great Detective perhaps I may turn out to be a Great Golfman.

They walked on to the next starting point, which Ghote suddenly remembered should be called a tee.

There, rather to his surprise, the caddie having taken out the club he had first used handed it not to the Maharajah but to himself.

Evidently this time he had to be the first to play. He tried to remember exactly what the Maharajah, and he in imitation, had done last time. But he realized he would never manage to get the whole ritual correct. Was it, he wondered, strictly necessary? He decided to leave it out, put his ball on the red peg, placed himself with legs astride beside it, swung the weighty club up once and brought it swishing down. Its head met the ball perched up on its peg with much the same satisfying thwack as before. But it seemed not to have quite as much effect. The ball ran well but nothing like as far as before.

'Oh, very good shot,' the Maharajah said.

Ghote thought he sounded secretly rather pleased.

The Maharajah then took his own stance. This time he shrugged his shoulders, flexed his wrists and altered the position of his feet even more than the time before. But with not much greater success. His ball went nearly as far as Ghote's, but it was well off the line and ended up in the longer grass at the side of the long clear swathe.

They marched off towards it – clearly silence was still to be observed – and after the caddie had lifted the ball out of the awkward longer grass the Maharajah managed to get in a shot that put it within easy reach of the green circle surrounding the second marker flag.

Ghote was uncertain whether to say 'Jolly good shot' or not. And by the time he had decided that perhaps it would be best to offer congratulations the moment seemed to have passed. The Maharajah had set off grimly in the direction of Ghote's ball, lying fair and square in the middle of the approach.

Ghote followed, took the club the caddie handed him,

looked over towards the flag, not too far off, and prepared to swing, with some confidence.

'Yes,' came the Maharajah's voice, in something like a sharp yelp from directly behind him. 'Yes, damned if I could find a partner at all when I asked about yesterday.'

The even swing Ghote had begun to impart to his club was not proof against the jerk to his nerves the interruption had caused. He struck the ball with sufficient vigour but appallingly crookedly. It rose too high in the air and took a path well away from the neatly clipped grass in front of him.

He resigned himself to defeat. But, to his awed delight, as the ball descended it struck one of the tall, pale-trunked trees dotted about, bounced off it at an angle and landed well on course for the flag, if still behind the Maharajah's ball.

'I say, I hope I didn't put you off by talking,' the Maharajah said. 'I didn't think you were going to take your shot so quickly.'

'No, no, not at all,' Ghote murmured.

'Still, bit of luck for you your ball hit that eucalyptus tree.'

'Yes.'

'So it's your shot again.'

'Ah, yes. Of course.'

Evidently then the player furthest from the hole always took the next shot. He was learning.

'Yes,' the Maharajah said, as if he was continuing the conversation he had begun so explosively at that highly inopportune moment, 'not a damn soul in the Club wanted to come out today when I asked around yesterday. Poor old Surinder Mehta's much too old, of course. And as for that fearful Moslem, Habibullah, I doubt if he's ever played golf in his life.'

'No,' Ghote answered bleakly, 'I do not suppose that he has.'

He wondered, too, whether, if talk was now permissible,

he should attempt to steer it round again to the subject of visitors to Ooty and whether the Maharajah was seeing any particular one of them.

But as they walked up to where his ball was lying the Maharajah stalked ahead, wrapped once more in silence. It was only when Ghote had been handed his next club and after looking to see where he should try and put his shot was placing himself to make it that his opponent took up once more the conversation he had abandoned.

'Even asked that fellow Iyer to play. Met him prowling about late at night – never rests that chap, often see him about in the small hours, can't understand it – and asked him if he was a golfer. He said he was . . .'

Ghote decided that yammer-yammer-yammer or not he would have to play his shot.

' . . . but when I put it to him that he could come out with me this morning he said he had his duties. I should have thought a club secretary's duty was to play with a member when asked, but there you have it . . .'

Ghote forced himself to shut out the voice and took his shot. To his joy he seemed to have hit the ball absolutely right. It rose up in a sweet parabola and landed within comfortable reach of the waiting flag.

'Good shot,' the Maharajah said, though he might have been saying 'Good God'.

They set off towards his own ball. Ghote gave a little cough. If chit-chat was suddenly allowable it must be kept up.

'But could you not find Major Bell to play with?' he asked. 'He would make a good partner I am thinking. He must be good at games when he was winning the snooker trophy, with his name on that cup that has been stolen.'

'Ringer Bell?' the Maharajah replied. 'My dear chap, he's more of a crock than old Mehta. He'd probably drop down dead when he took his first swing.'

Ghote was thinking furiously how to carry on the conversation when the Maharajah spoke again.

'And I'd really be obliged, old boy, if you didn't talk,' he said. 'I have asked you once.'

'Oh, yes, yes. Most sorry. Most sorry.'

Yet it seemed that his indiscretion had not too greatly upset his opponent. When he took his shot he succeeded in getting his ball on to the green almost as near the hole as Ghote's own.

'Looks as though I've got this for it,' he said. 'Or at least to halve it if you happen to sink your putt.'

'Yes,' Ghote ventured to reply, risking that much speech.

The Maharajah made a considerable fuss about making his stroke, even placing his club full-length on the ground to establish the right line between ball and hole. Or was it, Ghote wondered seeing him press the club hard down into the grass, here seemingly as smooth as the billiard table on which Pichu's body had lain, was it in order to make a little channel for the ball to run along?

But at last the Maharajah, after much wiggling and looking, did take the shot. His ball ran along the thin depression in the grass as if on a railway line. But it had been struck just too tentatively. It came to rest one inch short of the hole.

Taut-faced, the Maharajah stepped forward and tapped it home.

'Well,' he said, looking over towards Ghote's ball, 'you've got this for it, I suppose.'

At least, Ghote thought, the fellow has not had the utter cheek to pretend his two strokes were only one.

He wondered whether he ought perhaps to attempt to get his own ball to finish up short of the hole. If the Maharajah felt that they had done equally well, would he be more prepared for revealing chit-chat? Or would it even be best to make a complete mess of his shot so that the Maharajah's feelings of hundred per cent superiority would be restored? Would that get him then to lower his guard right down?

Always supposing he had a guard to lower. Always

supposing it really was one of His Excellency's five suspects who had actually done the murder and that the whole thing was not just an old man's fancy.

He decided that the possibilities were simply too many. Their ramifications were just too complex. The only thing seemed to be to play this extraordinary game which he had got caught up in just, apparently, as it should be played.

He went over to the golf-bag in which the caddie had for some reason replaced the club the Maharajah had used. The long, heavy bag was lying on the ground and he had to crouch to see if he could find the flat-headed affair that was, it seemed, best for the business of sending a ball accurately across smooth grass.

'Stop.'

The Maharajah's voice barked out as if he had suddenly been winged by a gunshot.

Ghote tumbled back on to his haunches.

'Please,' the Maharajah said, with what might have been a trace of apology. 'I never let anyone mess around with my clubs.'

He spoke rapidly in Tamil to the caddie, who scurried across and produced the club Ghote needed.

Picking himself up, Ghote came to the conclusion that the whole odd little incident must be another of the Maharajah's attempts to upset him.

Really his tactics were altogether too much of stark and staring.

He decided firmly now that, since he did seem to have the knack of dealing with the little white ball, he would do his damndest to make sure he got it into the hole.

He drew in a single deep breath of the crisp Nilgiri air, took his stance, looked at the dark little hole in the middle of the ring of velvety green grass and firmly tapped the ball. To his intense inward pleasure, it ran straight and true and plopped down into the hole as if it had been pulled into it by a swiftly rolled-up invisible string.

He looked across to the Maharajah. His lips were compressed and his eyebrows sharply drawn together.

After a few long moments he spoke.

'I'm very sorry, old man,' he said, 'but the truth is I've just got the most fiendish headache. I think I'll have to go back and lie down. And I'd like to get back to my wife. She gets upset if I'm away too long.'

'Of course, most certainly,' Ghote said, aware of the lack of logic in the Maharajah's double excuse but doing his best not to let that appear on his face.

They returned in storm-heavy purple silence to the club-house and got into the jeep. The Maharajah drove even more ferociously than on the way out. They did not encounter any wandering sheep, but they did come across a group of half-wild ponies. And sent them scattering.

As soon as they pulled up outside the Club, with a vile screech of brakes, the Maharajah jumped out and plunged into the building, leaving Ghote sitting up in his seat.

He stayed where he was, thinking about the strange hour he had spent. He was still there when His Excellency appeared in the portico.

'Ghote, Ghote,' he called out in his high, fluting voice. 'A surprising turn of events. They've found the missing trophies.'

He came trotting over to the jeep.

'Yes,' he said, 'they'd been hidden quite near the Club. Very near really. Very near. And you know what that means.'

10

Not the Great Golfman, Ghote thought in an abrupt swirl of depression. No longer the Great Golfman, but the Great Detective once again. Here is my Dr Watson, only he is a Watson who is somehow always the guru never the shishya, stating that finding the stolen silver so near the Club must be meaning something. And here am I, Sherlock Holmes, Hercule Poirot and all the rest, and I do not have any idea whatsoever why this should be so.

Wearily he scrambled down from the high seat of the jeep.

'I am not quite catching what it is you are telling, Your Excellency,' he said, hoping enlightenment might still come.

'The silver, man. It's been found, and guess where?'

'No, sir, I am not able to guess.'

'Not a hundred yards from where we stand at this moment. Or not much more. See the significance?'

Ghote decided that silence was his only possible course.

'Yes, exactly. Simply confirms what I've said all along. The theft wasn't a real theft at all. The whole thing was a piece of diabolic deception. The murderer simply took the silver, pretended to force that window, no doubt scrambled out through it and then hid it all in the nearest convenient place.'

'And, please, where is that?'

'Corner of the churchyard at St Stephen's. Scarcely more than a hundred yards from here, across country.'

'That is the church we can see?'

'Yes, yes. Parish church of Ootacamund. Been here since the early years of the last century, 1829 to be exact. Go there every Sunday myself, see the plaque. *Built at the expense of the Right Honourable Stephen Rumbold Lushington, Governor of Madras State.* Timbers of the roof taken from the ruins of Tippoo Sultan's palace after the Siege of Seringapatam. Cruel man, of course, but a fine scholar. Makes one think, that. Fine building, too.'

Under cover of this spate of historical information Ghote had been sorting things out.

'And what you are believing, Your Excellency,' he said, 'is that, if the murder had been just only the work of a dacoit, the fellow would have taken with him his loots and not placed same in hiding?'

'Of course, of course. Especially not so damn near. We'll see that fool Meenakshisundaram laugh out of the other side of his face now. He's coming over, by the way. We'll go and meet him at the spot.'

Ghote did not much like the idea of being seen by Inspector Meenakshisundaram, that believer in the wily ways of all Bombay CID wallahs, in the company of his overbearing Dr Watson. But there seemed to be no help for it.

'How was it that the silver came to be discovered?' he asked. 'If the murderer was wanting all this to look like a dacoity, he would have taken utmost care to hide safely, no?'

'He?' His Excellency said unexpectedly. 'Aha, caught you out there, old chap. He or she, surely? Mustn't get led astray by the unlikeliness of a woman committing the crime. Old trick that.'

Ghote tried to envisage Mrs Trayling climbing out of the broken window of the billiard room with a sack of heavy silver and making her way across country to where the missing items had been hidden. He did not find it easy.

Yet, he admitted, perhaps it would not be altogether impossible. Trayling Memsahib was a wiry-looking woman, and until quite recently she would have certainly taken her dog Spot out for walking each and every day.

'Ah,' His Excellency said, breaking into excited speech again, 'that's the dashed extraordinary part of it. Do you know how the silver came to light?'

'That is what you were telling, sir,' Ghote said, checking his exasperation.

'Ah, yes. Yes. Well, it was Dasher, you see.'

'Dasher, the dog of Major Bell?'

'Quite right. And pretty well as far gone as his master. In fact, old Bell was saying when he came round here to tell us what he'd found that poor Dasher hasn't smelt a thing for years. But today he took it into his woolly old head to rummage about behind one of the tombstones in the churchyard and there was the silver, just glinting in a shaft of sunlight.'

'Altogether a fine piece of luck', Ghote said.

But luck did happen, he reflected. In the wild jungle of the world the most unlikely things did occur sometimes. Though he had somehow not expected the unlikely in the ordered calm of Ooty. Perhaps, however, Ooty was not so ordered after all.

Filled with a vague sense of disappointment, he set off with His Excellency on the short walk round by road to St Stephen's Church where, His Excellency said, Major Bell had gone back to mark the spot.

As soon as they entered the churchyard, a sea of feathery grass interspersed with tall dark trees mounting sharply up from behind the very English-looking church, Ghote saw Major Bell. He was standing beside one of the square old tombs, very like those in the ancient Sewri Cemetery in

Bombay – Ghote thought – where he once had waited fruitlessly in ambush for a black-money seth buying smuggled gold.

The hero of the silver find, the suddenly rejuvenated Dasher, was invisible down among the depths of the tall grass, only evident from the way the Major occasionally shouted 'Stop it, sir, stop it.'

But, unexpectedly, the Major and his ancient dog were not the only ones standing guard. Seated on a tomb at a little distance, looking like a great ball of white seed-fluff that might at any moment be blown away by a puff of wind, was Mr Habibullah.

His Excellency seemed just as surprised to see the big Moslem.

'What's that fellow doing here?' he exclaimed. 'Poking his nose in. Not wanted. Not wanted on voyage, not one bit.'

'You are not thinking it is significant that the gentleman has come to the place where the murderer was hiding what he took?' Ghote asked, just a little out of malice.

'Hah. Revisiting the scene, eh? Hadn't thought of that. You may well be right, Ghote, you may well be right.'

His Excellency glared across at the former railways officer.

'Go and talk to him,' he said. 'Tackle him on the spot. Dare say he'll give something away. Rely on you.'

Ghote acknowledged inwardly that he had been properly paid out for his tiny, secret challenge. But he supposed that at least Mr Habibullah would be easier to talk with this second time.

They pushed on through the tall, purple-headed grass, warm in the sun and abruptly chilly when the dense shadow of a tree let the sharp Ooty air have its own way.

'So this is where it was,' His Excellency greeted the Major.

'Tucked in here, just where the tomb's crumbled away,'

the Major replied, pointing. 'Behind that bit of gorse growing there.'

The old tomb had indeed crumbled away at one of its corners, Ghote saw. There was quite a deep hole, partially concealed by the dark-green, prickly bush scattered with golden yellow flowers. Behind it a much-used gunny sack could be seen and, where a ray of sunlight came and went as the breeze moved the branches of a tree nearby, there were glints of silver.

On the tomb Ghote could just discern, where the sun struck its surface, letters that spelt out *Sacred to the Memory of Annie, Wife of Captain Henry Browne, Bengal Artillery, in the Twenty-fourth Year of Her Age.*

He felt a dart of pity.

But there was work to be done. Perhaps.

He turned and tramped off towards where Mr Habibullah was sitting, his heavy, black, silver-topped stick lying beside him.

From a tree further up the slope there came suddenly the call of a bird Ghote had not heard before. *Cuckoo, cuckoo*, it seemed to cry.

Of course, he thought, it must be a cuckoo bird, like the ones we used to read about in English poems at school. There would, naturally, be such an import from England in Ooty.

Cuckoo, cuckoo.

But a cuckoo, that was surely an expression meaning a fool. An owl, as we would say. Was the bird mocking him for going about here in Ooty on some sort of a fool's errand?

Now, though, he was standing directly in front of the huge Moslem.

He coughed.

'It is a most astonishing discovery Major Bell's dog has made, no?' he said.

Mr Habibullah turned his large face towards him and broke into a smile of simple delight.

'Oh, yes, yes. Altogether a freak of chance. I find that

most pleasing. I came up here, indeed, when I heard, just to see the place with my own eyes. After my years of attempting to regulate the complexities of the Indian railway system anything that has about it the wildness of chance appeals to me beyond measure.'

Ghote found all this somewhat hard to swallow. Yet on the other hand, he thought, people do have the most strange ideas. Perhaps this great fat fellow sitting up on the tombstone swaying a little from side to side is genuinely no more than a worshipper of the god of pure chance. After all, if he is instead that absconder under the MISA, it would be absurd for him to be putting out such a story.

But then – a new thought struck him – what if the murder of the billiards marker was not, as His Excellency kept insisting, the carefully plotted work of a diabolically cunning criminal, but a killing on a mere whim only?

Could this be so? Could this happy-go-lucky, smiling fellow in front of him have taken it into his head to go and stab to death an innocent old man?

'You seem pensive, my dear sir,' the Moslem's voice broke in on his thoughts. 'I trust you are not pursuing some implacable chain of logic. You have met Professor Godbole, of course, that so serious new visitor to my unlikely Ooty? Well, I understand he is an authority on the subject of Great Detectives, and he tells me, at some length, that such persons do not at all work in a methodical fashion but rely on some mixture of intuition to reveal all in one single blinding flash.'

Ghote experienced a jet of fury. It was bad enough to be called and called again a Great Detective by a murder-book-obsessed person like His Excellency, but to be hailed as this by an utter outsider was altogether too much.

'Please to understand, sir,' he snapped out, 'I am not any sort of a Great Detective. A detective officer, yes. Of the Bombay CID, and here on secondment to inquire into some special circumstances arising from the death of one

Pichu in the Ootacamund Club. But no more than that. No more at all.'

'Well, I am disappointed,' Mr Habibullah replied. 'I tell you frankly, Inspector, that I am much disappointed. The picture you put before me is sadly humdrum, and I do not like the humdrum. Not at all. I have fled from it all the way to Ooty, and now you pursue me with it once more. Yes, pursue me.'

'That is as may be, sir,' Ghote answered, still nettled. 'But I must tell you that, if the murderer of the said Pichu is to be apprehended, it will be by the humdrum and regular methods of criminal investigation. You can be sure of that.'

But how sure was he himself, he asked in sudden inward doubt. Here in Ooty, how sure was he?

He was spared arriving at an answer.

A shout from behind made him turn his head, and thus only half-see the quick look of – what? – suspicion, wariness, or mere displeasure that had passed over Mr Habibullah's large, placid face.

It had been His Excellency who had called out. A police jeep had appeared at the gates of the churchyard, coming to a halt in a cloud of rising dust. Inspector Meenakshisundaram had arrived on the scene.

Grimly Ghote marched off to where His Excellency and Major Bell were standing beside the newly discovered silver. He did not at all look forward to this meeting with his Tamil colleague.

They waited in silence for Meenakshisundaram to come plodding up to them in the crisp sunshine.

But after a little Ghote felt obliged to say something. He gave a little cough.

'You must be greatly pleased, Major, that the cup that is bearing your name as snooker victor will be once more restored to its place of honour.'

But the Major turned his puce-red face to him with a gun-battery glare.

'Feller doesn't want to go on and on about something like that.'

Ghote felt altogether disconcerted. His chance words of conversation had clearly angered the Major. It must be that he had unwittingly broken some unwritten Ooty rule about not showing enthusiasm. Had he been unBritish? Shown himself to be part and parcel of that swirling muddy tide rising up to engulf the proper Ooty of old?

He hung his head.

So he was doubly put out when Meenakshisundaram, his bloated cheeks beaded with sweat, coming within hailing distance, chose to greet him rather than either of the two senior Ooty hands beside the tomb of youthful Mrs Annie Browne.

'Hello, hello, Ghote bhai. Still enjoying the good life of here, I see, even when there is no more work for you.'

'But finding this silver at this place itself is meaning that work is still there,' Ghote declared strenuously, as he fought down a flush of shame.

'Oh ho, you are still holding and holding to that idea of Mehta Sahib's here, is it?' Meenakshisundaram answered, his voice booming over the tall grasses and tumbledown tombs all round. 'Well, I am not blaming. Ooty is most pleasant place to stay, no?'

Ghote was saved from defending himself from this hardly subtle allegation, as he was about to do with some anger, by the intervention of His Excellency himself.

'Come, Inspector,' he said to Meenakshisundaram, 'you cannot possibly claim for one moment longer that this affair is the work of a mere dacoit. Why would a thief promptly hide what he's stolen within a few yards of the place where he took it from? Answer me that.'

'Yards-fards,' Meenakshisundaram replied cheerfully. 'Here is a damn fine place to be hiding the loot till hue and cry is dying down.'

'Nonsense, man. In the churchyard of the principal place of worship in Ootacamund?'

Meenakshisundaram grinned.

'Temples are there also,' he said. 'In plenty-plenty. And how many are coming to your Christian place of worship? Let me be informing you. Twenty-thirty only each Sunday, no? I tell you, Mehta Sahib, I am knowing what goes on in Ooty. Every bit-pitt. Even if you are not at all liking.'

And His Excellency, very evidently, was not pleased to hear that even the attendance figure at the parish church was something that came under the Tamil inspector's eye.

'That's as may be,' he said. 'But you cannot get away from the facts. I told you at the time, Inspector, that the theft of the Club silver was no more than a ruse conceived by a devilishly subtle mind, and finding the so-called stolen goods now as near to the Club as this, whether it's one hundred yards, or two, or three, simply proves my point. If you don't believe me, ask Ghote here. India's Sherlock Holmes.'

Ghote suddenly understood to the full the meaning of the expression 'wishing like Sita to disappear into the bowels of the earth'. But this was not the world of the *Ramayana*: his opinion had been demanded and he would have to give it.

'Sherlock Holmes or not at all Sherlock Holmes,' he found himself answering, 'there is one thing I am long ago learning. It is no good whatsoever to come to theories without having at your disposal the facts.'

To his surprise, since he felt acutely that this temporizing answer was a betrayal of the man who had, for better or worse, done him the honour of calling him to Ooty, His Excellency burst into appreciative laughter.

'Very good, very good,' he said. 'Holmes to a T. "It is a capital mistake to theorize before one has data." I think I quote exactly.'

'Yes,' Ghote chimed in, as much to snub Meenakshisundaram as to gain further approbation from his Watson. 'Yes, and up to now we are not having enough of datas. Definitely.'

But his pronouncement did not seem to quash the Tamil inspector.

'Some datas at least we are having,' he said, stooping suddenly and tugging the gunny sack from behind the untidy, self-sown gorse bush. 'And I will take into my custody.'

From the grass beside him Dasher gave a feeble throaty growl and made as if to fasten his almost toothless jaws into Meenakshisundaram's distinctly too fat right calf.

A push rather than a kick put an end to the attempt. And in another moment Meenakshisundaram was tramping back down the slope towards his jeep, the Ootacamund Club silver in its clanking old sack held in a carelessly swinging hand.

'Well,' said His Excellency, 'that seems to be that. We'd better get back to the Club, I suppose. You coming, Major?'

'Er—No thanks, no. Generally take Dasher up to the top for his walk. Better stick to routine, long as my old ticker will let me.'

He turned and began trudging slowly away. Dasher followed, looking mournful.

His Excellency, contriving totally to ignore Mr Habibullah, led the way down towards the church and the way back to the Club via the road.

'Thought you handled that very well,' he said to Ghote as soon as they were out of earshot. 'Put that plodder Meenakshisundaram nicely in his place.'

Ghote preened himself a little.

'Get anything out of that fearful Habibullah?' His Excellency promptly asked. 'Fellow seemed to be talking away to you all right.'

Ghote thought. He had clearly not got anything in the way of a firm clue from the Moslem. Rather, instead, a series of disquieting ideas had been put into his head. Certainly none of them suitable to present to His Excellency.

'Well,' he answered, feeling his way, 'something perhaps I was learning. But—But it is not at all easy to put a finger on just only what.'

'Aha, yes. Poirot often felt the same, of course. Did so in *Mrs McGinty's Dead*. About two-thirds of the way through, it would be. When he compares the mystery to a pattern woven in some material, only the stuff's all in the same colour making it almost impossible to pick out the pattern. Got that far yet?'

'No,' Ghote said. 'No, I have not had much of time to go through that book up till now.'

Then, feeling that he ought at least to show an interest in something as close to His Excellency's heart, he asked a question.

'This cut-piece that Shri Poirot saw himself as examining, was he in the end seeing the pattern therein?'

'Oh, yes, of course, my dear fellow. Of course. Wouldn't have been a Great Detective otherwise, would he?'

'No. No, I am supposing not.'

'But you, old man,' His Excellency went relentlessly on. 'Surely by now you in your turn must have begun to glimpse the pattern? I mean, after all, we have just established beyond doubt that the crime is bound to have been committed by one of those five in the Club at the time. So can't you just hint at a name? I promise it'll go no further until you have absolute proof.'

The Sherlock Holmes silence, Ghote wondered. Was this a time to play that card again?

And then something that had been lying at the back of his mind, recorded but unnoticed since some time earlier in the afternoon, abruptly surfaced.

Perhaps it is part of the woven pattern, he thought. And at least it will keep His Excellency occupied for a little.

'Sir,' he said, halting their walk just at the turning to the Club where the yogi still sat unmoving as the discreet warning notice beside him. 'Sir, you were saying when we were first discussing that there are always in such cases as this, in the books that is, six suspects or seven. Well, sir, here and now there are not five just. There are six. Six suspects, sir.'

11

'Six suspects?' His Excellency said with sharp displeasure. 'But, my dear fellow, I explained to you. There is no question but that the murder must have been committed by one of the people inside the Club on the night. One of the five. Unless, of course, you're going to believe that bungler Meenakshisundaram and say the murderer was a dacoit who happened to break in.'

His Excellency darted him a quick, anxious look.

Ghote, wondering if he was seeing his whole concocted detective story on the point of falling to pieces, contrived not to let the least glimmer of any inner thoughts appear on his face.

'No,' His Excellency went on, reassured, 'as I said at the beginning, the billiard room was absolutely snowbound at the time. No doubt about it. The whole Club building was locked up tight. Iyer sees to that every night, and he's completely reliable if nothing else. No, it has to be either that fellow Habibullah, the Maharajah or the Maharani, or Lucy Trayling or, least likely of all, Professor Godbole. One of those five. Definitely.'

Ghote swallowed. Was he, after all, right in what he was about to claim?

'But sir,' he said. 'But, Your Excellency, I was just only

finding out. It was while I was talking with the Maharajah on the golf course.'

'Ah, yes, Poirot always said—'

'Mr Iyer. It is Mr Iyer,' Ghote banged in, tired to his bones of hearing about Poirot.

'Iyer? But—But Iyer doesn't sleep in the Club. Lives down in the lower town. Has a wife and children, and all that.'

'Nevertheless,' Ghote said, 'last night at least, in the middle of the night itself, Mr Iyer was seen upon said premises by the Maharajah. He was asking him at that time to play at golf with him today. He was saying also that Mr Iyer was often and often working until the small hours only. He must be locking up sometimes when it is almost dawn.'

An expression of shining delight came on to His Excellency's leathery face.

'Hah,' he said, 'I knew I was right. Knew the only thing to do in an affair like this was to go straight to the top. If you've got a really baffling murder on your hands, I said, only the consulting detective will do.'

'Well, sir,' Ghote said, 'it was just only something I was happening to hear.'

'Too modest. Too modest altogether, my dear chap. That's one point where you do differ from Poirot: no one could ever accuse him of being too modest.'

'No, that is so, Your Excellency, yes, indeed,' Ghote chimed in, seeing an easy way of establishing that he had more of an acquaintance with *Mrs McGinty's Dead* than two or three sleepily read pages.

'But you're well up to all the Poirot tricks,' His Excellency went on excitedly. 'The moment you told Iyer you had come to Ooty to investigate the murder, told him deliberately, he looked so upset I thought he was going to burst into tears. Full marks to you, Ghote, for that.'

'But, sir, that might have been because he was just only thinking that a Club member—'

'No, no. Guilt, my dear fellow. Plain as a pikestaff. So now we'll have him up in front of us and question him till he confesses. Break him down.'

'That is what Shri Poirot would do?'

His Excellency looked disconcerted.

'Well, no,' he admitted. 'No. Actually, Poirot never seems to go in for that sort of thing. None of his like do really. Prefer to rely on the sudden seeing of that which has never occurred before, as little Godbole was saying. Clouds of pipe smoke and all that.'

'Yes,' Ghote said, 'I was thinking that such questioning was the method an ordinary police officer would employ. But if you are wanting such, you must be going to Inspector Meenakshisundaram. I am having no official status here in Ooty.'

'Meenakshisundaram. The fellow wouldn't even listen.'

'Yes, that is what I am thinking also. So if Pichu was murdered by one of those six persons inside the Club, whether it is Mr Iyer or not, then we have got to have some damn fine proof and after go to Meenakshisundaram.'

'Yes. Yes, I suppose you're right.'

His Excellency sounded so despondent that Ghote, before he had time to check himself, came out with a suggestion.

'Sir, we can consider what is to be found out about Mr Iyer later. But this afternoon only, when you were requesting me to play at golf with the Maharajah, I was on my way to see whether the film star Sarla Kumar was definitely continuing to have illicit relationship with the said Maharajah. Sir, I think it would be best now if I was to resume checking up such line of inquiry.'

'Yes, by Jove, Pratapgadh and that film girl. Mustn't forget that. Iyer can wait. You go off there, Ghote. Fast as you can.'

Twenty minutes later Ghote spotted his possible witness, the manager of the Willingdon Talkies, standing in the cinema's foyer beneath two large and impressive, if dusty, photographs of Lord and Lady Willingdon, Viceroy and Vicereine at the height of the British Raj. The fellow, a little paunchy man wearing a European black bow-tie and a not very clean white shirt, was watching the audience arriving for the last performance but two of *Prem Putla* starring Sarla Kumar. But, in spite of the personal appearance she had made the night before, ticket-buyers were only a mere trickle.

Ghote began to make his way across.

As he did so, another ancient photograph caught his eye, and he stopped to read the legend beneath its faded sepia. *The Ooty Beauties – Grand Concert – Planters' Week 1937.* Above, the group showed rows of feebly grinning white faces, the men in tennis flannels, the girls in flowered frocks. It all seemed to sum up for him the ordered, distant past of this still just existing relic of a less muddled age.

And then he saw that one of the men, one not wearing flannels, was none other than His Excellency. The recognition gave him a curious little sense of shock. But there could be no doubt who it was, despite the long lapse of time and the fact that he was dressed as a Scotchman, complete with dangling leather purse in front of his kilt and a dagger-like knife in his stocking.

He stood looking wonderingly at this fragment of a past time, the true Ooty time, that he felt now connected to.

'Sahib, may I help?'

It was the manager. His witness.

'Yes. Yes, you can. Yes, I am wanting to know: is it that Miss Sarla Kumar is continuing to stay in Ooty after her personal appearance?'

The manager's attitude of oily willingness vanished in an instant.

'What for are you asking this? Always and always people are asking.'

But Ghote had dealt with too many truculent witnesses in his time to be set back by any such attitude as this.

'Police,' he barked. 'Answer up.'

It was all that was needed. Yes, the manager admitted in a rush of babbled information, Miss Kumar was still in the district. She had rented a bungalow. It was called Sunnyside Cottage. It was in a colony, a new colony, just outside the town. She had not told him why she was staying on. He did not know. No, she had not had any visitors while she was making her personal appearance. Yes, she would most probably be out at Sunnyside Cottage now. Where else would she be?

Ghote took a taxi.

The manager, he thought, might decide he had more to gain by warning Sarla Kumar about this mysterious police officer than he had to lose from that police officer's wrath.

The collection of new houses that comprised the colony disturbed, he was surprised to find, his notions of what was proper. They were set as close together as their gardens would permit and built in the most modern style, clean-looking and white-painted. But somehow in the course of the short time he had spent in Ooty he had developed a strong feeling that Ooty cottages ought to be like the ones that had been built a hundred years ago and more. They ought to be English, with roses round the door. And to stand apart from one another by a good distance, aloof and reserved like proper Englishmen.

Sunnyside Cottage, when they located it, proved to be even smarter than its neighbours with a very posh diamond-shaped window with coloured panes looking out across a garden dotted with flowering shrubs.

Telling the taxi driver to go a little further along and wait, Ghote opened the neat, white-painted wooden gate in the wire fence surrounding the place and made his way up a stepped concrete path to the front door.

He had decided his best plan would be to pretend he had been informed that they took in paying guests at Sunnyside Cottage. If it was indeed a love-nest for Sarla Kumar and the Maharajah, he would quickly be told that he was mistaken. But, with a little skilful manipulation in asking whether any of the nearby cottages would take him in, he might be able to learn at least something.

He knocked at one of the thick glass panes set in the door. After a moment he heard steps inside.

Would he see Sarla Kumar herself? Could he pretend to recognize her and burst into praises for her performance in *Prem Putla?* Tell her he had seen the film a dozen times in Bombay and that it was the best he had ever sat through? Would he even know who she was if she did answer the door?

The door opened. The woman who stood there was definitely not Sarla Kumar. She was a large, pillar-like, dumpy sixty-year-old, wrapped in a dull blue sari with a pair of rimless spectacles plastered across her pudding of a face. She was probably, he thought, from her air of placid authority, some old auntie of the star's, brought to Ooty as a companion.

'Good evening,' he said. 'I—That is—Are you having —Please, are you taking paying guest?'

'No.'

He licked his lips.

'But, please, this is Sunnyside Cottage?'

'Name is on gate.'

'Yes. Yes, I was seeing. But they were telling me you were looking for paying guest.'

'No.'

'No? You are sure? I mean, I am very, very much in need of somewhere to sleep tonight.'

'Then where are your baggages?'

'They—They—I was coming by taxi. The fellow was not knowing just where is this cottage. I have just only arrived in Ooty.'

'No.'

'No? But why . . . ?'

'Bus is not getting to Charing Cross until one half-hour's time.'

'Yes. I mean, no. No, I was coming by private car.'

'You said taxi.'

'Taxi, private car, it is all the same.'

'No. Taxi you are taking from the town. Private car you are hiring in Coimbatore. If you can pay.'

For an instant Ghote wondered whether he could claim to be rich enough to have done this. But at once he knew that, even with his new Ooty jersey, he did not cut such a figure. He decided that, confronted by the old auntie's unyielding opposition, all that was left to him was tactics of some brutality.

'Miss Sarla Kumar is staying here?' he demanded. 'She is inside now?'

But the podgy, stern face looking back at him did not change by so much as a quiver.

'That is what I am all along thinking,' came the retort. 'You are some sort of film fan only. Perhaps you were bribing manager at Willingdon Talkies.'

'No. Yes. Yes. That is, I am very, very much admiring Miss Sarla Kumar. I would like autograph. That is my inmost desire. Is she here?'

'Go away.'

The door was closing. Should he put his foot in the gap? Even if he did there would be nothing to be gained.

He turned away.

Darkness had begun to fall.

Gloomily he made his way back down the concrete path. But as he reached the last of the steps leading to the lane outside there came the sound of a burst of music from the cottage behind him. Western disco music.

He stopped still.

Yes, if that sort of music from the noisy, strident world far beyond the ordered calm of Ooty was blaring out, then Sarla Kumar was definitely in the house. And if she was there at home, waiting, was it not likely that the Maharajah, as soon as he had gone through the ritual of dinner at the Club, would jump up, leave his wife there nursing her pekinese and come out to join the star who had stayed on after her personal appearance at the Willingdon Talkies was over and done with?

He looked round the garden in the swiftly gathering darkness. Several of the bushes in it were reasonably big, though none of them seemed quite large enough to hide him. Then at last he spotted a sprawling hibiscus. It was not very thick, but he thought it would do well enough.

He went hastily back to where his taxi was still waiting, and dismissed it. Then he quietly re-entered the garden and stationed himself in his chosen hiding-place.

He thought that he would in all probability have a long wait. He would certainly miss dinner at the Club himself. But to sit in that dark panelled room again surrounded by the pictures of Masters of the Ootacamund Hunt, rock-like on their rock-like horses, with His Excellency persistently comparing him to Shri Poirot, was something he would be quite happy not to have to do.

But if supposing this evening will end, he thought, with cent per cent proof that the Maharajah of Pratapgadh is still the lover of one Miss Sarla Kumar, then I would be a good step nearer to showing that the said Maharajah was the blackmail victim of the billiards marker Pichu. And therefore was having damn good reason to dispose him off.

And that would be good, hard, police-work proof, not some piece of mystification suddenly unknotted, as in His Excellency's favourite form of fiction.

But before long he began to wish that he had brought with him his Agatha Christie, or any other book His Excellency might care to lend him, and then had found a hiding place distant enough from the cottage to be able to risk reading by torchlight. He had started his observation much too early. The Maharajah would only just have begun on his celery soup.

And, who knows, he thought, I might after all be finding in that Mrs McGinty affair some hint of a reason why

Pichu's body was laid out so squarely in the middle of the billiard table.

Certainly His Excellency would believe that Hercule Poirot could show the way to solving the mystery here. Look how he had been reading the book once more in the Nilgiri Library.

Time crawled by.

The Maharajah would be tackling his lamb cutlets or roast chicken now.

Now the roly-poly pudding would be being placed in front of him. Would he take coffee also, sitting on one of those blue and white sofas somewhere? No. Surely he would be more urgent to come out to Sarla Kumar. But what excuse for disappearing would he make to his wife? Well, no doubt he must have some story ready. He would have thought it out when he knew Sarla Kumar was going to set up this love-nest.

In the darkness a jackal howled from somewhere in the hills, safe now from Major Bob Jago and the hounds of the Ootacamund Hunt.

It was cold. A chill striking even through his jersey, under the tiny blinking diamonds of the stars.

But better not to flap his arms or jump up and down to restore some warmth. Someone might chance to look out from the cottage.

If only it would all turn out to be worth it. If only it was the Maharajah who was responsible for the body in the billiard room. The Maharajah and not a master criminal absconding under the MISA. Or a wiry old English memsahib avenging the death of her husband. Or the Maharani, blackmailed over her young Bengali lover. Or Mr Iyer, the Efficient Baxter, perhaps caught out by Pichu falsifying the Club accounts. Or a talkative professor from Bombay side, just because it was the most unlikely explanation.

Faintly in the cold night air there came the sound of a

car engine. The Maharajah. He must have downed that pudding at top speed.

But the sound died away. Some other person coming back to another cottage at the far side of the colony . . .

He allowed himself the luxury of a good shiver, and settled down to wait once more.

And what if it was Meenakshisundaram who was right? True, he had not so far put his hand on any dacoit who might have broken into the Club. But all the same his account of the business was really the more likely of the two. Even if, as a rule, professional robbers did not commit murder in the course of their crimes.

One thing was certain, though. If in the end it should turn out that His Excellency's idea of what had happened was correct the two of them would have to have a watertight case to put to Meenakshisundaram.

Abruptly he realized that he was not staring as he had done for the past hour or more at the unvarying shapes of the bushes in the garden in front of him and the pale strip of the concrete path up which the Maharajah would come. Instead he was seeing a moving figure. Someone was creeping towards the cottage and for silence and secrecy was keeping to the grass beside the path.

Who? Who could it be? Was it the Maharajah? Had that distant car, though its engine had not sounded like the roar of the jeep's, been his after all? But why should he approach like this? It was his mistress – a film star – he was going to. He should bound up the path like a film hero.

So who?

And why?

The figure had come to a halt now beside a smaller hibiscus bush nearer the cottage, one he himself had rejected as cover earlier on. With only the faint haze of light from the curtained windows of the cottage it was difficult to make much out. But it looked as if the intruder was settling down to crouch there.

Another watcher? But who? And what for?

After a minute or two more of fruitless speculation Ghote set off towards the smaller bush. On the grass his feet made not the slightest noise.

In a few moments he was within jumping distance of the crouching watcher.

Should he jump?

Yes, he decided. After all, this was definitely an intruder. Nefarious purposes were clear. And, however far he himself was from his proper territory in hugger-mugger, noisy, crowded Bombay, he was still a police officer. He had a duty.

And, besides, he was very curious.

He took a deep breath and launched himself.

It was only as his arms closed round the crouching intruder that he realized he had in them a woman. And, smelling suddenly a tangy, musky European perfume, he knew that the woman he had in his grasp was none other than the trouser-wearing Maharani of Pratapgadh.

12

Ghote whipped his encircling arms away from the utterly unexpected figure they had enveloped.

'Madam, madam,' he said.

The Maharani, who had let out a single whistling gasp of fright when he had leapt on her, began to recover. She got to her feet and peered forward in the darkness.

'Madam,' Ghote said, 'it is I, Mr Ghote, the guest of His Excellency Mr Surinder Mehta.'

'What—'

Her face came closer in the dark. He smelt again her tangy European perfume, and wondered abruptly what she had done with her pekinese. No doubt left in charge of some servant in the Club.

'Yes,' she said at last. 'Yes, it is. You're the Great Detective. That's what my husband said.'

'Well, madam . . .'

In the darkness he saw her straighten her back and move half a pace away.

'Then let me tell you this, Mr Great Detective. You are not wanted here. Not wanted in Ooty, and certainly not wanted in the Club. Why the hell they let you in in the first place I don't know.'

Ghote felt a burst of resentful anger. Who was it, after

all, who was illicitly present in this garden? And who was it, too, who had been stated as being a person who would not have been allowed in the Club in old days? Stated by Mrs Lucy Trayling. None other than this Maharani.

And, he thought, he had learnt the reason for that, even in the short time he had been there. A lady who could let herself have a love affair in a third, no, fourth-class hotel in the Bazaar.

'Madam,' he said, 'I am staying at Club as guest of Mr Mehta. He was calling me from Bombay. It is his belief that the billiards marker Pichu was murdered by some person within the said Club, and I am here to find such.'

'What nonsense. My husband was saying something like that, and I told him he was talking tommyrot. I don't believe Surinder Mehta asked you here at all, not even if he is practically gaga.'

'Madam, you are accusing myself of uttering falsehoods? I tell you, I am here in Ooty to investigate the murder of the billiards marker, and I have good reason to suspect that his murder was committed by one of the persons sleeping in the Club on the night in question. And among such persons, madam, you are there.'

The onslaught appeared to have had some effect. The Maharani stayed silent.

Silent and thoughtful.

'Oh God,' she exclaimed at last, 'let's go away from here. That bloody woman will come out or something if she hears voices, and I certainly couldn't face her just now.'

'Very good, madam,' Ghote said. 'I also would not wish to be found here.'

They crept to the gate, opened it and stepped down into the lane.

'I've got a taxi waiting along here,' the Maharani said. 'Do you want a lift?'

'You are most kind.'

'Don't be too sure of that. I don't feel very kindly disposed to anyone just now.'

They walked on in silence for a little. The air felt penetratingly cold.

Suddenly the Maharani turned towards him.

'And what were you doing hiding there yourself?' she demanded.

Ghote wished he had not laid himself open to the inquiry by retreating from Sunnyside Cottage in the way he had. He sought rapidly for some plausible lie. And decided there was none to tell.

'Madam,' he said, 'I will answer the simple truth. I was there in that garden, I am thinking, for the very same reason as yourself. I was wishing to have proof that your husband was in the habit of consorting with Miss Sarla Kumar.'

For a moment the Maharani was frozen in silence. Then she responded.

'Damn. Is he so obvious? Does every bloody soul in the Club know what's going on?'

Ghote, blinking a little at the vigorous language, pushed on with his truth-telling.

'Madam, I am not thinking so. It just happens that there came to my notice one out-of-date item of filmi gossip connecting your husband with Miss Kumar, and I learnt also she is staying on in that cottage after making her personal appearance at Willingdon Talkies.'

'Did you indeed? And what do you deduce from that, Mr Great Detective? That Vikram is renewing the affair and – what? – that that creepy billiards marker got to know of it, tried a bit of blackmail and that Vikram silenced him? Is that what you think?'

It was. Or it was, Ghote acknowledged to himself, certainly one of the things that Mr Detective, great or small, had thought. But he did not find it easy to say as much to the wife of this suspect.

'Madam, an investigating officer has to examine each and every possibility.'

'Loves to poke his dirty nose into each and every possibility, you mean,' the Maharani retorted, her former rage returning.

It brought up an equal anger in Ghote.

He had not wanted in any way to poke his nose into the affairs of these people up in the clear air of Ooty. He had been ordered to do so, and he had never relished the task.

'Madam,' he said fiercely, 'let me state this also: when I am saying each and every possibility I am not at all forgetting the possibility that you yourself could have been victim of Pichu's blackmailing.'

She came to an abrupt halt in the darkness. Some way further on Ghote could see the dim light coming from the interior of the taxi in which she had made her way out to the colony.

'Victim of that nasty old man's blackmail,' she said, 'and I suppose you think his killer too.'

Ghote drew himself up.

Why not? Why not accuse this suspect to her face here and now?

'Yes, madam. The killer of the billiards marker in the billiard room.'

'What bloody nonsense.'

Ghote felt he had dived head first into swirling, muddy waters. Where their buffeting would carry him he could not tell. But he had taken the plunge. He had told this woman he believed she had killed a man. That she had murdered him. Not that she was a mere playing piece in some bloodless game, the game His Excellency so delighted in. Not that she was just the "Suspect" who, it had turned out, had done it.

No, not that, but that she was an actual murderer, a killer.

'Not at all nonsense,' he said. 'Can you deny that you are having as much of secrets as your husband?'

'What do you mean? You dirty-minded little tick. I said you shouldn't ever have been let into the Club, and, by God, I was right.'

'I am meaning the Bengal Vegetarian Hotel,' Ghote said.

It stopped the outburst like a blow from a bludgeon.

A silence fell in the starlit darkness.

'How much do you know?' came the Maharani's cold voice at last.

'I am knowing the name of Mr Amul Dutt,' Ghote said.

Another silence.

Then another question.

'How much do you want so as to keep your mouth shut?'

'Madam, I am not at all wanting. I may not be any sort of a Great Detective, but this much at least I am sharing with Mr Sherlock Holmes: I am not taking bribes.'

'Then you're the first policeman I've met who doesn't. If enough's offered.'

'But you, you were not able to offer enough to Pichu? That is what I am asking myself.'

The Maharani laughed then.

'A billiards marker in a club? He wouldn't have wanted a tenth as much as a Great Detective.'

In the dark Ghote saw her turn sharply away.

'And as for you,' she called out, 'you can get back to your dotty friend Surinder Mehta on your own two feet.'

He stood where he was as she strode away. In a few moments he saw her outlined against the feeble light from inside the taxi, then came the choked splutter of its engine as it moved jerkily away. Soon there was nothing but the silence of the night.

Stubbornly he set out on the long walk back.

*

It was not until breakfast time next day that he saw His Excellency again.

Then, tucking into porridge with all the more appetite for having gone hungry to bed the night before, and much too tired even to attempt one more page of *Mrs McGinty's Dead*, he dutifully recounted to his influential Watson the events of the evening in the garden of Sunnyside Cottage.

It was only as he put his spoon down in the empty porridge bowl that a thought occurred to him. If the murderer was truly a Club member, now that it was believed by one and all that he himself was the only person who could solve this baffling mystery, then it would not have been impossible for a secret adversary to have added to his porridge white arsenic. No doubt rat poison could easily be obtained down in the Bazaar.

'So what do you think?' His Excellency was asking. 'Did the Maharani do it?'

Ghote, who when his softly-brought bed-tea had come had woken to find he had arrived at a firm conclusion about the dark-of-night confrontation, wagged his head.

'She must go low down on the list of suspects, Your Excellency,' he said. 'What she was pointing out about how easily she could have bribed Pichu is altogether correct. Why then should she kill him?'

'Yes. See that. And, if I may point it out, you didn't exactly succeed any better last night in adding to your case against Pratapgadh himself. I mean, I realize you did more or less have to leave your place of hiding. But, you know, when Sherlock Holmes followed somebody who said afterwards that he hadn't seen him he was able to reply "That is what you may expect to see when I follow you." '

Ghote was tempted more than ever to shout aloud 'But I am not Mr Sherlock Holmes.' However, he refrained.

'So,' His Excellency went on, 'our friend Iyer goes to the top again, eh?'

He leant forward, lined up salt-pot, pepper-pot, mustard-holder, Dipy's Tomato Ketchup bottle, sugar bowl and milk jug.

'Hm,' he grunted. 'Well, let's say the salt's the Maharani and the pepper's our friend Iyer. Now, we'll make the mustard the Maharajah – "keen as mustard", what? – and the ketchup Habibullah, why not, and then the sugar can be old Lucy Trayling – lady sweet as sugar, of course – while right at the end, the milk, that's little Godbole, so absolutely innocent I can't help wondering every time I think of him whether he must be the one.'

Ghote debated with himself whether to say, yet again, that complete innocence was surely complete innocence. But he knew that any such argument would be labour in vain.

'Right,' said His Excellency.

And down from the head of the line to its very end, even below impossibly suspect Professor Godbole, went the Maharani, the salt-pot. Ghote, recalling the night before, thought that the mustard-holder would have better represented the swearing, hot-tempered Maharani.

But the pepper-pot was now at the head of His Excellency's line. Looking at it, Ghote realized that he was as little anxious to interview the assistant secretary as he had been to tackle any of the sahibs and memsahibs, white or brown. Mr Iyer, after all, coming from the turbulent world below, would be much more likely to see that he could refuse to answer possibly incriminating questions from anybody other than Inspector Meenakshisundaram. Nor would the fellow, knowing who he himself was, be as easy to bounce into giving answers that might betray him as he had been when he had been bullied into opening up Pichu's quarter.

'And there's another thing now that you've brought Iyer into the picture,' His Excellency went on. 'He was, you know, the first to see the body.'

'Ah, good. Good. I can perhaps talk with him giving such only as my reason.'

'But, no, old boy.'

'What? That is not a good enough reason? You are thinking Inspector Meenakshisundaram has already asked him what he was seeing then?'

'No, no. Meenakshisundaram didn't bother with Iyer at all. Iyer told me so himself. No, that brainless plodder simply took it for granted that the signs of a break-in meant the affair was a dacoity and went on from there.'

'But if Inspector Meenakshisundaram has not put any questions to Mr Iyer, then I myself should do so forthwith.'

'No, old fellow, that's not my point at all.'

'No?'

'No. Thing is: the Efficient Baxter was the first to see the body. And you know what that invariably means, don't you?'

Ghote thought. No, he did not know what that invariably meant.

Luckily, His Excellency took his silence to convey just the opposite.

'Quite right, quite right. It wasn't, I think, Poirot himself but one of those shrewd regular policemen he sometimes worked with who said: the first person to find a dead body is often the same as the person who last saw him alive.'

Ghote blinked.

'That is what the British police are believing?' he said. 'But it cannot be so. Many, many times we at Crime Branch in Bombay are having cases where the body was reported by old, old women or by small children even, and they are never ultimately being charge-sheeted under Section 302.'

His Excellency looked down at his plate of bacon and eggs.

'Well, I dare say I may have quoted it a little wrong,' he muttered. 'Probably the chap said "quite often". "Quite often" or something of that sort. But you can take it from me: it's a damn suspicious circumstance. A damn suspicious circumstance against our friend Iyer.'

'Very well,' Ghote said, rising from the table. 'I would go at once and talk with Mr Iyer.'

He thought, as he strode out of the dining room abandoning all ideas of toast and Dundee marmalade, that His Excellency had half-risen from his chair as if to call him back and suggest a joint interview with this juicy suspect. But he ignored him.

To his pleasure, when he thrust open the door of the

Club office without knocking, he found the assistant secretary sitting at his table, his glinting spectacles deep in an assortment of bills and receipts. He looked up with some astonishment at the unheralded intrusion.

'Mr Iyer,' Ghote said without preliminaries, 'I am understanding that you were the first person to see the body in the billiard room on Tuesday morning.'

The Efficient Baxter put one lean finger into his floppy sheaf of papers to keep his place.

'Well, yes, that is so,' he agreed with evident caution.

'Ah. Then—'

'And yet it is not so.'

Ghote foresaw the need to be tough, and gathered up his forces.

But Mr Iyer was smiling placatingly.

'Please,' he said, 'it is just like this. While I was the first person properly to see Pichu's body, in fact before me a sweeper woman had been into the billiard room.'

'A sweeper woman? But she had not noticed the body, is it? Yet, so Mr Mehta was telling me, it was altogether in the very middle of the billiard table.'

'Yes. Yes, that is so. That is as I myself saw it.'

'But the sweeper woman did not see?'

'Oh, yes. Yes, she saw. She came shouting and calling to tell me myself. And, of course, I made prompt investigation.'

For a moment Ghote stood looking down at the Efficient Baxter, the necessity of keeping his place in the pile of bills preventing him for once from washing his hands together.

'So you yourself were not actually the first to see the body?' he said.

'No. Not if you would count the sweeper woman.'

'Yes,' Ghote said. 'I do count this sweeper woman. What is her name, if you please? And where would I be able to find?'

'Name? Name? I do not—Oh, yes. Yes, now I have it. It is Gauri. I think, Gauri. But I am not at all able to tell you where you would find her this a.m. She would long ago have finished her work here, and I do not know where she stays. Most probably in one of those hutments the poors are always building.'

'I see,' Ghote said.

He turned to go.

And put the question he had been careful to keep until this moment.

'Mr Iyer, on Monday night, when Pichu was killed, you were in the Club till a late, late hour. Why was that?'

The suddenness of the demand seemed to have had all the effect he could have hoped for. The Efficient Baxter swallowed, started back in his chair, took his long finger out of his sheaf of papers, stared at them blankly as they flopped into confusion.

'Well?' Ghote demanded.

The Efficient Baxter licked his lips.

'Please,' he said croakingly.

'Mr Iyer, what were you doing in the Club building in the middle of the night when Pichu was killed? And I am warning: no wool-over-the-eye business.'

'I—You see—Sir, it is—It is like this. In the town I have the smallest of houses only. And children. I have five children. No, six. And if I don't get sleep my work-standard is altogether deteriorating. So, often I am dossing down in this office itself. But Major Bell would not—'

But then suddenly in place of the look of gathering desperation on his face there came a broad, dawning smile.

'Six children,' he said. 'Six children. I have six children now.'

'What is this?' Ghote barked out, unable to see how the fecund turmoil of the Efficient Baxter's domestic life had any relevance.

'But it is simple,' Mr Iyer replied, still looking almost idiotically pleased. 'Last Monday night my sixth child came into the world. She is a daughter. We are calling her Radha. And there was a question of a difficult birth. So naturally I fetched Dr Fatbhoy, and he was there to see that I spent all that night in my house. I boiled a great quantity of water with my own hands.'

'And you did not once leave? Not for a short time even?'

'No, no. I would not. When my wife was at a death's door perhaps.'

'Yes. Yes, I see. Well, thank you. Yes.'

Ghote retreated.

But he still felt that he ought not to take this unexpected alibi totally on trust. So, without stopping to do anything else, he walked straight down to the Collector's Office, all arcades, glassed-in balconies, upspringing arches and the rattle-rattle-bang of all the typewriters that kept the administration of the district wrapped up in bureaucracy. From one of the clerks there he learnt where it was that Dr Fatbhoy had his dispensary.

It was down in the Bazaar, as he had expected, and once more he descended from the openness, Englishness and peace of the old town into a familiar packed conglomeration, strident with the sound of voices raised in huckstering invitation, in sudden argument or even in mere talk. Vigorous hootings from every form of motor transport added to the clamour together with the incessant clanging of bicycle bells and the wail of half a dozen different sorts of music, from transistors, tinny tape-machines and not a few elderly record-players.

He saw, as he passed, Mr Biswas standing outside his Bengal Vegetarian Hotel, with the knife-grinder still busy with his screaming trade beside him, and was offered an obsequious smile and a folded-hands greeting. For a moment he wondered whether he should stop and inquire into the relationship the Bengali had had with Pichu, the blackmailer, as revealed by the greasy visiting card he had discovered.

But he felt he had more urgent business.

He soon found the dispensary, a rather more prosperous

looking place than he had expected. A squatting, chattering circle of patients waited in its outer room.

He paused in the doorway, thinking what line he could take with the doctor. Back in Bombay as 'a Government Officer authorized to question', in the words of the Indian Penal Code, he would not have had any hesitation. But here? Here where he was what? The merest private detective, and without even a card to say that this was what he was. It was all very well in His Excellency's detective stories for a Hercule Poirot simply to go up to a suspect or witness and ask whatever he wanted to know. But he here was, no more than one Mr Ghote, staying at the Ootacamund Club, and wanting to know from a particular medical practitioner whether it was true that he had attended a certain Mrs Iyer last Monday night and whether her husband had been present and had remained so all during the night. How could he demand answers to such questions?

Could he pass off as a journalist, he asked himself. But even then his questions were hardly those a journalist would be wanting answers to.

At last he decided simply to make his way in, ask to see Dr Fatbhoy and trust to luck, or perhaps to a certain air of authority.

Certainly, the air of authority, together perhaps with his expensive Ooty jersey, at once gained him admittance to Dr Fatbhoy ahead of the patiently waiting squatting crowd in the outer room.

Sitting behind an ancient, dark-wood table, he saw an elderly Parsi, grey hair sparse across a high-domed skull, eyes deep-set, luminously brown and hungry looking.

'Good morning, sir,' he began. 'My name is Ghote, and I—'

'Ah, the Great Detective. The Great Detective in person.'

'But—But how—But how were you knowing who I am? Or, rather that . . .'

'Oh, my dear Mr Ghote, it is plain you are hardly

acquainted with Ooty as yet. Everything is known to everybody here, tucked away as we are up in the Hills.'

He smiled.

'Of course, I exaggerate. Here in the lower town not everything is known of what goes on in the Club, for instance. The majority of people here, my daily patients, would scarcely follow the rules of snooker. Snooker, is it? But there are some links between us. Yes, some indeed. The Culture Circle, for example. I myself, as something of a music lover, have the honour to be a vice-chairman of the Culture Circle, and, of course, its monthly meetings are largely attended by what I might call the old hands of Ooty. Yes, the old hands of Ooty.'

He leant across his dark, scratched table with its two or three tattered medical books at one corner and a stethoscope that seemed yet older lying beside them and rubbed his hands sharply together.

Ghote wondered whether it was to halt the distinct trembling he had noticed in them. But he soon decided it was not. It was a sign of eagerness.

'And, my dear Mr Ghote, this is a coincidence beyond expectation. Because, you see, you are just the person we want for our meeting tomorrow evening itself. Professor Godbole, whom you must know, has consented to give us a talk, and the subject he has chosen is none other than "Sherlock Holmes, Alive or Dead?" So, you see, to have a Sherlock Holmes actually present, palpably alive as I may say, would be nothing short of a triumph of the first magnitude for us.'

'But—'

'Now, Mr Ghote, do not deny me.'

And Ghote saw then that he could not refuse the request. He would have to allow himself to be Sherlock Holmes palpably alive. Because as a simple investigator he wanted from Dr Fatbhoy information that he was in no way bound to give.

'Very well, Doctor Sahib,' he said. 'Yes, it would be my

pleasure to attend your meeting. But, please, there is a small matter you could be helping me with.'

And he put then to the doctor the questions he had thought about so dolefully standing in the doorway of the dispensary. And received answers. Yes, Mrs Iyer had given birth, with some difficulty, a forceps delivery, to a daughter on the night of Monday – Tuesday last. And, yes, of course, the husband had been there. Throughout.

'In fact, my dear Mr Ghote, he was a positive nuisance. In the end I had to send him off to boil water. An old dodge among us medical men in such circumstances. And he boiled and boiled water during most of the night.'

'Thank you, Doctor Sahib. And now, if you would kindly excuse me . . .'

He left as hastily as he could, before the doctor began wanting to know why a Great Detective had been asking questions about innocent, alibied, off-the-hook Mr Iyer.

So, he thought as he trudged despondently up to the old town again, it is back to five once more. Back to five suspects, and nothing decent or definite to choose between them. Unless you opted for Meenakshisundaram's unknown dacoit.

He groaned aloud.

13

Outside the Nilgiri Library Ghote encountered among the earnest dog-walkers, overcoats over saris or Britishy tweeds in the cool, fresh air, His Excellency. He decided at once that the evidence that had finally been confirmed by Dr Fatbhoy was something that Sherlock Holmes would pass on to Dr Watson.

Or, more in the realms of the everyday, here was something of a gift for the influential, if rather ridiculous, personage who had brought him all the way from Bombay to Ooty.

But he found, when he laid out the facts of the matter, that Mr Iyer's alibi was no proof of guiltlessness – in some eyes.

'My dear chap, you know what a watertight alibi means?'

'It is that the professor of such is not at all the guilty party?' Ghote ventured without much hope.

'No, no, my dear fellow. Remember the words of the Sage of Baker Street: "Only a man with a criminal enterprise in hand desires to establish an alibi." '

Ghote felt a rush of almost overwhelming fury. That a watertight alibi meant the person with it was guilty of the very crime he could not have committed: it was absurdly against reason.

The world of detective stories, he thought with a jet of bitterness, how damned idiotic it was. Where simple logic, which was what the real world creaked and stumbled along by, seemed at once to be turned right-about. Where – God, what nonsense – if a man had an alibi, as he himself had fully established that Mr Iyer did, then he was to be set down as the most likely suspect of them all. Bukbuk, utter bukbuk.

In the seething bubbling of his mind he asked himself how he could put this simple fact to the man who had had him transported into this upside-down world. How he could? Rather, whether he could?

He supposed sadly that all he could really do was to agree. Or at least let the ridiculous notion somehow slide over him.

But, damn it, how could the alibi be faulted? Dr Fatbhoy, who had no possible reason for backing a lie, had stated plainly as plainly that the husband of his forceps-delivery patient had been in his house in the Bazaar for the whole of the night in which the murder had taken place in the distant Club billiard room. The doctor had seen him, had seen too much of him. There could be no getting round such testimony. Could there?

Then, in the state of depression in which his burst of fury had left him, another gloomy thought surfaced. The Culture Circle. He had pledged himself to attend it next evening, to be paraded at it as a living Sherlock Holmes while Professor Godbole launched into doubtless more and more abstruse and fanciful speculations about this story-book figure.

Non-existent, he thought with a renewed spurt of bitterness, in real life certainly.

Wearily, rather than endure any further discussion of alibis and their alleged ineffectiveness, he offered the

Culture Circle and that promise of his as another gift to His Excellency. Who, of course, was delighted.

'I generally put in an appearance there myself,' he said. 'Must support worthy causes and all that. But I hadn't realized Fatbhoy, who's the most terrible fellow by the way, had got hold of Godbole. And to talk about Sherlock Holmes, too. I most certainly will come with you, my dear fellow, and listen keenly to your own contributions to the subsequent discussion. Yes, indeed.'

Ghote was even more put out by this assumption that he would make contributions to a discussion which he had not in any case foreseen as taking place. So much so that he quite forgot to ask why Dr Fatbhoy was 'a terrible fellow', though when His Excellency had pronounced the condemnation he had meant to question it. The Parsi doctor had by no means seemed a terrible fellow to him.

The thought was pushed even further from his head by a sudden loud bird-like call from the steps of the Library.

'Mr Mehta! Mr Mehta! Your Excellency! Your Excellency!'

It was the guardian lady of the entrance counter. She was waving a book, in a bright dust-wrapper, and seemed in a state of high excitement.

His Excellency turned abruptly and set off towards her. But she was much too delighted with her news to wait for him.

'Mr Mehta, it has come,' she called out. 'The dak from UK. And in it is just what you were hoping for.'

The ex-ambassador broke into a trot, for all his years, and on the library steps positively seized the bright volume.

'*Into the Valley of Death* by Evelyn Hervey,' twittered the guardian lady. 'I have never heard of Miss Hervey, but it certainly is a first-class corker.'

'You—You haven't read it?' His Excellency asked in sudden suspicion.

'Oh, no, no. I would never. We all know that you like to be the first, Mr Mehta. We all have respect for that.'

'Hah. Well, yes. Yes, thank you, dear lady. Very decent of you.'

And, tucking the boldly coloured volume under his arm, His Excellency made his way back.

But he was not to add to his disquisition on alibis and how they were in themselves highly suspicious. As he reached Ghote, he happened to look along the road, and what he saw sent him into an evident state of panic.

He darted glances left and right as if seeking sanctuary. He took the book from under his arm and held it behind his back. Then, realizing that this manoeuvre had made him look particularly conspicuous, he endeavoured to tuck the volume closely to his side at thigh level. And nearly dropped it.

Ghote, wondering at the performance, looked along the road, calm in the sunshine, dotted with old Ooty hands and their dogs of various sorts and sizes, aged alsatians all tugging long past, terriers that had once been bouncy and yapping, a Scottie grey-faced as a whiskered elder. At first he could not make out at all what could have caused His Excellency to behave in such an odd manner.

Then, as much from the direction of those panic-stricken glances as anything, he hit on it. Mrs Trayling. Mrs Lucy Trayling, widow of the brigadier, the sugar bowl perhaps of His Excellency's breakfast-table line-up.

She was coming towards them, hair escaping as always from a wide sun-hat, ancient empty shopping basket in one hand, huge flowered knitting-bag in the other.

Why should such an everyday sight put someone usually so sure of himself into such a state? Could it be that he had somehow fixed in his mind on this unlikely figure as definitely the murderer? Well, if unlikeliness was the chief reason for considering someone as a murderer, then perhaps it could.

But, no.

'Ghote, Ghote,' His Excellency began to whisper piercingly, sidling near with the volume from the library still held tight against his tweed-covered thigh.

'Yes, sir? What is it, please?'

'Take this book, man. Take it, but don't let Lucy Trayling see you.'

It was not easy to do as His Excellency had asked. To begin with, he still continued to maintain his rigid grip. Then it was necessary to get between him and the waftily advancing Mrs Trayling, and there seemed to be no reason to stand closely face to face in the public road. And finally there was the question of what to do with the book when he had got it. He could, he supposed, push it inside his jersey, but that was so well-fitting that the square bulge would be particularly noticeable.

As he tugged away trying to slide the volume out of the vice of His Excellency's hand and thigh, he muttered his doubts.

'Sir, when I have got I have nowhere to hide.'

'Just tuck it under your arm, man. She won't suspect you.'

Trayling Memsahib not suspect him? But surely he was meant to be suspecting her?

Overwhelmed by confusion, he got the book free of its imprisoning grasp at last and, turning, attempted to hold it in a carefree manner under his arm.

'Good morning, Lucy,' His Excellency called out the moment he was free of the object that seemed to embarrass him so much.

He sounded to Ghote hopelessly false.

Trayling Memsahib, although by now she was not far from them, appeared not to have heard the greeting. Ghote felt a sense of absurd relief. Whatever it was that His Excellency had wanted to hide, aided by himself, he had apparently achieved it. More by luck than any adroitness in their manoeuvrings.

'Lucy! Lucy! Good morning!'

The fool. What for did he want to go and do that? If he had had the sense to keep his mouth shut only . . .

And, of course, this time she did hear.

She stopped, looked this way and that, recognized His Excellency and began with evident reluctance politely to come over.

Ghote, unostentatiously as he could, contrived to step somewhat behind the tall, tweed-clad ex-ambassador and to slip the brightly jacketed book more deeply under his arm.

'Hah. How are you this morning, my dear? Miss your presence at the Club. Ayah fit and well again, eh?'

But Mrs Trayling replied to none of his questions.

'Sorry, fearfully sorry,' she said. 'Got to go and take the dog for his walk. Must rush. Must rush.'

And she swung away and strode off at such a cracking pace and with such marked determination that Ghote began to wonder if, after all, she could have indeed scrambled out of the window of the Club billiard room and made her way with the silver to where Major Bell's decrepit Dasher had found it.

Then, perhaps with the image of the wheezing, ancient Dasher in his mind, something else struck him.

Mrs Trayling's Spot. The animal had expired some time ago. His Excellency had mentioned it, and so had the homoeopathic dog doctor. So why had Trayling Memsahib said that she had got to take her dog for a walk? Why had she told a blatant lie?

He turned to his Watson.

'Sir,' he said, 'urgent business.'

And he left at a run till he had made sure Mrs Trayling was within sight again.

It was only as he began to follow her at a calmer pace that he realized he still had His Excellency's book under his arm.

As he walked past a succession of Ooty cottages with their trim hedges and neat if faded name-boards, Woodbriar, The Lupins, Glenview, Cedarhurst, he began to think about the ridiculous episode he had just been involved in. It was clear, when he considered, that the book His Excellency had been given with such a show of excitement by the lady from the Library must be the latest detective story from England and that, with the freaks of behaviour apt to occur in any small cut-off community, His Excellency must have a bee in his bonnet about reading the newest story before anybody else. Plainly, too – His Excellency had even spoken about this – Trayling Memsahib was a rival reader. Perhaps she had once guessed an answer before His Excellency. Yes, that would be it.

So one mystery was explained.

But another was not. Ahead of him Trayling Memsahib was marching along with unflagging determination. And no sign of any dog.

Where was she going then? Would what she was doing prove to be a clue to the mystery of Pichu's death?

It did not seem very likely. But then unlikely things seemed to flourish in the unlikely air of Ooty. And, if His Excellency was right about the murder being some diabolically clever scheme such as you got only in detective stories, then the fact that Trayling Memsahib was a keen reader of such books might mean that she had taken the idea of covering up her crime from just such a novel.

Well, at least she was not so diabolically clever as to realize she was being followed. There she was striding ahead, tweed skirt, slightly baggy at the back, jerking rhythmically, knitting-bag swinging from one hand, shopping basket from the other.

Even Sherlock Holmes would not have to do whatever it was he did so as not to be seen following if he was tracking Trayling Memsahib.

They had got down to the neighbourhood of the Lake now. In the distance across its wind-ruffled waters the extraordinary countryside, high up, out of this world, lay twinkling in the bright sunshine. On the little rolling hills the terraces of cultivation looked neat and pretty as if drawn by some child-like god. Here and there a cottage or a larger house stood, free from clutter and clean-looking as if a minor god lived inside it.

Tall spiky eucalyptus trees, magnificent and alien, were scattered about. Where the land was not under cultivation dark green patches of gorse could be seen, looking like the scratchy plastic bushes round some model of a building before it had been put up and battered and defaced by grubby humanity.

And now it became evident that Trayling Memsahib was heading for the far side of the Lake, making for an unfrequented part of the stretch of artificial water first created – so His Excellency had said – by the very founder of Ooty, one Mr John Sullivan, Collector of Coimbatore, who had, if His Excellency was to be believed, both fallen in love with this airy paradise and simultaneously made a good thing out of it financially.

Ghote's mind turned for a moment to the thought of certain politicians, high-sounding in their pronouncements and ever more wealthy from their dealings. Perhaps the changing world did not change all that much.

Abruptly, some little distance ahead, Trayling Memsahib flopped to the ground and sat, an angular, hunched figure, on the fresh springy grass by the lakeside contemplating the glinting waters in front of her.

Ghote stopped in his turn and looked round.

There was a large gorse bush, spotted with dark yellow flowers, placed so conveniently for observation that it was almost too good to be true. Crouching a little, he made his way quietly and cautiously over to it and settled down flat on his stomach behind the cover it provided. If things always went so well for Sherlock Holmes, no wonder no one he followed ever saw him.

Down by the water Trayling Memsahib sat still as a carving, in marked contrast to the energy she had shown in haring away from His Excellency outside the Library and in marching to this spot.

And, of course, Ghote realized, this must surely be the very place where one dark night Brigadier Roly Trayling, wandering about in a state of alcoholic maziness, must have fallen into the Lake and drowned.

Perhaps he was witnessing an act of remembrance which Trayling Memsahib performed at regular intervals. Once a week? Once a month? On the anniversary of the sad day? Yet somehow he did not think so. There had been too much hysteria in the way she had hurried down to the Lake. But at least he knew now why in all probability she had paid so little heed to His Excellency when he called out to her. Plainly she had been in the grip of some strong compulsion.

Was she perhaps visiting the spot to 'tell' her dead husband that at last he had been avenged, that the man who had let him drown had met his own end, a body in the billiard room?

But how was he himself to find out if this was in fact so?

Presumably even if he went up to the brigadier's widow in her moment of final triumph – if this was her moment of triumph, if she had indeed killed Pichu, if the murder was not, after all, a simple act of dacoity – she would hardly pour out a confession to him here and now. No, if she had murdered Pichu she had planned the crime with care, had done everything His Excellency believed had been done in order to cover it up. She was not going to spoil it all now with any easy confession.

But, damn it, could she not do something? For how long was she going to go on sitting and sitting?

The gorse bush cut off the sun from a part of where he was lying and his head and shoulders were beginning to feel distinctly cold even though his legs were prickling with sweat.

His eye fell on the book His Excellency had transferred to him in that absurd manner, lying on the grass beside him. Well, if he had not got *Mrs McGinty's Dead* to go through, perhaps he could look at *Into the Valley of Death* instead. It, too, was a detective story after all. The lady at the Library had said it was a first-class corker. Perhaps from it he would get a clearer idea of the way such books worked. Of the way, possibly, Lucy Trayling's mind had worked.

And – a gleam of maliciousness lit up inside him – if he could find out who had done the murder in the book perhaps a chance would come of letting His Excellency know that he himself had arrived at the answer before him.

He took another look at Trayling Memsahib. Not a sign of movement.

He opened the book.

Time passed. The sun began to drop towards the horizon. It grew decidedly chillier. Every now and again he glanced up from the pages to make sure Sherlock Holmes's quarry was still there, and then he read on, fired soon by the simple desire to know who had committed this murder supposed to have taken place in some woods in the English countryside about one hundred years ago.

At last, having got the main facts clear in his head, he did something he vaguely felt to be wrong, though he could not exactly think why. He turned to the end and gulpingly read the final chapter.

Ah, so that was who it was. Very clever, if rather far-fetched. Still, not a bad reason for killing somebody. If you had been guilty of an act of cowardice during the Crimean War, not seemingly at the Charge of the Light Brigade displayed with all its mess-obliterated glory on the walls of the billiard room at the Ootacamund Club, but at some other battle in that war, and if, instead of being disgraced, you had by chance been awarded the Victoria Cross and somebody years later had learnt your secret . . .

Yes, true enough, blackmail could be a good reason for—

'Mr Ghote! What are you doing skulking here?'

He looked up, startled into heart-thudding dismay.

Trayling Memsahib was standing on the other side of the gorse bush looking down at him in fury and contempt.

14

Ghote, as his heart stopped thumping, felt a deep blush rising up all over his face. Sherlock Holmes had been caught out. His following of Mrs Trayling had been in the end appallingly incompetent. He had failed to obey the first rule of good detective work: to concentrate undeviatingly on the task in hand. Terrible words from the magisterial pen of Dr Hans Gross's *Criminal Investigation* echoed in his head: 'The Investigator must have a high grade of real self-denying power.'

And how had he denied himself? He had abandoned observation of a suspect in favour of reading a trashy detective story only.

He looked up at the stern, outraged face of Mrs Lucy Trayling under her wide hat with its surrounding wisps of iron-grey hair.

And he realized that, despite having been caught at such a disadvantage, he must assume command of the situation.

He rose to his feet in one single movement, ignoring a jab of pain that shot up his left thigh.

'Madam,' he said, 'what I was doing in this place was to keep strict observation upon yourself. You must be aware, isn't it, that the murder in the billiard room at Ooty Club is not certain to be the work of some dacoit. It may well have been instead a most careful crime committed by a person sleeping within the said Club premises on the night in question. And, madam, you are such a person.'

He certainly seemed to have turned the tables. Mrs Trayling looked decidedly discomposed.

'Madam,' he went poundingly on, 'kindly do not think that I am not very well knowing what it is that you are doing at this unfrequented spot.'

Mrs Trayling strove for words.

'Yes, madam, this must be the spot where your late husband, Brigadier R. Trayling, was falling into the Lake and drowning. You had come here for some purpose. But was it just only to mourn? That I am very much doubting.'

'Mr Ghote—'

'No, madam, was it not to tell the spirit of your late husband that the man who had allowed him to drown was now dead also? And at your hands?'

'No. No. Oh, no.'

Mrs Trayling seemed to lose in a moment all the iron backbone she had shown as she had loomed accusingly over the gorse bush.

'No, Mr Ghote,' she said. 'No, it isn't true. Oh, oh, I'm in such a muddle. I don't know what to do. I don't know where to turn.'

'But in this muddle you were killing the man Pichu?' Ghote said, not daring to unbend by the smallest amount.

'No, no. Oh, you see, I didn't come here to where Roly drowned – yes, you're right about that, this is the place – I didn't come here to tell him anything like that. Not at all. Not at all.'

'Then what for were you coming?'

Again Ghote forced himself to be unyielding as the Indian Penal Code itself.

'It was to ask him—' Lucy Trayling began. 'Oh, Mr Ghote, I know you'll think me silly, but it was to ask Roly's advice that I came out here. Truly.'

'You were asking the late Brigadier Trayling's advice?'

Ghote said, not feeling that this was altogether silly. 'But what for were you wanting advice?'

'About—About what I should do. I mean, while my old Ayah was still with me I knew I had to stay on here in Ooty and give her somewhere to live. All her family's long since dead. Of course, she isn't really much help in the house nowadays, but I don't mind that. Almost everybody in Ooty – I mean everybody like us – has to do things we would never have dreamt of doing in the old days. No, I didn't mind that, and I knew I must stay till poor old Ayah popped off. But she's hardly going to last another month or two, I can see that perfectly well. And when she's gone what ought I to do?'

'But His Excellency Mr Mehta was telling that you would go to Home.'

'Well, yes. I've said that to people. But should I go? I mean, what's it like at Home now? One hears such dreadful things. Lawlessness, and something they call muggings. Perhaps when I get there I shall find it's all too awful.'

'Yes, I can see that to go to UK if it is no longer an altogether law-abiding place would be a very, very bad risk.'

'Yes. But to stay on in Ooty? There's hardly anybody here I know nowadays. I mean, Surinder Mehta's from the old days but he's really awfully frail now. And dear old Ringer Bell's worse. Don't think I mind about people not being British. I got over all that long ago. But it's simply that there's nobody I really know. Scarcely anybody.'

'And you were coming here to seek the late Brigadier's advice upon this? To go Home or to stay on?'

'Yes. You see, Roly always knew the answer. It came from being an Army man. You had the regulations to go by. Parade at such-and-such an hour. Just one way to drill. Just one way to give commands. It was all fixed, definite, decided. And it made Roly decisive, too. I mean, I think that's why when we retired he—Well, I think . . .'

'It is why the late Brigadier was drinking very much of Indian whisky?' Ghote asked softly.

'Oh. You know? Well, yes, I suppose it's common gossip, and Ooty is a fearful place for gossip. Well, yes, that was why poor Roly did feel the need. He didn't have rules to go by any more. I mean, he tried gardening, but the damned hollyhocks would never grow in the lines he wanted. And it was the same with everything else really.'

'I see. And, please, when you were getting up and coming upon myself behind this bush, had you obtained any answer from the late Brigadier?'

Lucy Trayling sighed.

'Well, I shouldn't really have expected to, should I?'

'But, no. Some thought may have entered your head only.'

'Yes. Well, it didn't.'

'So what is it you are going to do when Ayah is popping off?'

'I don't know, Mr Ghote. I just don't know.'

Ghote looked at her.

Her hair, in the course of this intimate discussion, seemed to have become even more unruly and the contents of her knitting-bag, tilted forward in her agitation, had begun to spill out, a ball of fluffy pink angora wool, another of bright green, clashing horribly.

'Mrs Trayling,' Ghote said at last, feeling his way. 'Ooty is a very fine place. The air is so cool, yet the sun is shining with great brightness. There are many nice houses also, and other amenities. Do you not think this would be the place to stay?'

The brigadier's widow gave a huge sniff and wiped her hand carelessly across a lined, tanned cheek where a bright tear had glinted.

'Yes,' she said. 'Yes. I think perhaps you're right.'

She made an effort to scrabble back into her knitting-bag the tumbling balls of wool.

'Well,' she added, 'I suppose Roly has spoken to me. In a way.'

She seized a slipping metal needle and drove it fiercely down in among the other contents of the bag.

'And now, if you'll excuse me,' she said, 'I think I ought to be getting back. I think I may have left a kettle boiling and Ayah isn't very good at noticing such things any more.'

And away she went.

Ghote did not believe in the kettle. But he waited where he was beside the gorse bush until Lucy Trayling was well out of sight.

And he made up his mind that he would say nothing of this strange encounter to his burdensome Watson.

Not because he did not believe what Mrs Trayling had told him about her reason for coming to the lake, a great deal more than he believed in the ever-boiling kettle. But he realized that she had produced no hard facts to account for her not being responsible for the body in the billiard room. Indeed, the case against her was in some ways stronger. She was, after all, a great reader of detective stories, and the murder did appear to be a detective-story murder. And now there was her proven muddle-headedness. She could well be the sort of person, from what he had just seen of her, who would commit a murder for a jumble of reasons that would seem altogether insufficient to someone more rationally inclined.

Yes, no doubt His Excellency would insist, with some reason, on retaining Mrs Trayling as one of the suspects. So there were still five. Six, if you counted alibied Mr Iyer.

He had half hoped that, back at the Club, he would manage to avoid His Excellency somehow. But he was not so lucky.

As he sat under one of the aged stags' heads, consuming a large plate of cucumber sandwiches and a pot of tea by way of making up for the midday meal he had missed while lying watching Lucy Trayling, His Excellency descended.

'Hah. There you are. Had good hunting?'

Ghote got up from the deep sofa.

'Please, what hunting is this?'

'Lucy Trayling,' said His Excellency, with more acuteness than a guru's disciple ought to show. 'Don't think I didn't cotton on when you left at such a gallop after old Lucy had told that fearful lie about her dog.'

'Well, yes, I did wish to know where Trayling Memsahib was proceeding to in so much of hurry.'

'Good man. And where was she off to?'

'Oh, she was—That is—That is, I am sorry to state that I was not able in the end to follow her to wherever it was.'

'Aha, not quite up to the great Sherlock, eh?'

His Excellency dug him in the ribs. His thin old elbow felt extremely sharp.

All the same, Ghote reflected, it had actually been by failing to keep watch on Trayling Memsahib with the miraculous invisibility of a Sherlock Holmes that in the end he had found out all he had about her.

His silence, however, brought him further tribulation. It let His Excellency launch into a long comparison between Holmes and Poirot as sleuths, with particular reference to physical clues. Bicycle tyres came into it and little grey cells and why a dog had not barked in the night-time and some list of Poirot's that had included the smell of oil paint, a picture postcard, an art critic and some wax flowers, all of which put together had proved that a murder could have been committed only in one particular way.

Ghote listened to the confused recital with what patience he could muster. But at last he jumped up from the sofa down on to which his persistent Watson had dragged him.

'Sir,' he said, snatching at the first excuse that offered, 'very regret but I must be proceeding to Sunnyside Cottage once more.'

'Hah. Gathering evidence, eh? Keeping Pratapgadh and that secret amour of his well to the fore? Good man.'

He shook his head appreciatively.

'Yes, chaps of your sort never work on mere theories.

Just as I was saying. Hard evidence is what they want – the picture postcard, the wax flowers. Off you go then, Poirot. And be careful not to get those immaculate shoes of yours dirty. Hah.'

Ghote did not wait to find out what the last remark meant, but made his escape as fast as he could. Perhaps, he thought, when he came to read *Mrs McGinty's Dead* all would be made clear. If, after the trouble *Into the Valley of Death* had caused him, he had the heart to tackle another detective story.

Hurrying away from the Club as dusk began to come on, he thought that perhaps after all going out to Sunnyside Cottage again in fact would be no bad thing. If the Maharajah of Pratapgadh was the lover of Sarla Kumar, he might well have been so determined not to let his wife know this that he had simply got rid of blackmailing Pichu with the contempt of a Rajput of old for the merest menial. So it would be really useful to establish firmly that the amorous relationship did exist. And, out at the cottage this time, he would take very good care not to let his watch slacken by one jot. It would be Dr Hans Gross every second of the time, not that easily made invisible Sherlock Holmes.

So best to go out there on foot and not risk the sound of a taxi engine alerting that dreadful auntie.

He looked up at the sky, already fast losing its daylight brightness. He would have to hurry if he was going to get into a good hiding-place before there was any chance of the Maharajah leaping up from his dinner at the Club and into that jeep of his.

But, just as he reached the foot of the avenue leading down from the Club and was peering about to see if he could make out the pillar-still form of the yogi there, something else drew his attention.

It was the old watchman he had seen when first coming with His Excellency from the bus that had brought him to Ooty. The fellow was advancing waveringly to take up his duties for the night, long lathi in military fashion over his shoulder.

And it occurred to Ghote at once that there were questions he ought to ask him. Questions he ought to have looked for the fellow to ask as soon as he had learnt the basic facts of the situation. But, with the watchman appearing only during the hours of darkness, he had not remembered. It was the penalty of being a mere private detective.

On the other hand, the hours of darkness had now come, and if he was to get out to Sunnyside Cottage before the Maharajah he ought to be on his way at once. He had already left it a little late.

But, equally, the questions he had for the watchman ought not to be kept any longer. They might alter his whole view of the murder.

Reluctantly he branched off to greet the old man.

'Good evening, Watchman Sahib.'

In return he received a tremulously thwacking salute on the lathi, held up at somewhat of an angle.

'There is something you could tell. It is about the night poor Pichu was killed.'

A look of sudden distrust came on to the watchman's face, as far as in the rapidly gathering darkness Ghote could make out.

Had he been mistaken? Or was the distrust due to something other than the mention of Pichu's death?

'Perhaps,' he hazarded, 'Inspector Meenakshisundaram has already asked about what was happening on that night?'

'No, sahib. Inspectorji was not seeing myself.'

But the distrust – it was plain in the fellow's voice now – had not lessened. So it could not be that Meenakshisundaram – one more inefficiency – had in that bullying way of his set up any resentment.

Ghote thought for a moment.

Then he decided that there was only one way to tackle the matter.

He took half a pace nearer so that the watchman's face was as visible as possible.

'There is something you have not told,' he said.

A statement. One not to be denied.

There was a long silence. The scent from a nearby heliotrope bush sweetly assaulted Ghote's nostrils.

Then at last the old watchman uttered a short, deep groan.

Ghote waited.

'Sahib,' the watchman said, his voice so low that it was almost inaudible. 'Sahib, I was failing in my duty.'

But for all the pain in the fellow's voice Ghote knew that he could not let his grip on him go.

'You must tell all. Every detail.'

Another silence in the odoriferous air.

'Sahib, when that dacoity was happening I heard. I heard the sound of glass-pane breaking.'

Then a stop.

'Yes? You heard. You are the Club watchman and, it is true, you should have heard any strange sound in the night. That is why I came to ask you questions.'

'Yes, sahib. But after Meenakshisundaram Sahib was asking me nothing, I dared to hope no one would know what I had done.'

'What you had not done, what you had not done,' Ghote said implacably. 'Well, what duty was it that you failed in?'

'Sahib, I am an old, old man. Many years have I been watchman at Club. In old days the watchman before me was given retirement at age sixty years. While he was still hale and hearty. But, sahib, they were not giving me retirement.'

No funds, Ghote thought. No funds now, when the Club has so few members, to do what is proper. So this old man had been let go on as watchman until long past being able to carry out his duties as they should be done, until the lathi in his hands is no longer upright when offered in salute.

'Yes, you are an old man,' he said to him, unbending still. 'But nevertheless you were not doing what is right. When you heard that noise of the window of the billiard room breaking it was your duty to go there.'

'But, sahib, I was fearful and I did not.'

'And so you failed to seize the dacoit who was stealing the Club silver which it was your duty to protect.'

Only, Ghote thought, was it a dacoit the old man had failed to seize? Or was it someone from inside the Club, a member, laying that false trail His Excellency believed in so strongly?

'Sahib, I did not. But . . .'

'Yes? What is it? What is it?'

'But, sahib, I was not altogether disgraceful. Sahib, after some time I was recovering my fighting spirit, in so far as I was able.'

'Yes? And then?'

'Then, sahib, I did set out to see what was that noise of a breaking glass-pane.'

'Ah. And you found? You saw?'

'Sahib, I saw that a dacoit had entered the Club and had afterwards left.'

'You saw this dacoit? You got a good look at him?'

So Meenakshisundaram was right. So the crime at the Club was, after all, an ordinary affair, a simple dacoity, if one that had gone terrifyingly wrong. So, all that detective-story nonsense was just that, nonsense.

'No, sahib, I was not well seeing.'

Ghote felt a cascading descent of disappointment. For a moment he had had the pleasure of thinking that he would be able to go to His Excellency and report without any reservations that it was beyond doubt that Pichu had been killed in the course of an ordinary dacoity. That the affair was one that Inspector Meenakshisundaram was perfectly capable of dealing with, indeed with his local knowledge was the only officer fit to deal with it. And then he himself could have left Ooty, the treacherous paradise, and have gone back down to a world he knew, with all its difficulties, its half-answers, its muddles and mess. And there he could have got on with doing the best he could.

But after that one happy moment it had all been shattered.

'You were not well seeing?' he questioned the old watchman with dull hopelessness. 'Then just what were you seeing?'

'Sahib, in the dark I knew there was a man who was pushing through that hedge on the far side. But this I was more hearing than seeing.'

'And you stayed where you were even then?'

'No, sahib, no. When I was certain a dacoit had robbed the Club silver I was doing my level best to stop.'

'And what level best was that?'

'Sahib, I was calling and shouting. I was calling for others to come and start up hue-and-cry.'

'I see. And they came? Who came? Why was I not hearing of this hue-and-cry? Did anyone else see the thief?'

'Sahib, no one was coming.'

'No one? Of course. No one. So what next?'

'So next, sahib, I was myself going after this bloody dacoit.'

'But you saw no more of him?' Ghote asked, knowing what the answer was bound to be.

'No, sahib, no more. It was all dark and I was seeing and hearing nothing. Then, after, I began to hope no one would think I had heard one thing even.'

Ghote simply turned away then, for all that a tiny something inside him told him that he ought not to leave the watchman like this. He ought, he felt deep within himself, to say something. Whether it was to excuse the old man on the grounds of his age and feebleness or to rebuke him for dereliction of duty, it hardly mattered. But he ought to round off the business.

And he just did not have the strength of mind. Because it had all left him exactly where he had been before the thought had come to him that the watchman might all along be holding the answer to the whole mystery. But now he was back to the start once more. Back to it being as likely that the affair was some sort of detective-story murder as that it was a decent, messy, ordinary crime to be cleared up or not as chance and a thousand odd circumstances dictated.

Sapping gloom swirled and settled within him.

15

Drearily Ghote supposed that there was nothing else to do now but set out for Sunnyside Cottage to see if he could prove that the Maharajah, perhaps His Excellency's Number One suspect, was having that illicit affair with Sarla Kumar. And, he thought, I shall have to take a taxi after all, if I am to get into hiding before that fellow comes roaring and racing up in that jeep of his.

He set off leaden-footed to see if he could find a taxi, barely taking in that, night or no night, the yogi was there in his customary place, rigid as the Club signboard beside him.

As he passed he heard the sound of a vehicle coming towards him and a moment later saw its dim headlights poking through the darkness. Would it be a taxi he could hail?

A short distance away the car – it was a taxi – came to a sudden halt. Its rear door was pushed sharply open, and out of it stepped the Maharani, flinging a note back towards the driver.

To Ghote's surprise she came marching straight up to him.

'Good even—' he began.

She cut him short.

'The one man in Ooty I'd most like to see.'

'Please?'

Why, for heaven's sake, was this rich, Westernized, voluptuous creature, who less than twenty-four hours earlier had left him in anger to make his own way back from Sunnyside Cottage, why was she saying now he was the one man she most wanted to see?

'You were there with me yesterday,' she said, her voice ringing out in the cool night. 'You were there. You made me leave then before I'd done what I wanted. Well, you can be the first to know I did what I wanted tonight. I learnt just what I hoped to.'

'You mean . . .'

'Yes, the bastard had told me he didn't want any dinner. So I guessed what his idea was. And I rushed out and got a taxi and made the man drive out there hell for leather. So I was just in time, kneeling behind that bush again, to see Vikram go prancing up to the door and ring at the bell. And the bitch answered it.'

'The auntie?'

'Auntie, my foot. The bitch herself, bloody Sarla Kumar. Opened the door and flung herself round his neck. The whore.'

'Oh, I am most sorry. But, you know—'

'Sorry? What the hell is there to be sorry about? I've got him now. Got him wrapped up, tied hand and foot, just where I want him.'

'Where you are wanting him?'

Ghote was only half-following.

'Oh, yes. Now that I know for certain he's gone back to that bitch, sniffing round her like a pi-dog, he can't do a damn thing to me. Now there can't be any more of his talk about divorcing me without a rupee, not whatever I choose to do.'

'It is Mr Amul Dutt you are choosing?' Ghote said boldly.

'Yes. All right. It's Mr Amul Dutt. And, by God, I'll be

down there with him in just the time it takes me to change into some clothes that haven't been contaminated by the sight of that swine and kneeling in that bitch's disgusting garden. So goodnight, Mr Ghote, and wish me everything I wish myself.'

She swung away to march back up to the Club.

But Ghote was not going to let her go without learning as much as he could that might help him.

'Madam! Madam!' he called out. 'Madam, stop. There is one thing I must be asking.'

The Maharani did stop, turning impatiently to face him in the dim starlight.

'Madam,' he said, going up towards her, 'kindly tell me this thing. If your husband is having this illicit affair with Miss Sarla Kumar and taking each and every precaution so that you yourself would not know, then why, if he is a truly ruthless individual, is it that he did not remove the billiards marker Pichu from his path like a fly or an insect only?'

He heard her give a short angry puff of a sigh.

'Really, you're just damned obsessed with that frightful Pichu. Of course Vikram wouldn't kill him. I told you; he'd have bought him off if he had to and thought nothing of it. And, besides, Vikram isn't exactly your ruthless type, believe you me. No, sneakiness is Master Vikram's way, and don't I know it.'

'Very good. Thank you, madam.'

Ghote stood and watched her go striding into the dark. He shivered in the cold.

And felt at once fiercely irritated with himself. All his life he had cursed heat and humidity, and now when as if by a miracle he was up here in the delightful cool of the hills he was shivering and miserable.

Well, at least, he consoled himself, he no longer need keep a watch out at Sunnyside Cottage. Because one thing was certain: the Maharajah was the lover of Sarla Kumar. His wife, vengeful as well as voluptuous, would not have been lying about that, even if perhaps, keen to retain that meal-ticket of hers, she had not been telling the truth about the sneakiness or otherwise of his character.

So what to do? Go back and sit at dinner with His Excellency? After having filled himself up in any case with cucumber sandwiches?

No. He would certainly not do that.

What he would do – it came stealing over him like the spicy odour of rich food on a stove – was to creep back into the Club and go to bed. And, if he could not sleep at this early hour, he could always try reading *Mrs McGinty's Dead* after all.

Then tomorrow . . . Tomorrow after a long night's refreshing sleep he would be up very early and get hold of the other witness Meenakshisundaram had failed to interview, Gauri, the sweeper woman who had actually been the first to see the body in the billiard room. She might or might not have any new evidence. But at least some work on the case would have been done in the proper manner.

And he found, warm and happy beneath the blankets of his Ooty bed, even though getting into it so early he had had to forgo the hot-water bag a servant would have brought him, he had no difficulty once he had begun again on Agatha Christie in getting through his task. The words slipped by. Incident followed incident. There were glints of humour that made him smile but never caused him to pause in his reading. And all the while he could not stop himself wanting to know the answer to the simple question: who had killed the harmless charwoman, Mrs McGinty?

Somehow, sitting in the broad bed with its blankets drawn up to his chin – at home he never needed even one blanket – this cardboardy question seemed more gripping, more demanding, than the real question posed by the actual dead body that had been found in the billiard room under this same roof just a few days earlier.

And, it appeared, as he read on and the hours ticked away, that the harmless Mrs McGinty had not been so harmless after all. She had been, like Pichu, a blackmailer. Yet her blackmail, Ghote felt, was blackmail made out of moonlight. Shimmer stuff. Not touching anything or anyone.

In the smooth flow of it all none of the awkward queries that might have ripped at the surface of his mind like jutting sharp-edged rocks ever quite rose up. He read of Superintendent Spence wagging a heavy forefinger at Hercule Poirot and saying he had never seen an innocent man hanged and did not now intend to, and never a thought arose that Inspector Meenakshisundaram might be busy at this moment seizing on some dacoit, innocent at least of this crime, and preparing to beat a confession out of him. Or, worse, that His Excellency might push himself into getting charged under Section 302 some member of the Ootacamund Club who had not in fact committed any diabolically clever murder.

Poirot told his *cher Spence* that since Mrs McGinty was just an ordinary charwoman the murderer must be the one who was extraordinary, and, deep under the spell, it did not even occur to Ghote that His Excellency, who had probably read these words half a dozen times over the years, might have got his whole ridiculous notion into his head because of them.

One of the suspects remarked cheerfully that what he liked in detective stories were the clues that meant everything to the detective but nothing to the reader until the end when one kicked oneself for not seeing them. And Ghote knew that, yes, he too already, in flicking through the pages longing to know who had done it, had passed over half a dozen such clues. But he did not even for a moment rebuke himself, an officer of Crime Branch, Bombay Police, for being so stupid. He was in a world where the facts of ordinary existence counted for nothing.

Then, at last, Monsieur Poirot was taking off the shoes that pinched – the ones he had been upset to find dirtied with English mud – and was easing on the slippers which would allow him to enter undistracted into a state of trance. A state of trance, Ghote thought, just like the ones Professor Godbole had mentioned, except that his examples had been of Great Detectives who had reached not for slippers but for tobacco pipes. Shortly, then, Poirot would know.

Shortly indeed Poirot did know, and Ghote duly kicked himself.

But, to his mingled disappointment and relief, he found that the answer to the riddle of Mrs McGinty's death had not after all shed any light on what had happened in the billiard room at the Ootacamund Club.

And the time was 2 a.m.

A momentary panic swept up in him. He had pledged himself to be up before dawn to get hold of the sweeper woman, Gauri, at the hour which, as His Excellency had mentioned once, an army of sweepers came up from the Bazaar to keep the Club spick and span. Would he be able now to wake early enough? But he told himself sharply he would wake when he had to. Then he dropped His Excellency's book on to the floor and within two minutes was fast asleep.

He woke while the sky through the high windows of the room had in it hardly a trace of grey-white light. He got up, hurried into his clothes and let himself quietly out of the building.

To be astonished to find the springy grass of the wide lawns all round covered in white.

Frost, he thought. This is frost. It transforms everything. It makes Ooty into a fairyland from Western stories. As it is, as it surely is. A fairyland. An altogether unreal place.

Just like the book he had devoured before falling asleep.

That, too, had been something frost-transformed. On to the dull shapes of ordinary life a magic net of white crystal had been thrown. While he had been under its spell he had been wholly willing to believe there were people who did the things Dame Agatha Christie made them do. He had wanted to accept the circus hoops she held up for her people to jump through and the tangle upon tangle of mystification, no doubt in accord with some strict rules, she had arranged for them. And it was indeed a circus, her world. A circus where every trick came off.

But there was another world, he thought, his own world where very few tricks came off and where, when they did, something usually went messily wrong afterwards. A world where there was no transforming frost.

Then, looking up, he saw the raggedy band of sweepers approaching across the grass, and noticed that behind them it was no longer frost-glinting but a muddled trodden black.

He scrutinized the group as they got nearer.

'Gauri?' he called out when they were close enough to hear without his having to raise his voice and disturb the dawn hush. 'Which of you is Gauri?'

For a moment he thought he was not going to get an answer. It could be that Gauri had not come this morning. She might have fallen ill. She might have died even. Or just have vanished into the teeming masses down below in the plains.

But, no.

From the group an old woman stepped forward, wary but proud. She was a gaunt, age-battered creature, her hair grey-streaked and combed back hard to her head, her skin dark – how much must her parents years and years ago have fought against facts in naming her after the goddess famed for her fairness – her arms almost fleshless and sinewy, her neck corded and scrawny where it emerged from the faded orange choli she wore under a creased and sleep-crumpled cheap purple cotton sari.

He went up to her.

'Gauri,' he said, 'I have only a little Tamil. Do you speak English?'

'I speak, sahib. To work at Club is good to have.'

'Very well. Then let me tell you I have come from Bombay-side to investigate the death of the man Pichu. You were the first to see him dead, yes?'

'Oh, yes, sahib. I saw that old devil on billiard table, dead, dead,' Gauri replied, with an unembarrassed grin. 'Just like he drunk again, face pink-pink like flowers only and mouth all full up of spit-spit.'

With a warm rush of relief, Ghote realized that here was someone he could talk to with ease, despite the language difficulty, someone simple, cheerful and life-accepting.

But would she have anything for him worth hearing?

'Old devil you are saying?' he asked. 'You were knowing Pichu well then?'

'Oh, that one. When I was coming to billiard room always-always he would be snoring in front of silver-cups almirah. From all his drinking-drinking.'

Pleased to have at least gained this much confirmation of Pichu's bad character, Ghote plunged on.

'Yes, this drinking. You are knowing where in dry Tamil Nadu State he was getting drink to drink?'

Gauri wagged her grey-streaked head.

'Oh, no, sahib. Who can say where such fellow is getting drink? From Club stealing? Or buying-buying in Bazaar where they make out of rotten fruit and dead dogs only?'

'You saw him just in the mornings? Or did you see him at other times?'

'Oh, I am not being in Club after the burra sahibs are waking and walking up and down. No, no. It was in the morning only I am seeing that devil. Finishing sleep and wanting to put his stinking mouth to my face.'

'Oh, he was that sort also, was he?'

'He was all bad sorts, sahib. Goat-goat, thief, drunkard man, all-all.'

'And when you were finding him dead it was on the billiard table, not where he was always sleeping in front of that almirah?'

'Yes, sahib, that day he was not in that place. But I saw. In middle-middle of billiard table. Like this only.'

And the lively, gaunt-faced old woman threw up her arms and spread them wide, jumped her legs astride, opened her mouth and stood there in front of Ghote in the crisp morning air.

Their twin breaths in long plumes met and mingled.

Ghote felt he had almost seen now with his own eyes the body in the billiard room.

'And you saw the wound that killed him?' he asked, as Gauri brought her mime to an end.

'Yes, yes, sahib. I saw. On white-white coat one little ring of red-red blood.'

'And the weapon? The knife, the dagger, whatever it was, did you see that also?'

'Gone, sahib, gone.'

Well, it had been only the chanciest of hopes that His Excellency's famous 'sharp instrument' might still have been in the body when Gauri had seen it, or even somewhere in the room, and that she had in pure ignorance simply tidied it away.

If the missing weapon was indeed that sharp instrument and not the ordinary dacoit's sword the murderer-thief had taken away with him in Inspector Meenakshisundaram's version of the crime.

'So there was just only that patch of blood on poor Pichu's jacket?' he asked for confirmation.

'Poor-poor, no, no, no. A devil fellow, I am saying. Good he gone. Bad rubbish.'

And, yes, there was something to be said for this sharp view of violent death. It was certainly more real, more down-to-earth, more to do with life than the murder with paper blood that His Excellency saw as having happened, that Dame Agatha Christie put into her books.

'Now, in that room you are sweeping every day, did you see any single thing different that morning?'

'But, yes, sahib.'

'Yes? Yes?'

'Pichu on billiard table, not on almirah.'

'No, I was meaning . . .'

But, as he had been putting these last routine questions,

from which he had expected to learn nothing more, he had been obscurely aware of the sound of a car engine growing louder and louder. And at this point it had increased to such a roar that his attention was completely distracted.

He looked away and saw, coming racing up towards them like something in a film, a police jeep with Inspector Meenakshisundaram at the wheel leaning out and waving like a crazy man and a pair of uniformed constables clinging on hard behind him.

Meenakshisundaram brought the vehicle to a halt just beyond the group of curious sweepers who had been watching Ghote as he had talked with Gauri. Its braking tyres sent the stones of the driveway spurting.

'Inspector!' Meenakshisundaram yelled. 'Jump in. That dacoit, he is just here. Two – three minutes and we will nab.'

Ghote ran across, no time to think, and jumped up beside Meenakshisundaram. With a fearsome howl of the engine they shot away.

16

To Ghote's surprise Inspector Meenakshisundaram did not sweep the jeep round and go roaring back towards the Club entrance. Instead he charged straight up on to the grass and drove them bumpily along beside the extended stretch of the building itself.

Behind, Ghote saw, the frost-white grass was wealed by two broad black tyre tracks.

He turned and leaned closer to Meenakshisundaram's jowly face.

'Where are we going?' he shouted.

'Round to back. Pick up one informant.'

Informant? What informant? And what could he have informed about? At this dawn hour of the day?

Ghote wondered whether it was worth trying to yell these questions at Meenakshisundaram above the roar of the jeep's engine. And decided it was not.

In any case they were very soon answered, and altogether unexpectedly.

As they rounded the Club building, standing there in the pale morning light was Mr Habibullah, looking not unlike a circular white tent propped up by the thick black pole of his ever-present silver knobbed cane.

'Ah,' Meenakshisundaram shouted, 'now we would see.'

He brought the jeep to a jerking, forward-thrusting halt.

'Get in, sir,' he called to Mr Habibullah. 'Get in damn quick and say where to go.'

Mr Habibullah, moving with surprising rapidity and lightness, hoisted himself on board, to sit like a giant puff-ball between the two squat, tough-looking constables in the back.

'In the churchyard, Inspector,' he shouted into Meenakshisundaram's ear above the still thunderously vibrating engine. 'I spotted him there.'

'Can we get the jeep through?' Meenakshisundaram shouted back.

'No. no. I am afraid not.'

With a look of boiling fury, Meenakshisundaram turned to his two burly constables.

'Get over there on foot,' he yelled. 'At the double. Cut the bastard off. We'll go round by road and get him the other way.'

The constables tumbled out as Meenakshisundaram slewed the jeep round. Bumping and lurching, he hurtled back to the front of the Club again, leaving two more dark cuts across the whitened surface of the grass.

In another couple of moments they were thrumming down the slope towards the lane leading to St Stephen's Church. On the better surface the vehicle made less noise and Ghote felt reasonable speech might be possible.

He leant back towards Mr Habibullah.

'How was it you were spotting this fellow only?' he asked.

'Oh, my dear Mr Ghote, I have become in my retirement something of a birdwatcher. It is my hobby. I like to see the little creatures hopping here and there at their own sweet will.'

'And you have a binocular?' Ghote said. 'You observed this fellow at the place where they unearthed the Club silver?'

'Exactly so. The Great Detective sees all.'

Ghote lapsed into silence. Sulky silence.

Meenakshisundaram swerved and skidded the jeep along, and within two minutes they swung into the wide stretch of road leading up to the church, squat-towered and pinnacled against its background of densely green trees.

Then, just as Ghote had begun to wonder if Meenakshisundaram was going to drive headlong through one of the pairs of neat wooden gates in the churchyard wall ahead, a man dressed in khaki shorts and a white singlet came haring down the slope beyond and jumped clean over the low wall.

'By God, it's him,' Meenakshisundaram yelled. 'And I think I know the fellow.'

As the runaway pounded along the edge of the road towards the small white chapel outside the churchyard built originally for native servants, he seemed more aware of the distant pursuing constables behind than of the approaching vehicle. Meenakshisundaram gave a furious twist to the wheel and headed straight towards him.

'Got the bastard.'

He nearly had, too. Just at the corner of the wooden fence surrounding the chapel he touched the dodging, darting man – the jar was plain to feel – but immediately had to make a violent swerve to avoid crashing into the solid chapel wall beyond.

Their quarry did not seem much injured, however. As Ghote turned to look back, he saw that the fellow was still able to run and was heading down towards the tall shape of the Nilgiri Library.

'Next time, yes,' Meenakshisundaram bayed, flinging the jeep into reverse and backing off ready to launch forward once more.

'No,' Ghote shouted, almost without knowing he had done so.

An instant later he found himself down in the dusty road, pelting off as hard as he could go in the direction of the fleeing man.

The chase was not long. The runaway, it soon appeared,

had been more hurt than it had looked. He kept going, but he was leaning hard to his left and Ghote had little difficulty in drawing up to him before he turned the corner.

'Stop,' he panted. 'Stop, if you don't want to be hit again.'

Whether the fellow understood or not, Ghote did not know. But he certainly dragged to a halt, turned and stood, head hanging, mouth wide and gulping for air, face streaked with sweat, blood oozing from the place on his thigh where the jeep had struck him.

Ghote decided there was no need to take hold of such a wreck.

In a moment he heard the jeep draw up behind him and a thud as Meenakshisundaram jumped to the ground.

The Tamil inspector plainly had different ideas about apprehending suspicious characters. He came straight up to Ghote's captive, knocked him flat with one swipe of his arm and at once bent down, grasped him by his singlet and hauled him to his feet again.

'You I am knowing, you bastard,' he yelled. 'Name? What is your damn name?'

The panting, dust-covered captive, his left cheek now grazed bright red, struggled to produce a word.

Clack.

Meenakshisundaram brought his open palm smacking across the fellow's face.

'Name I am asking.'

This time, eyes white with fear, the captive managed to answer.

'Balakumar.'

'Balakumar, sir.'

Another heavy slap.

'Sir. Sir. Sir. Balakumar, sir.'

'Yes, Balakumar. Balakumar, that's it. One on my Bad Character Roll, by God. Now, you stole many silver cups from Ootacamund Club. Yes?'

'No, Inspector. No.'

The slap that followed sent Balakumar reeling to the ground again. At once to be lifted bodily up once more.

'You stole that silver.'

The hand was raised again, clenched now into an all too threatening fist.

For an instant Balakumar was silent. But his eyes flicked towards Meenakshisundaram's clenched hand.

'You are saying it, Inspector,' he muttered. 'Yes. Sir. Sir. Sir.'

'I am saying, yes. I am saying you stole, and I am saying you killed a servant there.'

'No—'

But the protest was hardly out of his mouth when Meenakshisundaram brought his knee sharply upwards.

Balakumar gasped in agony and doubled up. Meenakshisundaram reached forward and jerked him upright.

Ghote, a silent spectator, knew that this was no time to intervene. Interrogation was in progress. Perhaps not interrogation according to the strict limits of the Criminal Procedure Code, laid down first long ago in British days. But interrogation according to the rough-and-ready ways of life. And it might be producing the truth, or some of the truth. And if it was, then how much did it matter that the wretched fellow at Meenakshisundaram's mercy was having a bad time? Did it matter a little? A lot? Very much? To some extent?

There was nowhere to draw an exact line.

'Yes,' Meenakshisundaram growled, putting his heavy face to within an inch of Balakumar's sweat-stained, fear-filled one. 'Yes, you killed the servant there.'

It was hardly a question. But it demanded an answer.

'Sahib, sahib. Sir. Yes. Yes, if you want.'

'Not if I want. You killed that servant. Say it. Say it before these witnesses here.'

Ghote became aware that Mr Habibullah had clambered down from the jeep and was standing somewhere just behind him. He wondered what he might be thinking.

Perhaps, freed now of the railway rules and regulations that had dominated his working days, he was freed, too, of all concern.

But Meenakshisundaram was pursuing the answer he wanted with unswerving determination.

'You killed that servant. Say it. Admit. Murderer.'

The knee which had already once come up into Balakumar's groin with such crippling force twitched in anticipation.

'Sahib, I killed. I killed her.'

'Enough.'

Meenakshisundaram seized his victim by one arm and almost threw him into the jeep. He turned to Ghote and Mr Habibullah.

'Gentlemen,' he said, 'in due course I shall want signed statements in strict accordance with all procedures. You are wanting lift back, yes?'

'No,' said Ghote.

'Oh, no, no. No, thank you,' Mr Habibullah echoed.

Standing together they watched in silence as Meenakshisundaram roared off in the jeep, his battered prisoner collapsed on the back seat. In a little while the constables who had flushed the fellow out from the churchyard came plodding by. Still neither Ghote nor Mr Habibullah said anything.

But when the two exhausted pursuers had eventually limped out of sight round the corner of the Library building Ghote turned cautiously to his balloon-like companion.

'You were hearing what that fellow Balakumar was saying?' he asked.

Mr Habibullah sighed. A great drawing in and puffing out of breath, still turning to vapour in the chill morning air.

'Yes,' he said. 'My dear Mr Ghote, I heard.'

'Just what were you hearing?' Ghote asked unbendingly.

Another sigh, not sending out this time quite such a puff of vapour.

'I was hearing what you were hearing.'

Ghote recognized that his attempt to get the retired railways officer to make an unprejudiced declaration was not going to succeed.

'The man Balakumar was saying *her*,' he stated. 'He by chance assumed the servant Meenakshisundaram spoke of was a woman. Was it not so?'

'Yes. Ah, yes, my dear fellow. And we know, do we not, that the victim was by no means a woman.'

It was Ghote's turn to sigh now.

'But Balakumar confessing to same does not one hundred per cent mean that he was not truly killing Pichu in the billiard room,' he said. 'With such methods of interrogation the fellow might have said, I think, almost anything.'

'Well, yes, one has heard that the police—But, my dear fellow, perhaps I am rushing in where I should not. You, too, are, are you not, a police officer? But then you are more than that, of course, also. You will have other ways of finding out the truth of things.'

For a moment, for perhaps the hundredth time since his arrival in Ooty, Ghote thought of vehemently rejecting the mantle put on his shoulders. But he realized that, once again, it would be little use. Instead he asked Mr Habibullah another question.

'When you were spotting this fellow just only now, you were, you say, using a binocular for the purpose of some birdwatching activities. But what exactly were you seeing?'

'Well,' Mr Habibullah said, 'I like to rise very early on some days now, and on others very late. And today happened to be a day for earliness. But I had scarcely left my bed when it occurred to me to wonder what my little friends the birds did at this most early hour. So, still in my nightwears, I took those glasses you so cleverly deduced I must possess and looked out at the white, frosted world.'

'And you saw?' Ghote asked with some sharpness.

'I saw in the churchyard, not quite at the tomb sacred to the memory of Annie, wife of Captain Henry Browne, but not altogether far away, the individual now in the hands of the formidable Inspector Meenakshisundaram. And that individual was behaving in a suspicious, not to say definitely surreptitious, manner.'

'What suspicious?'

Mr Habibullah paused for thought.

'In a stooping, peering, looking hither and thither manner,' he said.

'But he could have been, for instance, just only searching for some edible berries or suchlike?'

Mr Habibullah sighed yet more heavily than before.

'Yes,' he said. 'Yes, that could be so, though at the time the thought did not at all occur to me.'

'I see. And you were at once then telephoning to the Urban Police Station?'

'Yes. Yes, I thought this was something that called for resolute action. Yes, resolute action. And that I took.'

'Yes. Yes, you did that.'

They set out to go back to the Club. In silence.

And Ghote let the thoughts run through his mind.

Did what had happened prove that Meenakshisundaram's account of the murder was correct? Yes and no. Yes, in that Meenakshisundaram had got his hands on a known Bad Character who had been seen behaving in a suspicious manner near the place where the missing Club trophies had been found. No, in that the confession beaten out of the fellow had sounded plainly false in one vital particular at least. No, also, in that the activity in the churchyard Mr Habibullah had described might have been simply innocent. And yet the confession could still be true, bar that one detail extracted in the face of threats.

Yet if the answer was indeed no, then was His Excellency's version of events the true one? And the murderer then one of those five sleeping in the Club? With, just possibly, added to them Mr Iyer?

But there was yet another possibility . . .

As they walked along, with the rising sun beginning to

take the frost off the patches of grass at the edges of the lane, Ghote took a sidelong glance at his companion.

Was he really the old retired railways officer he appeared to be? A wind-blown, rootless man who, it was quite possible to believe, would get out of bed at the crack of dawn and promptly start to birdwatch? Or was he, as from his physical description he well might be, an absconding master criminal? A person well capable of spotting an innocent fellow somewhere at the back of the Club grounds and seizing the opportunity of laying the crime of murder on to another's shoulders, guessing too perhaps at Meenakshisundaram's rough and ready way of investigation?

The big Moslem ambled along beside him, smiling gently to himself. An inscrutable figure.

They reached the entrance to the Club grounds and began to make their way up the tree-shaded slope to the building itself. The notion of breakfast, an Ooty breakfast of steaming porridge, of toast and Dundee marmalade, making up for the bed-tea missed by his very early rising, entered Ghote's mind.

Then, suddenly, a figure came flapping out of the Club portico towards them, waving and gesticulating like some wild, feather-fluffed bird. His Excellency.

His state of high excitement almost palpable.

Ghote's spirits sank. He guessed that his breakfast might not be as near as he had anticipated.

'Ghote! Ghote! My dear fellow!'

The elderly ex-ambassador came half-running up to them.

'Yes, sir? Yes? What is it, please?'

His Excellency came to a halt, stood for a moment getting his breath.

'Ah,' he said. 'Ah, just the man. Just the man. Glad I saw you. You see, it's the second murder.'

17

A second murder? Who could it have been who had been made away with? And why? Does this mean finally, Ghote thought, that His Excellency is right about the whole business? Or can it be that somehow Balakumar, Meenakshisundaram's detenu, actually got into the Club before he was seen by Mr Habibullah and for the second time killed – who? Who?

Then a worse thought, a grimly terrible thought, came into his head.

Gauri. Had someone, one of His Excellency's list or Balakumar, seen him himself out in the open talking with Gauri and, fearing her as a witness, done her to death? Was he responsible for that?

'Please,' he stammered out. 'Please, who? Who is this victim?'

'Ah, that's what I hoped you could tell me,' His Excellency replied, with much less consternation in his voice than seemed right.

'Myself? But how can I be knowing who?'

'Well, I thought if you had a pretty good idea by now of who the murderer is, then you'd know who their second victim is likely to be.'

Has the fellow gone mad, Ghote asked himself. Is he a case for locking up in the pagal khana?

'This second victim,' he asked cautiously. 'Is it that you are stating that you just only expect there will be such?'

'Of course, my dear fellow. It comes in a good many Christie books after all, the second murder. Poirot or Miss Marple begins to get close, and the murderer gets rattled. Commits the second murder, sometimes to eliminate a dangerous witness, sometimes to lay a false trail.'

Ghote took a deep breath and looked up at the tall, tweed-clad figure in front of him.

'You are saying that in real life, in this life which we are living now, even if it is here in Ooty only, that a person is going to commit murder just only to lay a false trail?'

His Excellency looked suddenly down at his well-polished brown brogues.

'Well, don't forget,' he said, 'Dame Agatha was a remarkably shrewd woman. Remarkably shrewd. I mean . . . Well . . . Well, it could happen, you know. It really could. Sometimes.'

'But it has not happened here at the Club now?'

'No. No, that's what I came to say to you: if it is going to happen, it may happen quite soon.'

Abruptly he perked up.

'And that's another thing I wanted to say,' he went on. 'I mean, if we're going to avert the second murder – and Poirot manages that in some of the books, of course – then isn't it time you held the Grand Confrontation?'

'A confrontation? One that is being grand?'

'Well, yes. I mean, isn't that pretty well standard form, after all? Summon all the suspects, generally into the library or the drawing-room, and then go round one by one pointing out how each of them could have done it, and finally say, no, of course, it wasn't any of them and round on the actual murderer, someone you've already seemed to have let off the hook, and make whoever he or she is – mustn't forget the ladies, bless them – break down and confess when there isn't really enough evidence to bring a charge. You must know about doing that.'

Yes, Ghote thought in a flash of comprehension. Yes, of course I know about this. That frost-unreal book *Mrs McGinty's Dead*, it all happened in that.

'You are talking of books itself?' he asked. 'It is like the ending of the McGinty case?'

'Exactly, my dear chap. Exactly. And glad to hear you've finished the book. It'll be an enormous help to you in running your Grand Confrontation tonight.'

'Tonight? What tonight?'

'Oh, didn't I say? Well, you see, it struck me that your agreeing to come to the Culture Circle for Professor Godbole's talk was too good an opportunity to miss.'

'Opportunity for exactly what?'

'Why, for getting them all together in one place. Then, as soon as the few other people likely to turn up have gone, with the exception perhaps of Dr Fatbhoy who's always pretty difficult to dislodge even from the Club here, we'll have just the circle of suspects left. And you can go round them one by one and eventually unmask the real murderer.'

Ghote would have liked at this moment to utter with all the force at his command the simple syllable 'No'. But, despite his semi-triumph a few minutes before in somewhat shaming His Excellency over the absurd notion that anyone in the real world would go to the point of committing bloody, messy, awkward murder just to lay a false trail, he did not feel that he could challenge so influential a figure as flatly as this.

He would have liked to have said that the whole idea of Pichu's death being anything other than the chance side-effect of the theft of the Club silver was ridiculous. He would have liked to have said that his own presence in Ooty was altogether unnecessary, and had never been necessary. He would have liked to have turned round and marched straight down to the place they called Charing Cross and jumped aboard a bus waiting there with its engine throbbing ready to take him twisting and turning down, down, down to the hot plains below and the complications and half-successes and three-quarter failures of police work in the real world.

But his suitcase and the few possessions he had brought with him were there, barred from him by His Excellency, in the Club itself. And, besides, no bus would be going down to Coimbatore for many hours yet.

Worse, it was by no means certain that His Excellency's mad idea was not, basically at least, right. After all, Meenakshisundaram's solution was far from being without flaw.

'Well,' he said, nerving himself up, 'I was promising to Dr Fatbhoy that I would attend the Culture Circle, and there I will go.'

But, he added in the secrecy of his own mind, about any Grand Confrontation we would be seeing.

'Good man.'

And then, as he thrust aside the implication of His Excellency's congratulations, a thought planted itself suddenly and sturdily in his head.

He was not sure why it should have come to him at this moment. It may have been that, turning a little so as not to be looking at His Excellency full in the eye as he told his half-lie about the Culture Circle, he had caught a glimpse in the distance of the pillar-like yogi sitting by the Club entrance board unmoving in the early morning cold. Or it may have been sheer chance. Or it may have been that the mention of Professor Godbole had recalled to his mind that strange half-hour in the deserted upper room of the Nilgiri Library when the excitable little brahmin had propounded his theory about how Great Detectives were unique in that at their height they combined in a tobacco-wreathed trance the insights of the poet and the mathematician into that which has never occurred before.

But, for whatever reason it was, the thought had come to him: if they are always and always calling me as a Great

Detective, let me see if that is what I am. I will enter into a trance. But not any Western Sherlock Holmes trance. No, I shall just only do what I was all along trying to achieve at home in Bombay. I will put myself into the hands of Dr K. S. Joshi, MSc, MA, PhD, of *Yoga in Daily Life* fame.

'Well, Your Excellency,' he said with briskness, 'I must not stand here all the day idle. First, I should eat a good breakfast, then I will have work to do in my room. No disturbance, if you please.'

He must have achieved a note of sharp authority, because His Excellency stepped aside at once and Mr Habibullah made no attempt to accompany him as he marched off into the Club.

Soon, fortified by a breakfast that was all he had hoped for, creamy sustaining British porridge, boiled eggs each warmly protected under its own woollen cosy, and finally toast with amply spread Dundee marmalade, dark, tangy and somehow breathing rich assurance, he retired to his enormous bedroom. There he rested a hand momentarily on the bright yellow, pink and black cover of Dr Joshi's paperback – no need to dip into its well remembered pages – and getting down on to the floor, assumed the lotus position.

Yes, surely, he thought, the floor of a bedroom at the Ootacamund Club, cleaned daily by servants drilled to preserve the highest standards, is a fit and proper spot on which to perform the techniques of yoga. A place, in Dr Joshi's own words, well protected from the menace of animals, rodents and insects. And, if he was disobeying another of the precepts of the author of *Yoga in Daily Life* by setting out to undertake the asanas with a loaded stomach, well, surely this was a special case. Yoga in Ooty. It should have different rules. And at least he had avoided, as Dr Joshi urged, too much of chillies and spices.

Then resolutely he turned to attaining the state of dharana that had so frequently eluded him before. This time, he pledged himself, he would concentrate unswervingly on that point at the tip of his nose. He would eliminate every sign of the restlessness of mind, the idle thoughts, the whims and fancies that so often before had run about rat-like in his head.

He would attain dharana. And from there – who knows? – he might find he had entered into dhyana, that his mind, in Dr Joshi's words, would become very stable like the flame of a lamp in a very calm atmosphere. And then . . . Then would he know what the answer was to this messy riddle that had been thrust at him? Was what Meenakshisundaram—

No. No, forget Meenakshisundaram. Forget His Excellency. Forget Ooty. Think only of the tip of his nose. And, however much later it might be that this meditation came to an end, see what had happened in his head then.

The tip of his nose. The tip of his nose. The tip . . .

*

There seemed to be thunder. Fire God Agni hurling his massy bolts. The rage of the heavens.

It was the door. Banging on the door of – where was this? Yes, of his room. In the Club. The Ootacamund Club. In Ooty.

'Yes?' he heard a croaking voice call out, a voice that must be his own. 'Yes? What—Who is—Come, please.'

The door opened.

He looked round towards it. In the doorway stood a thin, tall, leathery-faced figure. It was—Of course, of course, His Excellency.

He scrambled to his feet.

'Please, yes, good morning,' he said.

'My dear chap. Good evening. It is evening, you know. Been asleep, have you? Well, even the great Sherlock is recorded as sleeping, though he was usually up before Watson, eh? At his bedside with "Cocoa in the next room and the game's afoot", what?'

'Please?' said Ghote.

'Well, I came to look you out, old man. Culture Circle's due to begin in half an hour, and I thought I'd have seen you about somewhere before this, raring to go.'

'In half an hour? In just only half an hour? But . . . But what has happened to the time?'

'You've been asleep, old chap, I suppose. I must say when you went off in that very determined manner this morning, saying you were not to be disturbed, I thought you were going to get down to it and work out who'd done it. Like Poirot in *Mrs McGinty* when he took off his tight shoes, remember?'

Ghote did remember. He remembered that he had seen himself as taking off, not any tight shoes, but perhaps the tight rules that had prevented his seeing what might have been in front of his face all the time. And he remembered the particular way he had thought he would achieve this, a different and even a better way than those of Poirot and Holmes before him.

But how could he tell His Excellency, that former ambassador to some country in Europe, that man steeped in Western ways down to the very detective stories he spent his time in admiring, how could he tell such a person that he had tried to put himself into a state of dharana, had hoped even to achieve dhyana?

He was saved from the embarrassment by the sound of His Excellency's clipped voice.

'Well, come on, man. Don't want to be late, do we? Guest of honour and all that. Better put on that tie I lent you, and then we'll be off.'

'Yes, yes. Two minutes only, if you please. I will come to the portico. I will meet you there. Two minutes only.'

As soon as His Excellency had gone, Ghote hastily dipped his face in a cooling basin of water, seized his comb and dealt with his hair, wound His Excellency's tie round his neck and knotted it, pulled on his Ooty jersey, cursed, did his hair again and left the room at a trot.

His Excellency was waiting for him.

'Thought we'd take my car,' he said. 'The Circle meets at the Indian Union Club, of course. Old Fatbhoy's territory. Not that we don't see all too much of him up here.'

The car, an ancient, stately Morris, imported from England perhaps as many as forty years earlier, still immaculate and shining in its polished grey paint and bluey-silver chromework, stood in the driveway.

Ghote obediently hurried across and got in. His Excellency climbed behind the wheel. A servant appeared, on cue, and swung the starting-handle dangling from the vehicle's front. The engine caught with a warm, instant purr. The servant, well used to the routine, ran round with the starting-handle and clipped it into its place.

Ghote was just alert enough to register with astonishment the performance of this procedure from the past before His Excellency let in the clutch and they rolled forward.

The journey to the other, lesser club where the Culture Circle met, one originally established for Ooty's Indian inhabitants of social standing, did not take long. Ghote sat through it in a silent daze.

Culture Circle, Culture Circle, he kept thinking, repeating and repeating the words like a mantra. But a mantra not of aspiration but of doubt.

How had he been so foolish as to get trapped into going to this meeting? And, worse, worse, worse, into going as the Great Detective personified? And had His Excellency, to add to it all, done what he had said he would? Had he contrived to persuade all those he suspected of the murder of Pichu to attend? When Professor Godbole's talk was over was there going to take place that absurd Grand Confrontation?

For a moment it actually occurred to him that the wretched Bad Character Roll fellow, Balakumar, would somehow be there as well under the fiercely brutal charge of Inspector Meenakshisundaram. But, no, he thought. At least the suspects – if suspects they actually were – would be confined to His Excellency's breakfast table line-up. Pepper-pot, mustard-holder, Dipy's Tomato Ketchup, sugar bowl, milk jug and salt-pot.

And was he really in accordance with His Excellency's wishes – no, His Excellency's orders – was he at the evening's end expected to challenge each one of them in turn and finally to pick out the one who had actually committed the murder in the Club billiard room? How could he? He had no idea who it was. He was not even sure that the murder had anything to do with any of them. Certainly his effort to arrive at an answer through yoga seemed to have led nowhere. Had he achieved dharana even? Or had he, as His Excellency had assumed, simply fallen asleep? Had that huge British breakfast been the undoing of him after all?

But now they were drawing up outside the Indian Union Club, a long, low bungalow at the end of a short, potholed drive, surrounded by a garden that, in distinction to the grounds of the Ootacamund Club, had been allowed to run riotously to seed.

'Come along, come along, my dear fellow,' His Excellency said, briskly leading the way into a lofty room, the corrugated iron of its ceiling criss-crossed by painted beams. Thirty or forty canvas stacking chairs were drawn up in front of a low platform on which stood a table covered with a patterned orange cloth with on it a water carafe and a solitary upturned tumbler. On one of the two chairs behind there was draped a marigold garland. Even down the length of the room Ghote caught a tang of its odour.

But from the collection of individuals scattered in ones and twos among the drawn-up rows of chairs his eyes at once picked out five in particular, as if each was spotlighted by a dazzling arc lamp. The Maharajah of Pratapgadh and his Maharani, seated with a grey, paint-chipped chair between them. Mr Habibullah, seeming to spread over two of the ranged chairs, dressed as usual in spotless white muslin, his heavy walking-stick between his knees, hands folded over its silver knob. Mrs Trayling, sitting a little apart and knitting furiously at some indeterminate garment in bright fluffy yellow wool. And, lastly, Mr Iyer, also sitting at a distance, in the very back row, casting quick glances from side to side through his peering spectacles as if he felt that he ought not to be where he was.

There needs now only Professor Godbole, the Least Likely Suspect, to make the gathering complete, Ghote thought with dank resignation. His Excellency had, of course, succeeded in getting every one of them to attend. He was the man for that.

And, as if the very thought of Professor Godbole had caused him to appear, at that moment a door at the back of the room opened and the little brahmin came scuttling in, urged on from behind with gentle flapping gestures by the lank form of Dr Fatbhoy, grey-haired and hungry-eyed.

Well, Ghote thought, at least while the professor is talking – and he will talk, surely, for a long, long time – I will be able quietly to go over every aspect of the case, working strictly in accordance with the precepts of Dr Hans Gross and the rules I learnt at Detective School. And by the end I may have been able to work my way through all the mess and muddle and fairy-tale strands with which the affair is covered and perhaps see an answer. Or perhaps not.

He settled down in his chair beside His Excellency. Dr Fatbhoy launched into his chairman's introduction. At its end he dextrously unhooked the garland from the chair behind him and slipped it over Professor Godbole's head.

Professor Godbole grinned hugely.

Not so much, Ghote guessed, at the honour done to him as at the prospect of being able to talk uninterruptedly on a favourite subject for many, many minutes to come.

And at once, bearing out his guess, Professor Godbole began.

'Ladies and gentlemen, tonight I have the honour to introduce to you one of the major figures of our age. Sherlock Holmes, the Great Detective, and to ask whether he be alive or dead. The Great Detective, a myth of our times, no less. A myth, certainly, come to life among us. Or come at least to that semblance of life which is literature. Because, let us be clear about this at the outset, the Great Detective cannot of his nature exist in reality.'

Ghote, at these last words, felt such a surge of gratitude and relief that all ideas of not paying attention to the professor's words while he wrestled instead with the facts of the case of the body in the billiard room deserted him in an instant.

18

Freed of the chasm-creating thought that it was up to him to represent some impossible creature, Ghote found himself listening with fascination to what Professor Godbole had to say about the investigator from the world of books, the world of books and nowhere else. Soon he began to think that the professor's ideas, which had seemed when he had originally heard them to be altogether fantastic, had in them a good deal of sense.

'We are, are we not,' the little brahmin said, favouring his scattered audience with a sharply wicked grin, 'each one of us trapped? Trapped within our own personalities. Over the years we build up in our minds a picture of ourselves. A picture of a person we can bear to live with, perhaps often a person of whom we are secretly proud.'

Well, Ghote thought, one thing I am knowing: His Excellency is damn proud of the picture he has made of himself, of a detective story-loving man living in some sort of England translocated. That is one thing certain.

'But,' Professor Godbole went on, giving each one of them a quick and ferocious glare, 'but a picture that we create for ourselves in this way has a most terrible effect. It places round us limits. It lays down for us rules, rules we dare not break even though they are rules we alone have devised. But the Great Detective . . . Ah, the Great Detective, he – or sometimes she – in the pages of those books we delight to read can by the force of genius show us these self-imposed rules being broken. He can show us that the prisons we make for ourselves can be escaped from.'

Yes, Ghote, thinking hard, conceded, what he is saying is very true. I myself am in such a prison. I have all along been serving one life-sentence therein, as a man fixed in the shape of a police officer. And, worse even, in these last few days in paradise Ooty I have been in a yet more strict prison. One where the Gaol Superintendent laying down rules and regulations is not even myself but – he turned to steal a sideways glance – this influential fellow who has been inflicted upon me. So can I—

But Professor Godbole was still in full flow.

'Yes, the Great Detective, whilst we read with simple pleasure of his triumphs, can teach us by the secret ways of imaginative writing that it is possible to escape from the prisons, the locked rooms, imposed upon us by our own egoes. Now, what is one of the ways, perhaps the most striking, in which this lesson is presented to us? Why, by the simple yet always intriguing device of disguise. In that notable tale *A Scandal in Bohemia* we read of Mr Sherlock Holmes disguising himself as a drunken groom, making himself – note – wholly into a person smelling equally of the horse and the bottle. And we realize then, without realizing that we have realized it, that other people exist. That as a drunken syce comes to exist for, and in, Mr Sherlock Holmes, wholly to exist, so some person equally foreign to us can be seen as existing, truly existing, as real as ourselves.'

Ghote took a quick survey of the professor's small audience. Were they realizing they could become drunken syces? It did not from their politely dazed expressions look like it.

'Yes, we see, we are made to see,' the monkey-faced

professor rattled on, 'that it is possible for any one of us, however high-minded the life we lead, however powerfully intelligent we happen to be, to enter into the soul – the soul, I do not hesitate to say – of any fellow human being, however low.'

'Yes, Ghote gropingly thought, perhaps if now, or in just only a moment, I could enter into the five – six souls of the suspects in this room itself, I might possibly find the answer to the whole business I have been brought here to solve.

But, once again, Professor Godbole was pouring out his rich mix of ideas, and Ghote found himself listening willy-nilly.

'But notice, notice this, ladies and gentlemen, in that tale *A Scandal in Bohemia*, the story in which Mr Holmes rebukes Dr Watson with the ever-famous words: "You see but you do not observe", in that story the disguise which Holmes has plunged himself into is penetrated. It is penetrated by a woman. By that Madame Irene Adler, whom Holmes is said ever afterwards to refer to as The Woman. And because his disguise is penetrated Holmes himself fails in this adventure. Yes, the Great Detective shows that he is no more than a prophet: he is not God Almighty. He does not enter into everything there is, only into some souls, some drunken grooms. He has thus to recognize, for himself and for us also, that the whole outside world is there. A world beyond him, a world of the other. So sometimes he fails. Yes, the great Mr Sherlock Holmes could fail, and in that failure lay his ultimate strength.'

He fails, Ghote echoed. And he realized that, even if His Excellency had not taken in enough of what Professor Godbole had been saying to relieve him himself of the burden of Great Detectiveness – and there was small hope that anyone with ideas so fixed would have done that – then it could still be permitted to him not to succeed in the case that had been thrust upon him. He could leave

Ooty eventually with the baffling business still unsolved and feel he had not failed in his duty.

He ventured another sideways glance at his Watson. His Excellency was looking just perceptibly worried by something. Was it at hearing his simple beliefs about Great Detectives upset? Or could he be trying to recall an occasion when Shri Poirot had failed?

'Ladies and gentlemen,' Professor Godbole resumed before Ghote could answer that question, 'these pieces of simple entertainment we read are, in fact, of very much greater importance than might be thought from the apparent nature of the books themselves. They are in one sense light reading, yes, fiction for the simple purpose of entertainment. But they are also, with or without the willing connivance of their authors, much more than that.'

For a naughty moment the diminutive brahmin allowed a silence to fall while he looked, twinkling-eyed, round his sparse audience. Even Ghote found himself churningly trying to think how books like *Mrs McGinty's Dead* or even *Into the Valley of Death* could be much more than the fairy-tale fiction he had thought them.

'What are they, these simple stories?' the professor went on, letting his listeners off the hook at last. 'They are nothing short of deeply symbolic constructions. Their heroes are figures of pure myth, albeit they became as time went on a myth diluted. But their stories are stories of the everlasting struggle between Good and Evil. And they are tales in which the weapon of Good is in the hands of the Great Detective half at least Reason. Reason fighting to restore in a world to which Evil has brought imbalance and chaos the orderliness which we, each one of us, cannot but desire.' And half also, of course, intuition, the poet's vision.

Seated on his droopy canvas chair, Ghote felt rising up in him a wave of crusading vigour. These investigators the professor had described, these fighters against evil and chaos, these strivers for orderliness: he was one of them.

They might be in books. He was in the world, which was harder by far to bring any orderliness to. But bringing order was what his task in life was, like theirs. And he was proud of it. To bring orderliness. Orderliness. Orderliness.

The word with its tumbling syllables repeated itself murmurously in his head. It sent him almost into that very state of meditation which, by directing all his thoughts to the tip of his nose, he had striven to reach for most of the day behind him. Unless he had been asleep.

Almost it sent him, but not entirely. He was aware still, dimly, of Professor Godbole's voice going on and on. Odd words continued to impinge.

Mr Sherlock Holmes.

Dr Watson.

Still, in that sense, alive.

Hercule Poirot. Lord Peter Wimsey. Superintendent Maigret. The Great Detective. The Great Detective.

Then, emerging abruptly from his semi-trance, he became aware that the handful of people in the room were decorously applauding. Professor Godbole had finally brought his discourse to an end.

Dr Fatbhoy was standing up. He was thanking the speaker, talking about a veritable feast. And announcing that after the coffee interval he was sure our learned friend would be most happy to answer questions.

Then two servants came in with trays on which there were cups of coffee and plates of glucose biscuits. Ghote took a cup when it was presented to him. The coffee was distinctly watery. But he sipped at it with as much simulated relish as he could contrive. While thus occupied he felt he was excused from engaging in conversation with His Excellency, something he was more than ever disinclined for. And neither could he be expected to chat with any of the other visitors from the Ooty Club, something he was utterly averse to.

Soon the coffee interval was over. The cups were collected. The almost depleted plates of biscuits were taken away. Dr Fatbhoy, to Ghote's relief evidently feeling that, since the Great Detective had authoritatively been declared to be only a figure in fiction, it would not be appropriate to draw attention to the presence among them of a simple CID wallah from Bombay, asked if there were any questions for 'our honourable speaker'.

There were none.

After a sufficiently long embarrasing pause, during which Professor Godbole alternately hopped up from his chair and hopped back on to it again, Dr Fatbhoy repeated, almost word for word, his earlier speech and then declared the meeting closed. Most of those present got up rather quickly and made their way out into the cool night.

Ghote thought the professor's torrenting ideas must have been rather too much for them. But they had not been too much for him.

He contemplated going up to the little brahmin to tell him so. Until he realized that the people who had not yet left were precisely His Excellency's collection of suspects, added to only by the spare, bald-domed, unshiftable figure of Dr Fatbhoy.

The Grand Confrontation. With an ice-chill descent, Ghote realized that this was what was going to take place now. At once. Directly. By whatever manoeuvres and authority had been necessary His Excellency had set the scene.

The suspects had been assembled, waiting for him.

There was Mrs Lucy Trayling, who might have murdered the man she believed had allowed her drink-fuddled husband to drown. There was Mr Habibullah, who might not be Mr Habibullah at all but a master criminal somehow betrayed to the over-inquisitive billiards marker. There was the Maharani of Pratapgadh, who was certainly having a love affair with one Mr Amul Dutt, student, and who at all costs did not want to be divorced by her extremely well-off husband. There was the Maharajah of Pratapgadh who, turning the situation the other way round, might be very determined that his wife should not learn that he was picking up his old affair with the sultry Sarla Kumar and who might have thought it easier to kill blackmailing Pichu than to buy him off. There was Mr Iyer, so efficient in his handling of the Club accounts that it was by no means beyond the bounds of possibility that he had been milking them dry.

Or there was even Professor Godbole himself, with no conceivable reason to have killed an old Club servant whom he had not set eyes on until recently, but who nevertheless had been one of that handful of people in a position to have murdered him on the fatal night. The Least Likely Suspect.

Unless – a sudden thought – that doubtful honour should go to Dr Fatbhoy. He had, after all, been somewhat unaccountably allowed to remain in the room which His Excellency had transformed into the library, or drawing room, in which by tradition Grand Confrontations took place. His Excellency had, of course, said that Dr Fatbhoy was a hard person to get rid of. But on the other hand he had also said he was a terrible fellow and, more to the point, that he was frequently to be seen not at his own club but at the Ootacamund Club itself, scene of the crime. Could he have been there, somehow lurking unseen, on the night of the murder? It was not quite impossible.

Or there was, in the most outside of chances, Mr Biswas, proprietor of the Bengal Vegetarian Hotel. He had a link with Pichu, that card of his. But was that link only that Pichu perhaps sold him from time to time drink stolen from the Club? Or was it, just possibly, something else?

And here he himself was, expected by his ever-hovering Watson to conduct this confrontation. But he had no idea, not the least glimmer of any idea, of what order even he should take each of the suspects, make it look as if he or she had committed the murder and then show that after all this was not so until he finally picked on the one among them all who was the real murderer.

His Excellency, he saw, had made his way up on to the

deserted platform and was toying with the tumbler and water carafe on the orange-clothed table. Now he replaced the glass on top of the carafe with a sharp clink.

All of them sitting in the body of the room below looked up at him.

'Ladies and gentlemen,' he said in a voice that reverberated under the lofty, cross-beamed roof, 'I believe Mr Ghote, our visitor from Bombay, has something to say now. Something highly important.'

Ghote got to his feet.

He had nothing to say.

And then he found, as if a jewel-bright object had been thrown into his hands, that he did have something to say. A revelation he had had, unknown to himself, during his long withdrawn day of trance in his bedroom at the Club. It had at this last moment made itself clear to him. It had fallen into his mind. Or perhaps risen up there.

It must after all have been dharana, not sleep, that had overcome him. It might even have been dhyana. But, whichever it was, somewhere inside him it had linked together things he had seen but not observed, or had not realized that he had observed. He had done just what Professor Godbole had said Mr Sherlock Holmes did: he had fused into a new whole the products of reasoning and the jumping lightning-strokes of intuition. He had discovered *that which has never occurred before*.

He knew now just how it had come about that Pichu, the billiards marker and blackmailer, had been done to death.

He had known it, he realized, from the very moment that His Excellency, by knocking on his bedroom door, had filled his head with irrelevant images of Agni, god of fire, and his thunderbolts. And, because His Excellency had been there, urgently demanding that he should attend the Culture Circle, the knowledge of what had come to him in his trance had been temporarily driven from his head.

It was rather as if he had forgotten some unimportant little task because something more pressing had suddenly come up.

But what he had forgotten, and had now remembered, was not unimportant. It was as important as could be. A matter of life and death. Of a murdered man's death, and perhaps at some future time of a murderer's life.

He pushed aside the grey stacking chairs impeding him and strode up on to the platform. He took up a position behind the table and leant forward across it.

'Ladies and gentlemen,' he said, 'I think His Excellency was expecting for me to accuse each and every one of you in turn of murder, and after to find each of you but one not guilty. But I am not going to do any such thing whatsoever. I cannot do such. I am not at all knowing who was committing the murder of Pichu, the billiards marker.'

He was aware of His Excellency stepping back in affronted dismay. But he went determinedly on.

'No, that I am not knowing. That I am not knowing, yet. But what I am knowing is the manner of Pichu's death. For, you see, Pichu was not murdered once. He was murdered twice.'

19

The eight of them in the high-beamed room looked back at Ghote after his announcement with a shifting variety of expressions. Shock, deep puzzlement, something approaching incredulous contempt, something that might have been fear. Was there among them, he asked himself, somewhere as well a fiercely concealed enmity?

He forced the thought aside and continued.

'Yes, it is a most astonishing matter. But I am assuring: Pichu was murdered on two occasions. Let me tell you how I came to know that such was the case.'

He paused, gathering into as logical a chain as he could the various scraps of knowledge and observation that he had been able to forge together in his hours of trance into the real explanation of Pichu's death.

'It was in the following manner,' he began again. 'The first thing I was noticing, though at the time it did not strike me as it should, was the billiard table upon which the body of Pichu had been lying. That table was not at all bloodstained. Yet Pichu received a blow to the heart from some kind of sharp instrument. Now, as perhaps you are knowing, such blow will, unless in some cases where the inflicting weapon is left in the body, cause great effusion of blood. So why was there just only a small red stain upon

Pichu's white servant's coat? His Excellency had told me this was so when he was examining the body quite soon after discovery. Also I had confirmation when I was after able to speak with the person who actually made that discovery, one Gauri, a sweeper woman.'

Now there was only one response among his eight listeners, close attention.

'So I am forced to the conclusion, impossible though it is seeming,' he continued, 'that Pichu was not killed by a blow from this sharp instrument, whatever it was. Yet there was in his chest a deep wound. Gauri had seen it. Mr Iyer, you also saw it. Your Excellency, you saw it. Inspector Meenakshisundaram saw it, and because of it, with every good reason upon his side, concluded that the murder was the work of a dacoit, the dacoit who had robbed many silver cups and trophies from the locked almirah in the said billiard room. How then did this almost bloodless wound come to be inflicted? The answer must be plain. It was after the blood in the body had ceased to flow. Or after it had almost ceased to flow. And what is it that is making blood cease to flow? It is death. Death itself.'

He took a quick survey of the eight faces watching him. Would one of them, at this stage of his revelation, betray something?

But, no. The faces he saw were all still pictures of mingled bewilderment and intentness.

He went on.

'It was from the sweeper woman Gauri that I was also learning some other most significant facts about the body, though I must confess that at the time she told me I was too interested in finding out other matters to pay fullest attention. But I remembered at last what she was telling. She was saying Pichu's face was pink-pink like flowers. Such were her words. She believed this was because Pichu had been drunk, as he often was she said. But, if the body had been dead even a short time, the colour from drink would have disappeared. No, what Gauri was describing in saying Pichu's face was pink like flowers was patches of pinkness and when she was stating also that his mouth was filled with very much of saliva, I should at once have thought 'Poison'. These are the signs of poisoning by cyanide. So it is plain that Pichu had taken a fatal dose some short time before in that billiard room where he lay on the shelf of the almirah, as was his invariable custom, and there entered feloniously the dacoit Inspector Meenakshisundaram had from the start suspected of committing the crime.'

'Meenakshisundaram right?' His Excellency, till now kept silent by the steady piling on of Ghote's explanation, broke out in frustrated amazement.

'Yes,' Ghote replied. 'Inspector Meenakshisundaram is a trained police officer. It is most likely he would know how a crime has been committed, isn't it?'

'Then you are saying that the fellow I'm told he's got down at the police station is the murderer?'

Again His Excellency sounded incredulous.

'Well, I am not necessarily saying so much. A police officer can sometimes arrest a suspect upon good circumstantial evidence to find upon questioning that he has nabbed the wrong man.'

'With Inspector Meenakshisundaram's methods of questioning,' Mr Habibullah put in, 'I greatly wonder whether any detenu whatsoever would afterwards be freed.'

Ghote thought he had no comment to make.

'Whether the dacoit who undoubtedly entered the billiard room at the Ooty Club and robbed away the silver trophies therein is or is not the murderer of Pichu is a most difficult question,' he said. 'Because, you see, the person who was administering that cyanide must also be his murderer.'

'A nice point, a nice point,' Professor Godbole broke in, his eyes shining in pure glee. 'I'd enjoy putting that to my colleagues in the Faculty of Law. I fancy it would set them at each others' throats in fine style.'

'But would they at all be able to say which person should be charge-sheeted under IPC Section 302?' Ghote said. 'Because at some time that is what is going to be the problem for Inspector Meenakshisundaram.'

'Oh, the practical implications,' the professor answered with a darting shrug. 'Those I cannot help you with. And nor, I am sure, could any of my colleagues.'

The intervention seemed to have the effect of throwing the subject open to the meeting. If such it is, Ghote thought.

Now Mrs Trayling put in her contribution.

'I may be stupid,' she said, 'but what I haven't understood is how that wretched Pichu got on to the billiard table at all. I mean, if he was poisoned – and I don't really understand about that either – but if he was poisoned and then lay down in the place where he always slept, in front of the trophies almirah, as he never used to cease to tell us, then how did he move over to the billiard table? Did he hop or something? I don't understand.'

'Oh, there is no need to crack your head over that, madam,' Ghote answered. 'Pichu had to be moved by the dacoit who had come to rob the trophies. I have a suspicion that the fellow had learnt that Pichu was often drunk last thing at night and had counted on only gagging and binding him. But, when he came to touch, then the final one of the convulsions that are also a symptom of poisoning by cyanide was taking place. And so the dacoit, in fear and surprise, stabbed him with the sword he had with him in order to break open the almirah. He then, altogether in haste, was moving the body so that he could seize his loots.'

'Yes, but steady on,' His Excellency intervened, resuming something of his old authority. 'What about the way the body was, right in the middle of the billiard table? You yourself agreed when I first told you that it was laid out in that way that it was a damn significant circumstance. A blackmail victim's message to the world. Nothing less.'

'Yes,' Ghote admitted. 'Yes, I was agreeing then. But I was wrong to have concurred to one hundred per cent. Certainly such was one possible explanation, even one likely explanation. But, of course, it was not the sole and only explanation. In life, many factors can add up to provide one particular circumstance. What must have happened here, I am believing, is that the dacoit, in order to remove Pichu from in front of the almirah doors, was putting the body across his shoulder and then turning round and staggering a pace or two away. Then there in front of him was the billiard table. He tossed the body down. It fell by chance into that particular position.'

'Hm,' grunted His Excellency doubtfully.

But Ghote abruptly received some unexpected support. It came from Mr Habibullah.

'Oh, yes,' he said. 'Yes, yes, indeed. We are too apt in our everyday goings-on to neglect the oddities of chance. Altogether too apt. I can believe Mr Ghote's explanation. Perfectly.'

And from some of the others at least there came a murmur of assent.

But His Excellency had not done yet.

'That's all very well,' he said. 'But there's the way the silver was hidden, too. I pointed that out to you in the first place, Ghote. A dacoit would have no reason to hide his haul so near to the scene of operations. It's exactly the same situation in *Mrs McGinty's Dead*.'

'Please,' Ghote said, 'that is not so. *Mrs McGinty's Dead* is just only a detective story, a book wherein what is stated to be the only possible thing to have happened is the only possible thing. But the case of the body in the billiard room is not at all a detective story. It was a real body, except just only that it had been done to death in a highly unusual circumstance, such as may by coincidence sometimes occur in this world we are inhabiting.'

'But—'

'No, sir. What was taking place in this world we are in,

as could have been found out by one talk with the Club watchman, is that the said watchman was hearing the breaking of a glass-pane in the billiard room window but was not instantly proceeding to the scene, for perhaps good reasons. He did not in fact proceed until the culprit had just left the spot with his loots. Then he was calling hue-and-cry. So the dacoit was damn quickly hiding evidence of his nefarious activity, not knowing that the hue-and-cry on this occasion did not succeed to be raised.'

He looked directly at His Excellency. The ex-ambassador attempted to look him back. The whole theory on the strength of which he had summoned this supposed Great Detective was at stake. A stubborn determination not to be proved wrong was set in every line of his long leathery face.

Ghote gathered his thoughts.

'But, yes,' he said, 'it was a dacoit's sword that was inflicting that wound. It was not at all like in some detective story where each and every person concerned has in some way concealed an object that might have been the murder weapon. This is life, simple if not always most clear life. No, the murder was not committed with one of Mrs Lucy Trayling's long metal knitting needles, though I had noted the existence of such when I was thinking the business was just only some sort of detective-story affair. No also, it was not a case of murder with a long, strong ivory paper-cutter such as Professor Godbole is sometimes using. And, once more, no, Mr Habibullah's silver-headed walking cane is not a gupti with a sword blade inside.'

'Alas, I am afraid, no such romantic notion . . .' the balloon-airy Moslem murmured.

Ghote ignored him.

'Again, no,' he went on, 'although Her Highness the Maharani of Pratapgadh is sometimes visiting a part of the Bazaar where a knife-grinder is often working, there was no sharpened murder weapon coming from him. And, once more, no, in the golf-bag of the Maharajah, although he is so jealously guarding same, there is not the pig-sticking spear he was in youth so skilful in wielding.'

And at last his inexorable catalogue seemed to have done its work.

His Excellency's mouth under the neat white bar of his moustache contracted in a grimace of wryly bitter acknowledgement and his gaze dropped to the floor.

So it was left to someone else to take up the challenge Ghote's explanation had put to them all.

It was the Maharajah.

'I dare say you're right about poison and all that, Inspector,' he said. 'I mean, you're a Bombay CID wallah and should know your business. But, even if you are correct, you can't really prove anything. Not unless you can name the person you say gave that fearful old billiards marker cyanide.'

Ghote looked at the ring of faces round him once more. No longer were they bemused and accepting. There was, in every eye now, some hint of combativeness.

He swallowed.

'Yes, that is so,' he agreed. 'Unless I am able to state who was putting poison last thing in the night into the alcoholic drink that Pichu habitually took, as you, Mr Iyer, were informing me was the case, then I would not be able to prove what I have told you has happened. And, ladies and gentlemen, I am not able to name that name.'

Was there a sigh of relief from somewhere in the big room? If so, it was so faint he was unable to locate it.

He decided to see if he could produce a clearer give-away reaction.

'I am not able to name that name,' he repeated. 'But I am able to say one thing. The person who was administering poison to the said Pichu cannot have done so without having some strong need. His Excellency was summoning myself from Bombay to investigate into the murder because he was convinced that Pichu had threatened to wash some dirty linens and that some person unknown had taken a dramatic step to prevent. Some person within the Ootacamund Club on the night of the murder. And His Excellency's reasoning on that is still holding good to one hundred per cent.'

He tried then in one comprehensive sweep to bring into high focus every face in the room.

Would there be a twitched muscle, a momentarily held breath, that would be a betrayal?

But the room was too large, the faces too distant.

And the general lack of response to his attempted bombshell immediately renewed the opposition he had felt. It came now in particular from the Maharani.

'I think you're talking damned nonsense actually,' she said. 'I mean, cyanide. How would I – how would any one of us, come to that – get hold of cyanide? Or know anything about any sort of poison at all? Tell me that.'

Ghote fought back a hot flush.

'Well, yes, madam,' he said, 'that I can be telling you. You are all, I am thinking, at one time or another visiting Nilgiri Library. And there on the shelves, for any person whatsoever to lift down, is the book Alfred Swaine Taylor *On Poisons*, 1848. It is not altogether up to date, but therein you could be finding all you are needing to know about cyanide, or as it was sometimes called prussic acid.'

'Very clever,' the Maharani replied, hardly hiding a sneer. 'And when we have gathered all we are needing to know, where the hell are we going to get the stuff from? In Ooty, for God's sake?' But now Ghote was more prepared.

'Madam,' he replied, 'in Ooty itself many, many dogs are always being what is called "put down". I have heard those words more than once in the few days I am here. And what is most recommended for this putting down? A poison. A poison based, as is well known to every Crime Branch officer, very much upon cyanide.'

He felt then that the initiative was his once more.

'So,' he said firmly, 'nothing that I have seen or heard here has in the end made as meaningless the theory of His

Excellency which caused me to be called to Ooty. He has stated that the person who was murdering Pichu must be one of just only your small group. I have said I cannot as of this day and date put a name to that person. But it is nevertheless my bounden duty, now that I know that Pichu was a poison victim also, so to inform my colleague on the spot, Inspector Meenakshisundaram. And I have no doubt he would be wanting to question each and every one of you.'

Once more he looked at the array of faces, if now with not as much hope as before. And after a moment he had to acknowledge that, with the advantage of shock less and less on his side, his threat had not met with success.

He drew himself up.

'Ladies and gentlemen,' he said, sharply brisk, 'I am wishing you goodnight.'

He marched out past them all, out into the chill, starlit Ooty night and on along to the Urban Police Station where, a little to his surprise, he found Inspector Meenakshisundaram was still in his office.

'Ah, Ghote bhai, good to see. Are you also having a wife who is nag-bagging at you day and night only?'

Ghote, feeling he was betraying a little his Protima back in Bombay, contrived a reply that did not altogether deny the possibility. And its implied plea for male comradeship.

Seizing advantage of the warm atmosphere thus created, he launched at once into his account of what must have happened in the Ooty Club on the night of the murder, glossing over as much as he could points such as Meenakshisundaram's failure to question the old watchman.

The Tamil inspector took it pretty well, once he had been brought to understand the full details.

'Okay, Ghote bhai,' he said. 'First thing ack emma I am up at that Club-shub with questions-pestions for each one of those buggers.'

So at last Ghote made his way back to the Club, scene of the crime, and dodging any contact with any of the people he had had his non-confrontation with at the Culture Circle, he crept to bed and tried to compose himself to sleep.

But, despite the comforting hot-water bag he found in the bed, he could not stop his mind racing alertly round and round the facts. He tried, not once but half a dozen times, to launch himself again into that state of fruitful trance that had produced half the answer to his riddle. But, concentrate on the tip of his nose, the tip of his tongue, the mid-point of his eyebrows as he would, round and round his thoughts continued to scurry. The Maharajah. The Maharani. Professor Godbole, but how could he—Mrs Trayling. Balloony Mr Habibullah. Mr Iyer, the Efficient Baxter.

Nothing emerged.

He began to long simply for the oblivion of sleep. But even that would not come. Had he, after all, he wondered, been asleep most of the day? Had he not after all achieved dharana? Had his revelation come not in a yogic trance but in common or garden slumber?

And would that make him more or less of a Great Detective?

20

Professor Godbole proved to be the first suspect Inspector Meenakshisundaram wanted to see when, as early as he had promised, he arrived at the Club next morning. Whether this was by way of eliminating first the least likely person or on some other obscure principle Ghote did not inquire.

He found himself now distinctly at odds with his Tamil colleague. To begin with, Meenakshisundaram had at once made it clear that he would not welcome his presence during his interrogations of the poisoning suspects. Was he going to subject them, Ghote promptly wondered, to the same sort of treatment he had meted out to runaway Balakumar?

He found he viewed that with dismay. Had he, he asked himself, already become so much of an Ooty person that he was beginning to think of his fellow Club members as being somehow different from the rest of harassed, chance-afflicted humanity?

Whatever the answer, he had no hesitation when the door had closed on Mr Iyer's office, which Meenakshisundaram had commandeered, in stationing himself on the watch in the depths of one of the sofas nearby.

But what he heard after a little emerging from behind

the heavy, well-polished door of the office came as a distinct surprise. Meenakshisundaram's baying voice sounded tamed as if he had been transformed from unleashed bloodhound into one of the docile dogs of upper Ooty. And Professor Godbole's high, gabbling monkey chatter appeared to be every bit as irrepressible as it had been when in the Nilgiri Library he had first propounded his theories about the Great Detective.

Phrases penetrated the heavy teak door.

'... life, you might say, Inspector, is in this wholly exceptional instance writing a detective story in reality ... the naked truth for once without disguise ...'

Then, after an interlude of inaudibility, Meenakshisundaram's tamed rumble rising to loud astonishment.

'Please, let me be getting matter clear. You are stating that it was you, who as some sort of experiment, killed this fellow? Or not-not? Yes or no? Please.'

'Only an instance, my dear Inspector. I suppose, if such were the facts, you would hardly expect me ...'

A lapse into squeakings and rumblings.

Then the professor's voice coming through clearly again.

'... the poet, as I may say, and the mathematician combined in one ... '

'But me, I am never making verse-worse. Never.'

'... in clouds of tobacco smoke, a veritable three-pipe affair ...'

And at last the rumble mounting to final fury.

'Professor, I am not understanding. Not one damn-sham thing. Please to go. Go, please. Go. Now.'

And little Godbole spryly emerged, hands rubbing together in evident delight.

Ghote, unnoticed in his tucked-away post of observation, wondered what might be the true cause of such pleasure. Was it simply that Godbole had had another chance to air those theories of his? Or was he, possibly, just possibly, triumphing at having pulled very much of wool over Meenakshisundaram's eyes?

With a sigh he abandoned speculation as pointless.

Meenakshisundaram's interview with Mr Habibullah seemed at the start to be going on the same quiet lines as had Professor Godbole's in its beginnings.

'. . . did seem to be acting in a most methodical manner in the churchyard, my dear Inspector, reminding me of the fearful methodicalness I was for so long . . .'

A descent into mere murmuring.

But, after some time, a new note. The fat Moslem's voice definitely louder in response.

'Inspector, I am in no way surprised. Certainly you would not have found one A. A. Habibullah in the roll of names there.'

No Habibullah employed as an officer of Indian Railways?

Ghote jumped to his feet, crossed to the door of the office and, careless of whether he might be seen or not, pressed his ear hard against it.

Meenakshisundaram had put another question he had not been in time to catch. But the answer came clearly through the door.

'No, no, Inspector, it is quite simple. I wished, may Allah the merciful forgive me, to wipe away all traces of my servitude to Indian Railways, its many rules and its mountains of regulations. I did not wish to be pursued by its million-clawed bureaucracy. Inspector, I have taken a new name. I have taken a new personality even.'

Something low, menacing and uncomprehending from Meenakshisundaram.

'Well, my dear fellow, you must believe it or not as you will. But, no, I do not intend to tell you that name of shame.'

Growl. Growl.

'If you like, Inspector. I cannot say I welcome the thought of a police cell, but one never knows, it may have unexpected charms.'

There was the sound of a chair scraping back.

Ghote hurriedly retreated, right round the nearest corner.

In consequence when he crept back to his place in the depths of the sofa he was unable to make out who it was who had followed the airy, almost inconceivably inconsequential Muslem into Inspector Meenakshisundaram's spider parlour.

He listened with head cocked, but could make out no more than that than the voices behind the heavy door were exchanging rapid question and answer. Had Meenakshisundaram, even without his customary methods, got on to something?

After a while he began to feel sure that at least the other quiet voice was a man's. Mr Iyer? The Maharajah? Perhaps His Excellency. Even he might be summoned as a witness.

Then at last the voice rose a little just once and he realized that it was the Maharajah's. A maharajah, descendant of Rajput warrior princes, as uncharacteristically subdued as Meenakshisundaram himself.

He wondered whether to stand with his ear at the door again. But, even if he were to take the risk of being seen in that undignified posture by some passing soft-footed Club servant, he doubted whether he would be able to hear anything worthwhile, so quiet were the two of them inside.

So he waited.

He even began to wonder whether from the long exchange there would emerge at last a Meenakshisundaram beaming in triumph and a handcuffed Maharajah.

But when the door opened it was the Maharajah who came out alone.

For perhaps two seconds Ghote saw a chastened figure, one who put his hand to his forehead and wiped away the sweat which even in cool Ooty had gathered there. But almost at once the beaten man straightened his shoulders and could be seen pasting a careless smile on to his handsome, aristocratic face before striding off.

A few moments later his wife, for once not wearing brightly coloured trousers though still carrying her popping-eyed pekinese, swept past and entered the office. Her heavy silk sari, Ghote thought, must be worn to proclaim status and invulnerability.

He wondered how much of the interview he would be able to hear.

Soon enough he had his answer. The Maharani's confident voice came through the thick door as if it was paper.

'I'm not ashamed of it, not one bit. I have a lover. And, yes, he's younger than I am. And, yes, again, he's poor. Just a student. But he is mine, and no one is going to stop me.'

Meenakshisundaram's reply was altogether inaudible.

'Oh, I don't care if he does get to know. He can't do anything, not now. I've got every bit as much evidence against him as he could possibly get against me. The law with all its damn weighing and balancing can't alter that. My husband has been stupid enough to let himself get caught by that creature. He's given way to his damned urges once too often. And I've got him. Now I can do just what I like, and to hell with him. To hell with him.'

Once more Meenakshisundaram in putting his next question seemed completely subdued.

'And what if Amul could have bought some damned dog poison?' came the clarion voice in answer. 'You won't be able to prove he has. And I warn you, Inspector, try any of your tough stuff on him and you won't hear the end of it, not so long as you live. I know people who could have those pips off your shoulder before you could say Chakravarty Rajgopalachari. So be warned.'

The discreet murmur that followed this threat made it plain to Ghote that it had been accepted at face value.

But what about the threat itself? Had it been made simply to protect an innocent young man waiting for love down in the Bengal Vegetarian Hotel? Or had it been made to protect someone who had, in fact, when the Maharani had yet to secure that hold she had over her husband, gone to somewhere in the Bazaar and bought a quantity of dog-poison?

He heard the door of the office beginning to open and pressed himself hard back into the deep sofa. The Maharani, her eyes sparkling, the pekinese held triumphantly before her, spotted him at once.

'Ah, it's you. Do something for me, would you?'

Ghote hastily got to his feet, striving to make it look as if he had by chance been lounging there at his ease.

Was there some magic formula he could use to make this arrogant creature, flushed with her success, answer the questions he had been asking?

But inspiration failed to materialize.

'Yes? Yes, madam?' he was reduced to stammering out.

'Find Mrs Trayling, would you? Tell her that bloody inspector wants to see her. I'm not going to run his errands for him.'

She strode away.

Ghote stood for a moment, attempting to find some circumstance that would shatter the brazen façade he had been shown. But he could hit on nothing.

Sadly he set off to see if Mrs Trayling was waiting anywhere in the Club, as she must have been asked to be.

He found her sitting out in the portico and informed her that Inspector Meenakshisundaram wanted to see her.

She pushed herself up in a flurry from her long cane chair, sending her knitting-bag tumbling to the ground, made a grab for it and sent her handbag to the ground on the other side.

Ghote went round picking them up, restoring to the wide flowered knitting-bag a long metal needle such as he had once wondered might be His Excellency's famous sharp instrument.

'Mr Ghote,' Mrs Trayling said, 'tell me . . .'

'Yes, madam?'

'Inspector—Oh, I've forgotten his name again.'

'Inspector Meenakshisundaram, madam?'

'Yes. Yes, him. Is he . . . ?'

The question faded into silence.

'What is he, madam?'

'Well, I mean, will he . . . Will he, well, will he bully me, Mr Ghote? You see, I get muddled at times, and—And I don't know what I might say if he begins to shout and bang the table and . . . And all the rest.'

Ghote's first thought was whether he could do anything to protect this helpless, muddled lady. But at once he remembered it was still not impossible that she had wanted to kill the man who, she believed rightly or wrongly, had let her husband drown. She had certainly done her best once to get him dismissed.

So was she truly helpless? Or, under an air of helplessness, was there a steely will acting according to some decision arrived at in the confused secrecy of her own thoughts?

He looked at her.

'Well, madam,' he lied, 'I do not think an officer of Inspector Meenakshisundaram's standing would shout at a lady such as yourself. But in any case kindly allow me to stand outside the office where he is, and if you feel yourself to be in need of assistance please to call out.'

'That—That is most generous of you, Inspector.'

Inspector, he thought, as he escorted her to Meenakshisundaram. So Trayling Memsahib is very well aware that I, too, am a police officer. Is it by calculation she is wanting to take my help then? Is it, even, so as to build up a picture of cent per cent innocence?

He knocked at the office door for her. But when Meenakshisundaram called 'Come' he did not open it himself but stepped back and took good care his colleague did not see him.

But, listen out though he did, he heard no shouting nor table thumping nor bullying. And in five minutes Mrs

Trayling emerged, walked straight past clutching knitting-bag and handbag and disappeared.

So now, he thought, there is just only Mr Iyer.

But it seemed that Meenakshisundaram was not going to attempt to break down the alibi the assistant secretary had established, the details of which Ghote had dutifully reported the evening before. Because, without any warning, he himself came banging out of the office.

'Oh, so you are there,' he said, seeing Ghote.

'Yes, yes. I was sitting only.'

'Hm? Well, let me tell. Not one speck of good-should out of any one of the buggers. Sticking to their stories from start to finish. Or, worse-purse, trying to give me some damn-sham ideas I was not at all able to follow. And they are saying-saying one and all that, no, it was not them who was putting poison in any drink-stink that bloody Pichu was taking.'

Ghote had hardly expected Meenakshisundaram immediately to crack the case, with whatever sort of interrogation he chose to use. But he could not stop a feeling of leadenness from slowly sinking down into him at this renewed blank failure.

If all of the suspects His Excellency had lined up for him, salt-pot, pepper-pot, sugar bowl and the rest, were going to persist successfully in simply denying any connection with the poisoning, the mystery was never going to be solved. And, though he told himself that anyhow it was really no business of his, and that Professor Godbole had even declared that Sherlock Holmes had sometimes failed, and that if the matter had to be left on the file it would be on Meenakshisundaram's record not his, he was unable to suppress a simple desire in himself to know . . .

He paused in his thoughts to find the exact words he wanted.

Then they came to him.

To know who had done it. Just that.

'Well,' he said to Meenakshisundaram, 'I suppose you

can try questioning the servants. One of them may be knowing something, even if it is not more than how Pichu came to get that drink.'

Meenakshisundaram's eyes brightened.

'Yes, by God,' he said, 'I can beat something out of one of them. By God, I can.'

He turned, rejuvenated, to go on this happy errand. But at the corner he looked back.

'And you, Ghote bhai,' he called out. 'Give us some of that Bombay-style think-pink, yes? Make that brain-pain of yours work some more and find one of your explanations-complications like last night, yes? Yes?'

'I would try,' Ghote answered.

Without enthusiasm.

For a little he stood there, overwhelmed by depression. Yet again he wished with all his might that he was not where he was, in Ooty, cool and cut-off. He wished he was back in Bombay. He wished even he had been given some filthy, miserable, back-breaking task like a hunt for some mad mass-killer through a huge unmapped slum. He wished, above all, that he did not feel, inescapably, that he wanted to know who had done it, who had set out to poison blackmailing Pichu.

But – he slowly began to admit to himself – might there after all not be a way in which he could answer that insistent question.

Meenakshisundaram had requested him to think. And that was something he could do. Not in the way he had been used to thinking, sitting in his cabin in Headquarters in Bombay, working out by logic what might have happened in any particular case and then seeing if he could find evidence. But in a different way. The different way, here in different Ooty, that he had already once successfully brought off.

Could he not try again the Great Detective's way?

All right, last night, lying in bed, he had altogether failed to get into that state of yogic trance which had worked for him earlier. But . . . But there was another approach. The true Great Detective's way.

Professor Godbole had pointed it out, more than once.

He turned, marched out of the Club, marched down the hill and past the yogi without paying him the least attention, marched on into the town – and received an unexpected check.

Spencer's Stores, where he had seen himself as going, was Sunday-closed.

But, after a little hunting round, he found, down some steps opposite the Nilgiri Library next to the equally Sunday-closed Royal Hairdressing Saloon, a paan-seller. And from him he succeeded in buying, not a refreshing paan to chew, but a tobacco-pipe. matches – two boxes since they were probably very unreliable – and a large packet of unexpectedly cheap tobacco.

21

Ghote waited until he had got clear of the upper town, with its elderly inhabitants out in their heavy tweeds or snug overcoats for Sunday morning walks, dogs of all descriptions at their heels in well-trained obedience. Then he halted and experimentally filled the newly-acquired pipe with the coarsely sweet-smelling tobacco. He had never before smoked a pipe, and was anxious to commence unobserved.

After a little he got the bowl stuffed to his satisfaction, put the stem to his mouth, took out a match, struck it – it lit – and applied the flame to the tobacco. He sucked in hard. Smoke filled his mouth, stinging and sharp.

But, he thought, I have mastered this art, at the first attempt. One good omen. It must be.

He set off walking again, striding away, sucking and puffing. Past the outlying cottages and bigger houses, Glen View, Runnymede, Harrow-on-the-Hill – a house hardly on much of a hill, but its name echoed with old Britishness – Woodbriar, Stella Cottage, Dahlia Bank, Clifton Villa. He glanced at each one as he went by, waiting all the time for the pipe-smoking trance as certified by Professor Godbole to establish itself.

There they were these houses, he thought vaguely, pieces

of utter Ootiness, from another world than teeming, twisting India below, with their sloping roofs in those mild red tiles, their occasional little plaything turrets made out of warm terracotta bricks, their windows often with picture-book diamond panes, their neat verandas and their toy-town balconies.

Once he almost came to a halt at the sight of a particularly well-kept garden that was full of all sorts of pale flowers he had never seen before, grown years ago no doubt with seeds from England. Were those tall, thin ones the hollyhocks which Brigadier Trayling had failed to persuade to parade in lines? Perhaps.

And the name boards beside each gate, though they were almost all Indian, were so neat and ordered that he did not feel they took away at all from the general Britishness of everything – Col. and Mrs D. C. Saxena, Lieut.-Gen. and Mrs R. K. Singh, Dr and Mrs R. D. Pochkhanawala, Major J. K. Bell.

At this last he came to a halt. So this was old Major Bell's house, the place from which, so His Excellency had said, firewood hunters had made off with a whole tree. It was easy to see how. The garden had been let fall back into something not far from jungle and the cottage, glimpsed behind the overgrown, sprawling bushes, was every bit as neglected. There were tiles missing from its sloping roof, one window at least had a broken, unrepaired pane in it and on the cream-coloured walls huge patches of yellowish-green, the damp of many winters, spread in gloomy triumph. On the mossed-over path near the lopsided gate – the house name, My Abode, could only just be picked out thanks to the strong sunlight – it was plain that ancient old Dasher had long since ceased to be able to scrape himself a proper place for his natural functions.

This, then, was what an old Ooty hand could become reduced to.

Ghote sighed.

He did not particularly cherish the idea of the white sahibs of former times and their claims to superiority, still occasionally accepted. But somehow these signs of loss of status, of a former security fallen to nothing, saddened and disturbed him.

But he had not come walking out here to mourn the passing of the British Raj. He had come out with a purpose.

And his damn pipe had gone out. It must have done so as he had mused over the Major's house.

In a ruffling of irritation he refilled it, struck a match, struck another, and another, and at last got the thing going again. Then he strode off, once more rhythmically puffing, waiting for the wisdom that would come from the magical joining of poet and mathematician. The wisdom that would produce in a burst of light the answer.

Soon he was climbing steadily, entering the wide grassy area they called the Downs. In the distance, majestic, rose the peak of Mount Dodabetta. The views were magnificent. Behind him the clustered buildings of the town, the brilliant glinting of the Lake and, to one side, the long oval outline of the Racecourse with the enormous thatched coverings of its stables. Nearer, the mellow red roofs of the cottages he had passed earlier stood out in the universal green. Here and there the squared-off oblongs of the cultivated terraces on the hill slopes showed each a different colour from a different crop.

He strode. He puffed.

But nothing, as yet, showed any signs of happening.

He strode on.

He stopped again to recharge the pipe, this time leaving on the ground a huge circle of failed and broken matches.

He set off once more.

Should he try combining pipe yoga with Dr Joshi's? Concentrating perhaps, not on the tip of his nose, but on the smoke-curling bowl of his pipe?

What, he knew, he must on no account do was to let his thoughts return to the actual question of who was responsible for the body in the billiard room. If they did, he would be attempting to solve the mystery by the ordinary processes of logic plus haphazard guesswork, the customary police way. And this had ceased to be the sort of case that could be dealt with on those lines. No, Professor Godbole's path was the only one left to take.

But where – puff – was the entrance to that path?

He marched on. The smooth Downs gave way to more rugged country. There were wooded ravines, sholas he had been told they were called, where perhaps even today a leopard might be lurking, wild and unpredictable.

On he strode. On he puffed. Upwards he climbed.

He began to feel a little sick. Was it, he asked himself, the thin air at this height? Or the tobacco?

That had certainly been cheap. Or might it be the pipe itself? It, too, had cost less than he had expected and it had been the only one the paanwallah had for sale, grimed with sticky dust from years of remaining unsold. He had not, he had to admit, so far gained any pleasure from smoking it. Presumably Sherlock Holmes, however, did enjoy the business. Perhaps you could not get into a really revealing tobacco trance unless you were a fully accustomed, deeply enjoying pipewallah.

Quite suddenly he felt very sick indeed. He snatched the reeking pipe from his mouth and staggered down on to the nearest crag of grey rock. Below him, at the bottom of a small ravine, a silver stream trickled. He longed to go and dip his face in its cool water.

But he had a feeling that if he got to his feet to do so the worst would happen.

He tried instead deep breathing of the pure Nilgiri air.

This did have some effect. Only, after a few inhalations he realized that he was also breathing in the acrid remains of smoke from the pipe on the rock at his side. He picked it up, looked at it and then, with one gathered-up effort, swung back his arm and sent the stinking thing flying through the air.

It landed in the stream at the bottom of the ravine, sinking in its clear water with a hiss that made him think of a defeated, angry snake-demon.

But it was he himself who had been defeated, he reflected. Defeated in his struggle to become a true, pipe-smoking Great Detective.

Would he never now know who had done it? Who it was who had committed the murder in the billiard room?

He thought he would just stay sitting where he was for a long, long time. He would not go back to the Club and risk encountering His Excellency, full of his theories again and insisting on him performing impossible tasks. He would not go back to the town, sleepy in its Sunday calm, and risk bumping into Meenakshisundaram to learn either that he had or that he had not advanced matters a little by bullying and browbeating the Club servants. He would sit and sit and sit where he was.

So, instead, he rose to his feet, turned in the direction he had come from and went tramping back down.

It took him about three-quarters of an hour to reach the outskirts of the town, and as he did so he became aware that from St Stephen's Church there had sprung up the sound of bells, a gentle, lapping, melodious ringing that seemed to be repeating softly but insistently *Ootacamund, Ootacamund, Ootacamund.*

And, standing still so as to appreciate the – to him – extraordinary sound all the better, he realized something. He had, after all, experienced the true Great Detective's trance.

Somewhere in the course of his long walk back, without the aid of so much as a puff of tobacco, the knowledge of who it was who had been Pichu's poisoner had flowered in his mind. Everything had mysteriously come together at the very back of his head, in the innermost recesses. As he had tramped along he had – yes, he had – altogether without thinking of it done the thing Professor Godbole had spoken of just once. He had bent himself into the posture of the hunched and peering hatred of the poisoner.

Now he knew.

He walked on, under the sound of the lapping bells, stunned into mindlessness by the shock of his discovery. Then a voice hailed him.

'Ah, Ghote. Good man. Can't stop just now, on my way to church. But I'll see you after.'

His Excellency. Wearing a dark blue suit with a white shirt and a striped regimental tie.

'No,' Ghote said, waking from his somnambulistic state. 'No. No, no, Your Excellency, I would come to church with you.'

'Really, old man? You're a Christian then?'

'No, no, not at all.'

'Well, no need for you to come. Church parade and all that. Don't feel you've got to.'

'No. But I must come. Yes, I very much must come with you.'

His Excellency shrugged.

'Well, if you're sure. But we'll have to step out. Doesn't do to be late, you know. Specially if a chap's reading the lesson.'

'Yes,' Ghote said, not following this but not wanting a single word more of conversation.

Together they walked smartly along to the foot of the hill where Inspector Meenakshisundaram had forced a doubtful confession out of the wretched Balakumar, and on through the church gates, this morning invitingly open. In the deep porch Ghote caught a glimpse of the plaque he remembered His Excellency speaking about, *Built at the Expense of the Right Honourable Stephen Rumbold Lushington.* He had just time to recall that the timbers of the roof inside had been taken from the besieged palace of Tippoo Sultan before they were in the building itself.

What struck Ghote immediately and impressively was the hushedness of the atmosphere. Though in the rows of cane-backed seats there was a scattering of some twenty-five or thirty people, mostly Indian with half a dozen Europeans, not one of them was talking. There was the sound of music, wheezy, slow, turgid music, but it was so discreetly played – from some giant harmonium, no, an organ, it was called an organ – that it hardly seemed to be making a proper sound. It was more as if it was simply wrapping itself around the overall silence.

How different, he thought, from a noisy, chattering, bell-clanging temple, loud, too, with the sound of half a dozen different, heartily sung bhajans.

How those little girls in clean frocks and with braided pigtails, sitting so demurely with their stout mother and stouter father, had they been little Hindus, would have talked and run about and dodged round those tall white pillars and stopped every now and again to worship the god.

His Excellency had taken a place on one of the cane-backed benches. Ghote saw a free space immediately behind him and carefully stationed himself in it.

After a moment, seeing His Excellency pull out a sort of stubby cushion from under the bench in front of him and drop on to it in a posture of mild prayer, he in his turn pulled out his own hard cushion and knelt. Above all, he did not want anyone to realize he was not accustomed to this procedure, that he was not there as an ordinary worshipper.

His Excellency had put a hand to his brow as if to ward off rays of power coming from the god at the front. Only there seemed to be no god, no picture, no idol. Ghote imitated him, and from underneath his spread fingers took a careful look round.

Yes, as he had expected, Major Bell was one of the scatter of people sitting or kneeling there, as was Mrs Lucy Trayling. Had not His Excellency said, on that first evening, that the Major had been a 'sidesman' at St

Stephen's for many years? Only why then was he not sitting at the side?

He abandoned this Christian puzzle and let his covert glance roam further. He read a plaque let into the wall just within his view. *Sacred to the Memory of Helen Cecilia, Wife of John Sullivan.* John Sullivan, he had been the very founder of Ooty. And he had left his wife here, dead. But she had been remembered, it seemed, remembered through a hundred and fifty years by a little world that had retained in itself order and regulation enough to remember. That had them still, if only just.

Now there was a disturbance from somewhere at the back, but the mildest only of disturbances.

Ghote, seeing His Excellency seat himself and turn his head, did the same.

A small procession was coming up the central aisle, an Indian wearing some sort of white, lace-edged kurta over a long, black, dress-like garment, and four young girls similarly clad. The five of them made their way up to the front beyond a rail cutting off the, no doubt, holier part of the building. There the girls divided and went two and two to benches on either side facing each other. The Indian – was he a priest? – turned.

'We shall sing No. 165 in *Hymns Ancient and Modern,*' he announced. 'Oh, God, Our Help.'

The organ changed its quietly meandering music for something more rhythmical. Led by the four girls who had entered in procession, the scatter of worshippers raised their voices in song.

Rather doleful song.

'Oh, God, our help in ages past, Our hope for years to come, Our shelter from the stormy blast, And our eternal home.'

Ghote, as he succeeded in piecing out the words, began to reflect on them. Ooty was, true, a shelter from the stormy blast, and had been so for at least the past ages back to the time of John Sullivan, Collector. But it was not, sing as they all might, truly an eternal home. Things changed. Even here. And it was not altogether a monsoon-proof shelter either. Even here, even in the heart of sheltered Ooty, the ugly blast of murder had come striding in.

And, as the voices rose and fell around him like the dull surge of the sea back in Bombay when the monsoon threatened, he returned to thinking of the revelation he had had on his walk in the hunched and peering manner of the murderer of Pichu.

He paid little attention to the remainder of the service, automatically standing and kneeling and sitting when His Excellency in front of him did, and only just stopping himself in time from following when at one point His Excellency stepped out from his bench and went up to a tall reading-stand. There he proclaimed a passage from some Christian sacred book. It must, Ghote had supposed, have been the 'lesson'. But he learnt nothing.

He was aware, too, that at another stage Major Bell had gone round from bench to bench holding out a shallow dish for alms. He did remember afterwards, oddly, that the dish had a circle of soft green baize at its bottom, presumably so that the clink of coin should not spoil the general air of calm. But he could not remember whether he himself had found any money to put into the dish, nor whether it was at that time or a little later that he had wondered briefly if the Major, poor as he was, was ever tempted to take out any of the crumpled rupee notes others had put in.

But at last the ceremony was over. The worshippers filed out, exchanging in the porch a little conversation with the priest.

Ghote followed His Excellency as closely as he could, and when eventually he walked away down towards the ironwork arch over the churchyard gates he stepped up to walk beside him.

'Sir,' he said, 'I have something of utmost gravity to say to you.'

His Excellency have him a quick, startled look.

Then after a second or two he spoke.

'Well, say what you have to say, Inspector. Now must be as good a time as any.'

'Yes, sir.'

For a little Ghote kept silent as they walked gravely along side by side in the direction of the Club.

'I know who is the murderer,' he said at last.

'Yes?'

'Yes, sir. It is not your Least Likely Suspect, even if Professor Godbole might have been interested in the idea only of killing a person for purposes of experiment.'

'Not Godbole? Very well.'

'It is not the Maharajah of Pratapgadh, who as any individual who has been with him on a golf course would know, is devious and not direct, however much he is descended from Rajput ancestors. So he would not have resorted to any direct action in answer to a blackmail attempt.'

'I see.'

'Nor is it the Maharani, who is on the contrary too direct not to just only bribe a man as little rich as Pichu, as she was once trying to bribe myself, instead of murdering the same.'

His Excellency turned his head and looked Ghote straight in the eye.

'Suppose, Inspector,' he said, his voice edgy, 'you just name the name.'

'It is not Mr Habibullah,' Ghote replied composedly. 'He, if he was a notorious criminal absconding under the MISA, would also have been able to stop Pichu's mouth with hundred-rupee notes at least for as long as he needed to go elsewhere into hiding.'

'Lucy Trayling?' His Excellency said.

'No, no. It is not at all her. If she had wanted to put poison into the drink Pichu was having, she would have succeeded to put in wrong glass, or to put some harmless substance in correct glass.'

'I dare say you're right. Certainly Lucy's always been in some sort of a muddle, though I don't find your reasoning altogether faultless.'

'But let me assure: it was not Mrs Trayling. Because I am well knowing who it was.'

'Iyer's alibi? You're going to tell me it can be broken after all?'

'No. It cannot.'

'Then you have arrived at the point, Inspector, of clearing all six possible suspects.'

'Sir, there did not need to be six. There could be seven.'

'Seven? I don't—'

'Sir, there was always someone unaccounted for who has a bedroom in the Club and who must have been in same on the night in question.'

'But—'

'Yes,' Ghote said, 'as soon as you were fetching me one necktie to wear in dining room under By-law Number 13 on the first night I was here, I was observing to myself that you also, Your Excellency, could be upon the suspects' file.'

22

His Excellency stopped in his tracks. They were only a few yards from the entrance to the Club grounds. The yogi was, of course, still there, a stone pillar beside the Club signboard's wooden post.

'Yes,' Ghote repeated, 'seven suspects. Did you not once tell me that *Seven Suspects* was the title of a very, very famous book by a British writer?'

'Michael Innes, the American title,' His Excellency said automatically, his mind plainly elsewhere, thoughts racing.

Now Ghote felt his ever-hovering Watson had finally been put in his place.

'Of course,' he said, 'I did not truly consider that it had been you who had murdered Pichu. Even though I was knowing that you at one time had dressed up as a Scottish with a dagger in your long sock which might have been the weapon. And also that you might have had a motive.'

'A motive?'

'Yes, yes. You also could have had that motive which is in the story you yourself obtained in secret from the Nilgiri Library, namely *Into the Valley of Death* written by Miss Evelyn Hervey. There the murderer is blackmailed because he was winning one VC award under false pretences. And you are possessing one MC award.'

'But—'

'But you are right, it must be only in detective stories that a person who has committed a Section 302 offence would call a detective with some high reputation to investigate in order to establish his own one hundred per cent innocence.'

'Yes,' His Excellency said, with a weary sigh, 'I imagine such a thing would hardly happen in real life.'

He stood looking vaguely round for a few moments. Then a slight frown appeared on his leather-brown face.

'But if you've really eliminated all the six – all the seven people who could have . . .'

'But, you see,' Ghote said, 'once it was certain that Pichu was stabbed by a dacoit – whoever he was, Balakumar or some other – and that he was also poisoned, then the murderer with poison did not need to have been someone who was sleeping in the Club. The Club, you see, was no longer, as you were once calling it, snowbound. We do not yet know how Pichu was obtaining almost every night alcoholic drink, but it is not at all impossible that such was put for him at some time before the Club was shut up and the servants went to their quarter.'

'So, a fellow servant?' His Excellency said, visibly brightening.

Ghote felt that, now he had finally sent the Watson-Holmes business flying, he could spare the old man a reference to servants not being acceptable as murderers.

'No,' he said simply, 'it was not a servant. The reason Pichu had to be killed was because he was a blackmailer, do not forget. And he was not going to blackmail a fellow servant who could pay so little.'

'I suppose you're right. Who then? I gather it has to be someone connected with the Club?'

'Oh, yes.'

'Wait. Fatbhoy? It's that terrible pushful Parsi.'

'No. He was sometimes visiting the Club, yes, but what could Pichu have been blackmailing him for?'

'Then who, for God's sake? Who?'

Ghote paused for a moment.

True, he had felt that a jibe about servants in detective stories would have been unnecessarily cruel. But he was entitled to a little revenge at the expense of someone who had made his life such a misery.

'You were telling once,' he said, 'of Shri Poirot making some list of four significant things. I think it was one smell of oil paint, one picture postcard, one visit by some art critic plus one set of wax flowers.'

'You've an excellent memory, Inspector.'

'Oh, yes, I am able to remember many things. But it is not always that I am able to join them together in one, as today I have joined together the death of the dog by the name of Spot, plus one hand of bananas, plus the exact date on which Pichu died, plus the effect of the World War Two on the standard of snooker playing at the Ooty Club.'

His Excellency contracted his brow in intense thought. But not for long.

'No,' he said, with a sigh of frustration, 'you'll have to explain.'

'Yes, I would do that,' Ghote answered. 'Kindly think. Mrs Trayling's dog Spot was – what it is? – "put down" because of old age. And, Number Two, while Mrs Trayling, who is not a well-off lady, can still make many purchases at Spencer's Stores, there is one person who has to buy with much care just only bananas down in the Bazaar. As to the date of Pichu's death, it was immediately before the last Saturday of the month, the day when the Culture Circle is always meeting. Now, you are well knowing, I am sure, that everywhere people are always most short of money before the first of the month when salaries etcetera are paid out. So that is the time Pichu would have demanded blackmail money. And if he is killed then, it is because he has threatened to give out the secret he has perhaps kept for years should he fail to get regular requisite sum on due date. And, finally, what was the result of many, many good snooker players being away after the war? Why, that Major Bell, who was not very much of a good player and who has never played since, was that year winning trophy.'

'Ringer Bell?' His Excellency said, a look of distant understanding beginning to show in his eyes.

'Yes, Major Bell. Major Bell, who won that trophy when, as you yourself were telling, no one else was watching that match. But Pichu, as billiards marker, must have been there. And when the Major was cheating perhaps, when his opponent's head was turned by moving just only a little one ball, Pichu must have seen. And because of that, month by month for many, many years he would have had his sum in cash from Major Bell. So it was no wonder when I was mentioning his snooker success after we had met him where the silver was found he was very much glaring at me. And no wonder also he was refusing and refusing to give Pichu a sack at the request of Trayling Memsahib.'

'But, surely . . . No. No, I see you're right. A chap like Bell would pay as often as he had to rather than be branded a cheat at games. Yes, I see that.'

'And, as he was paying and paying, value of money was falling and falling while any pension he had was not rising so fast. So, in the end, he was forced, burra sahib though he was, to get bananas only from the Bazaar and, as you yourself again were telling, at one time there was question of Friend in Need Society. And at last there came a day when Major Bell could no more pay the sum due at or before the month-end, and then . . . Then he must have been making use of poison he had already bought for the purpose of ending the life of his old, old dog Dasher, who should have been put down like Trayling Memsahib's Spot.'

'Yes. Yes, I never somehow thought of that. But Dasher ought in all decency to have been put down well before this.'

His Excellency contemplated the ground at his feet,

thinking perhaps of the ending of lives, of time passing, of inexorable change and decay.

Then he looked up.

'So what happens?' he asked.

'Well,' Ghote answered, 'of that I am not altogether sure. That is why I was wanting to inform you of the facts. You see, although I am certain that this is what must have taken place, I do not have any court-of-law proof.'

'No. No, I see that. Awkward.'

'So what I am thinking is: should I go to Major Bell and put whole matter to him?'

His Excellency pondered for a little.

'Yes,' he said at last. 'Yes, I suppose that's the only thing to do. Can't say I envy you. Whole affair's an appalling business.'

'Yes,' Ghote said.

He gathered himself together.

'Well, I suppose now must be the time. I was seeing the Major going in the direction of his home after he was at church, isn't it?'

'Yes, yes. Always does that. Doesn't like to leave Dasher alone too long. Wretched beast howls, you know.'

His Excellency looked down again at the well-polished black shoes he wore with his blue suit.

'Dasher,' he said.

'Then I will be going,' Ghote said.

'Yes. Yes. Well, good luck. Good luck, old man.'

It did not take Ghote many minutes to walk out to the old dilapidated house called My Abode, even though he went at a leaden pace. At the gate he paused for a moment. But there seemed to be nothing to think over, and he pushed his way past Dasher's incontinent messes, and went up to the front door.

There was a bell-pull, brass and doubtless once carefully polished. He gave it a cautious tug, but at once realized that nothing had happened on the far side. So he rapped hard on the door's blistered paint with his knuckles.

After a little he heard – he had half hoped he would not – shuffling steps coming towards him. Then the door opened.

It was the Major, with Dasher looking more decrepit than ever at his heels.

For a long time the old man just stared at him, his mottled red face second by second going greyer and greyer.

At last he spoke.

'It's you. Inspector Ghote, Bombay. Thought at first it might be somebody else, though God knows no one comes to the door any more now.'

'Yes,' Ghote said.

For want of anything better to say.

'Yes. Well, I suppose you'd better come in.'

'Please.'

The Major turned and, followed by Dasher, shufflingly led the way through a hall bare of all furniture with only a sola topee resting on the floor.

There was a strong smell of mildew.

'Drawing room,' the Major said.

He pushed at a wide teak door, but was able to open it only by little more than a foot as, sagging from its loosened hinges, it scraped on the floor. He squeezed his way through. Ghote, turning sideways, prepared to squeeze after him but had to wait while Dasher made his way in step by dragging step.

'Must get that door seen to,' the Major muttered.

Then, quite suddenly, he turned round and faced Ghote, his patchily mottled face barely nine inches distant.

'Well, no,' he said more loudly and clearly, 'the time for that sort of thing's gone, hasn't it? Rest of my life in gaol, I suppose. If they don't hang me.'

Ghote, standing just inside, saw that the room behind was half-denuded and almost in ruins. The single remaining armchair had its stuffing trailing feebly out. From a long bamboo bookcase a length of edging cane swung forward. The few books on its shelves were uniformly greened-over with the damp of many past monsoons. A row of photographs in frames on its top had faded almost to plain rectangles of pale sepia.

'So I am right,' he said, in answer to the Major's declaration, wishing there was something else to say.

'God knows how you got on to it,' the Major replied. 'But, yes, in the end I had to get rid of the fellow. After all those years of paying, paying, paying. But when I thought it was all going to be wasted, I decided I had to do what I could. Of course, I knew he took whisky from Major Jago's Room each night. I tried to tick him off about it once, but he only said it was nothing like as bad as moving a ball on the snooker table. S'pose he was right.'

'That was just only breaking one rule of a game,' Ghote said.

'Well, but the rules are the rules, you know. No point in playing games otherwise.'

Ghote sighed.

'No, I am supposing not.'

The Major lifted his sagging shoulders a little.

'You know,' he said, 'I thought I was going to get away with it. Thought I'd managed the whole thing rather well, as a matter of fact. When I was down in the Bazaar, buying some bananas – more or less live on the damn things nowadays – I spotted a fellow I knew was a fearful blackguard. Dacoit, ready for any easy money. So I deliberately said something in a loud voice to the vegetablewallah there about the silver in the Club billiard room, and what a fearful old duffer our watchman was. And the hint worked. Fellow came up that night, stole the silver and even added to everything by sticking a sword into Pichu's body. But . . . But you saw through it all, eh?'

'Well, yes. Yes, I did.'

Dasher, Ghote noticed, was sniffing morosely at the corner of the bookcase which, judging by deep stains on the floor, he had often visited before.

'So what next?' the Major said.

'Well, I must ask you to accompany me to the Urban Police Station where I would inform Inspector Meenakshisundaram of the full circumstances.'

'Yes. Yes, s'pose that's the ticket.'

At the corner of the bookcase Dasher, perhaps somehow scenting catastrophe, suddenly flopped back on to his haunches and uttered a feeble howl.

'Dasher,' the Major said. 'Poor old boy. What shall I do about him?'

Ghote felt the complication as one last almost overwhelming burden thrust on to him.

'I—I do not know,' he said. 'Oh, wait, yes. Yes, I think I can see what to do. Mrs Trayling. If I am telling her, she would, I am sure, come and rescue Dasher. Yes, I am sure.'

'Lucy Trayling? Yes. Yes, she'd do it. She'll get him put down for me too, I expect. Thing I should have done myself, only . . .'

Ghote stood by then while the Major manoeuvred himself past the door, keeping it as little open as possible. Then he wriggled out in his turn, holding Dasher back with a carefully placed foot.

When they had got the door shut on the decrepit animal they both stood looking at it. From inside there was silence. Silence more nerve-wracking than any feeble moans of protest.

At last the Major turned, picked up his sola topee from the floor, placed it carefully on his head and gave Ghote a look.

'Well,' he said, 'better be off, hadn't we?'

'Yes.'

They went out into the rioting, overgrown garden.

'Shan't bother to lock up,' the Major said. 'Not a damn thing to steal now, and Lucy'll be able to get in all the easier.'

'Yes,' Ghote said once more.

They set off.

The Major walked with incredible slowness, head lowered, back stooping.

When they had gone about fifty yards along the lane, from the house behind them without any warning there came the sound of Dasher lamenting.

The Major came to a halt.

He stood where he was in silence. Ghote, after one glance, kept his gaze resolutely looking forward. He thought he had seen glistening tears on the greyish, mottled cheeks.

After what seemed a long while the Major spoke.

'Choclox' he said.

'Please?'

'Choclox. I could give the old fellow the last of the Choclox. His favourite, you know. Haven't been able to afford them for a long time now. But kept a few in the box. Treats. Christmas and all that.'

'Can I go back and give?' Ghote asked. 'You are looking most tired.'

'No, no. Better do it myself. Might force his way out and go on the rampage.'

Ghote thought how unlikely that was. And how unlikely it was that the Major, if allowed to go back into My Abode on his own, would contrive a daring escape.

'I will wait,' he said.

'Good of you. Shan't be long.'

'Do not hurry. Please.'

The old man shuffled off. Even before he had reached the gate of the house Dasher had stopped his lament.

Ghote stood where he was, trying not to think of anything. Especially of his strict duty as a police officer.

Minutes passed.

He looked at his watch. How long had it been since the Major had gone in search of Choclox?

He decided to give him another five minutes. He looked at the hand of his watch with scrupulous care.

At the end of the measured time there was still no sign of the Major.

Ghote turned and strode rapidly back. The lopsided garden gate had been left fully open. He looked at the house. The front door was slightly ajar.

Careless of Dasher's leavings, he sprinted up the path, pushed his way into the house, looked round the empty hall.

The drawing-room door was open, as far as it would go. He ran across and thrust his head in.

The Major lay, face down, on the floor. Near him was an empty carton labelled 'Choclox'. Dasher was standing beside him, slowly poking with his nose at a place by his master's neck.

Ghote went and knelt beside the dog.

He was not surprised to find, when he thrust a hand underneath the Major's inert body, that the heart had stopped beating. He recalled that at the time they had inspected the missing silver in the churchyard the Major had said something about his old ticker being likely to let him down.

He got to his feet.

'Well, Dasher,' he said, cursing himself for doing it as soon as he had begun, 'this must be the end. For your master. For you soon also. For me in Ooty.'

*

Inspector Ghote watched the little blue-'and-buff-coloured train come chuffing into Ramgar Station ready for its return trip down to the plains below.

When he had learnt from the ever efficient Mr Iyer that no bus left for Coimbatore for several hours the evident rage and disappointment on his face had prompted the assistant secretary to mention the train. There would be just time to catch it.

Ghote had actually run to his room then, hauled his suitcase out of the enormous almirah in which it had occupied a corner and almost frenziedly had stuffed his clothes and possessions into it.

The tail of a shirt, he saw now, was still sticking out at one side. He decided he had time to put the case up on to the concrete bench just behind him – it was underneath Tree No. 3 inside the spiked railing, the number painted on a neat yellow square cut in the trunk – open it and tuck the offending piece of red-and-white check out of sight.

Order restored, he picked up the case and made for the oddly tall, square-looking carriages of the waiting train. He selected the carriage labelled *Seats A 1–6*, one that no one else among the handful of passengers waiting to leave paradise Ooty had chosen, since he was filled with an intense desire to be alone with his thoughts.

To his relief he was not joined by any scurrying late arrival before there came the clang of one of the red-capped porters striking the dangling departure-signal iron bar. The guard then put his whistle to his mouth and blew a thin, piercing shriek. In answer the train's engine produced a hollow musical boom and they slowly began to roll forward.

I am leaving Ooty, Ghote said to himself in a sunburst of unalloyed delight.

Then, almost at once, he thought that there had been times in hell Ooty when he had experienced feelings of high pleasure. Not, certainly, during the past few hectic hours as he had reported the death of Major Bell to Inspector Meenakshisundaram, telephoned Lucy Trayling to arrange for her to take care of Dasher, informed His Excellency about all that had happened and had contrived to say goodbye to him without making it obvious that he intended to shake the dust of Ooty from his feet as rapidly as possible.

But he had felt intense, almost overwhelming, awesome pleasure in the out-of-the-world world he was leaving when he had succeeded, twice, in actually becoming, for a few minutes only, a Great Detective.

He had put himself into a yogic trance and had seen

how it had come about that the wretched Pichu had died: had died once and then died again, though which death was the first would never be known. And he had, if not by means of a Sherlock Holmes tobacco-filled pipe, entered into another trance and had found himself at last walking in the hunched and peering manner of that sad murderer, the Major.

And he had eaten porridge and Dundee marmalade.

The train was now descending rapidly, passing alternately through cuttings hacked out of the solid rock barely wider than its locomotive and winding down the mountainside with huge precipitous views of wild tumbling valleys and distant spiny ridges stretching out for mile upon mile. Soon the deep green of the hill forest had begun to change to a lighter colour. The stations of the route had been ticked off one by one, Lovedale, Wellington, Runnymede, Hillgrove.

Ghote had hardly noticed them and their out-of-place English names. A world that was not frozen in the pages of a detective story awaited him in the steamy heat below.